BOOK 3 IN THE
MAPLE RIDGE SERIES

Sweet
RIDGE HEARTS

SUSAN BAGBY

Also from Susan Bagby

MAPLE RIDGE SERIES
Christmas Wish Upon A Star
Home for Love

For Carl Jalesh Bendix, my dear friend and soul brother. You brought love and magic into my life, and I will forever be grateful for those gifts. You are missed— never to be forgotten.

Chapter One

Today is the day. The day her hard work would finally pay off. Katy rummaged through her jewelry box looking for the perfect earrings to go with the rest of her outfit. Yes, the creative director job was between two people, Simon Wadsworth, her present boyfriend, and herself. She and Simon had agreed that whatever the outcome, they would support each other, no matter what. *My work is superior.* But would William Lewis, co-owner of the company, see that? Based on merit, she should get the promotion. The Wadsworth family did have connections in the business world that could help the Martin and Lewis agency; she hoped that wasn't a deciding factor in Mr. Lewis's choice today.

She threw on her cashmere wool coat and leather gloves, then grabbed her purse and briefcase. Looking in the mirror, she said, "You've got this, girl. You deserve this position, and you've worked hard for it." Flipping her silk scarf around her bare neck, she took the elevator to the street below and treated herself by hailing a taxi, avoiding the subway.

With a lilt in her step, she hopped out of the cab, grabbed a coffee from the kiosk outside, and scurried into the office building, anxious to escape the frigid air outside. The elevator doors opened; she darted past the receptionist, greeting her as she rushed to her office. Passing by the boss's door, it suddenly opened, and Simon walked out, bumping into her.

"Oh, hi," he said.

Was that a sheepish grin? "Hi," she said. "Did you have a meeting?" A sinking feeling in her stomach rumbled, inciting a slight panic.

"Yeah. He wants to meet with you, too." Simon shifted his body weight, looking down. "I've got to make a phone call, but see you later?"

"Sure." An icy chill spread throughout her body. She had a premonition of what was to come and wasn't happy about it.

No sooner had she tossed her coat and purse on the chair in her room when William's secretary popped her head around the corner.

"William would like to see you when you're settled. Just knock on his door." The young woman whisked away and was gone before Katy could reply.

This was the moment she had been preparing for her whole career. She deserved this. She stood up taller, straightened her suit with her hands, reapplied lip gloss, and tidied any loose hair flying around in her bun. She walked towards his office and tapped on his door.

"Come in."

Her stomach flip-flopped, but not with excitement—only fear. She looked at the intimidation seated before her. "Good morning, Mr. Lewis."

"Please. Sit down, Katy. How are things going on the Barclay account?"

"Fine. They seem very pleased, and the campaign is bringing in more business." *But he knows that. Is he just making small talk with me?*

As if reading her mind, he abruptly got to the point. "As you know, since Val is leaving us, we are filling the creative director position after the holidays. Big shoes to fill."

"Yes." She readjusted her posture, sitting up taller.

"The position was between you and Simon. Your work is exemplary, Katy. I want you to know that."

Uh, oh. She didn't like where this was going.

"But we've decided that Simon will get the position. I'm sorry. But as I said before, your work speaks for itself. Excellent on all levels."

Dizziness congested her head, her belly aching like she had been gut-punched, the breath knocked out of her. *Pull it together, woman. Don't give up.* "Mr. Lewis, that is disappointing, but I think my work has been superior to Simon's. Can you be a little more specific about why he was chosen?" She wasn't giving up so easily.

"Let's just say, his access to future clients is more solid. And that idea he had of cause marketing with companies was stellar. This has nothing to do with the quality of your work, Katy. Like I said, it's been outstanding."

A maddening heat crept up inside her body, bubbling, ready to explode. "Cause marketing?"

"You know. Attaching a non-profit to a company's brand and using marketing in that way."

"Mr. Lewis, I hate to tell you, but that was *my* idea, not Simon's."

He stood up. "It doesn't matter whose idea it was, the board loved it, and I'm going to let Simon oversee building it. He'll need your help, of course. If you'll excuse me, I have a meeting across town."

She stood up, her wobbly legs teetering on collapse. She was pissed. "Thank you, Mr. Lewis." She shook his hand, trembling inside, and retreated to her office, slamming the door behind her.

What just happened? She sat down in her chair, counting her breaths so she wouldn't scream. Simon had stolen her idea, claimed it for his own, and most likely schmoozed the boss with all his father's connections and potential income. There was nothing she could have done. Once again, the big boys stuck together, and the woman with more talent and skill got pushed aside. She wanted to throw-up.

A gentle rap sounded at her door. Katy straightened her posture, attempting hard not to let tears fall down her face. No one at the office could see her disappointment; she could handle defeat. "Come in," she said.

Simon slowly opened the door, then closed it before he walked over to her. "Are you okay? I'm sorry you didn't get the position, but we both knew this could happen." He waited for her response.

She flicked a stray hair from her face and took a sip of her coffee, all the while trying to calm down the fury inside of her. "I'm fine." She raised her gaze to meet him eye to eye. "You stole my idea for cause marketing with the Krafton case and used it for yourself. How could you do that?"

"I didn't *steal* it, Katy. I just mentioned it in passing to William. We both had tossed ideas around with it, remember?" Simon shifted his stance, wiping a fleck of perspiration on his upper lip.

"Yes, after I had suggested it in our discussion." She wasn't backing down.

He reached out to touch her arm. "We're on the same team, Katy. Let me take you to dinner tonight. You're important to this company, and I wouldn't want to do this job without you by my side."

Aarrgh. Was he really suggesting she play the supporting role position? Katy squirmed in her chair. He was more arrogant than she thought. Her self-worth was at stake here, and she was fighting hard not to crash and burn right before him. "Okay. Text me a time and place and I'll meet you." She pulled away from his touch. "I've got a phone call I need to make. We'll talk later about this."

"Of course. I wanted to make sure you were alright. See you tonight."

As her door closed, she pulled a tissue from her purse and dabbed the corners of her eyelids, preventing any wetness from trickling down her cheek. Losing out to Simon was more devastating than she realized. Her client campaigns were superior to his, and her creative ideas at staff roundtables were more engaging and frequently used. Why had she lost out? It had to be Simon's connections; her stolen idea didn't help matters for her either. Suddenly, she didn't like her boyfriend very much, but would go to dinner anyway.

* * *

With less spring in her step, Katy climbed out of the cab and entered the restaurant. She would eventually get over the loss but hated that she wasn't getting the kudos she deserved. Katy had brought in more clients for Martin and Lewis than anyone else on the marketing floor these past few years; she could run circles around Simon when it came to social media and her branding ideas. And she always put in more hours than she got paid for when fine-tuning a campaign. Indeed, William should have seen that. She shook her head, trying to erase the day, and glanced around the crowd until she saw Simon waving to her.

He stood up as she approached, took her coat off, and kissed her on the cheek. "Thanks for coming. I know this day wasn't what you expected."

Try not to be a sore loser, Katy. "Yes, that's true." *Deep breath.* "But I'm happy for you." *Even though you don't deserve it.*

"Thanks. We'll still work together." He cocked his head, looking at her.

You mean you'll take credit for all my ideas and campaigns because I'll be working underneath you? "Yes, we will." She needed a drink.

"How about a drink?"

"Please." *Now you're talking.*

They engaged in small talk while they drank, and then Simon became serious.

"Look. There's something else I need to tell you."

Great. What is it now? "What's that?" Things couldn't get any worse, could they?

"Human resources called me into their office today and ..." He stammered and stopped.

"And what?" she demanded.

"Since I'm technically going to be your boss, they are discouraging a romantic relationship together. It's clearly written in the bylaws. Being equal associates, they were fine with it, but in this case, it's not possible."

She drained the rest of her cabernet, set the glass down, and stared at him. "Are you breaking up with me?"

"I think I have to, Katy." He fidgeted his fingers around the neck of his wine glass.

"But we have Thanksgiving plans in two days with your parents. We even discussed going to the Caribbean right after Christmas. Are you kidding me?"

"I know. I know. But there's nothing I can do about it. The same thing would have happened to you if they had given you the position." He shrugged.

Katy shook her head. Simon hadn't even bothered fighting for her or gone to William to see if they could come up with some exception to that stupid rule. He just took *her* position and bowed down to any corporate guidelines to keep it.

"I would have tried harder to salvage *us,* Simon. But I can see this is never going to work anymore. Thanks for the drink." She quickly grabbed her coat, stood up, and bolted out the front door before she exploded.

* * *

A hot shower and another glass of wine barely put her irritation on a simmer. She couldn't believe this day—nothing like she expected. *What am I going to do?* The thought of looking at Simon every day and following his orders made her insides want to hurl. The big promotion she had deftly pursued for these last five years—gone. Maybe she needed a break. Maybe she needed to look at her life from a different perspective. But how?

Her phone rang, and she saw her cousin's name, Christine, flashing on the front. *Perfect timing.*

"Christine! Just the woman I need to talk to," Katy exclaimed.

"Oh, yeah? What's going on up there?" Christine lived in the small town of Maple Ridge in the Berkshires and ran a successful business called, Sweet Ridge Bakery.

"You're not going to believe my day." She downloaded everything to her.

"It sounds like you need a break," Christine said. "Why don't you come stay with me for the holidays? And I mean, really stay. Come for Thanksgiving and stay through Christmas. Let that company see how they function without you. You haven't taken a vacation in years and probably have a ton of days accrued. Right?"

Katy sat up in bed, a flashbulb going off in her brain. She did have a lot of vacation days. "You may be on to something. I do have days to take off."

"And you can help me with my business. I'm thinking of expanding, and I'll need marketing and branding help—your specialty."

"Really?"

"Yes, really. Please?"

The thought of returning to Martin and Lewis sickened her. That wasn't a good sign. Maybe this was a sign from the universe telling her she was worthy of taking time for herself. She had been on a fast track for so long, she had no clue of what her innermost dreams were anymore. She thought she had—the creative director job. That didn't pan out. *Now, who am I?* She had to be more than just a marketing employee. There was too much creativity inside her, bursting at the seams with no direction to go.

"Maybe I do need a respite from the maddening pace of New York," she said.

"Of course, you do."

"Okay. I'll do it."

"Yippee! I'll get your room ready. You'll see. This is going to be so much fun. I can't wait to tell you about my next adventure."

That's what Katy needed—a next, new adventure. "I'll put in for my leave and text you my arrival time." *Am I really doing this?*

"You won't be sorry, Katy."

"No, I don't think I will be. See you on Wednesday." As she hung up, she stared out her window onto the busy streets of Manhattan. Country air and a slower pace would be a welcome reprieve. Perhaps she would find some inner peace and redirection for her internal compass in the trip to Maple Ridge. She hoped so.

* * *

As the subway chugged along, Katy gazed around at the full car of passengers, most on their daily commute to a job somewhere. She felt her phone buzz for the twentieth time and looked down to see Simon's name. She would see him soon enough. She was still dealing with residual anger from their sudden break-up and her frustration at work. But she had made a decision, and that part felt right.

She grabbed a coffee at the stand outside her building and jumped into a crowded elevator about to close its doors. With head held high, she waltzed into her office as if nothing had happened. She was determined to keep her pride intact and her self-esteem glowing. She deserved more than she was getting here at Martin and Lewis, and she was taking this break come hell or high water.

She tossed her purse on her desk, hung up her coat, and placed her coffee next to the computer. She swiftly turned around, heading for William Lewis's office without an appointment. If his door was open, she was going in.

She nearly collided with Simon as he was coming out.

"There you are! I've been texting you all morning. Can we talk at lunch today?"

Is he regretting his decision to break-up? "Possibly. Let me see how busy I am. I'll text you." She zipped by him, heading straight for William. "Can I talk to you a minute?" she asked.

"Sure. Close the door," he said.

Katy gave a smirking smile to Simon who was just staring at her now, and gently closed the door on him. *Oooh, that felt good.*

She proceeded to outline her plans to take her vacation days between Thanksgiving and Christmas. There wasn't much to say since she had never used any vacation time in the five years she had worked there.

"What about the Krafton campaign? What's left to do with that one?" William asked.

"My assistant can handle any details along with Simon, and I'll make myself available if needed remotely in case there are any issues." She stretched a little taller, asserting herself. She wasn't backing down. She was getting her way today.

"I hope this doesn't have to do with our decision to give Simon the creative director position, does it?" he asked. "You do know you will have to work together in the new year, and I hope you're not letting your feelings cloud your judgment about your career." His eyebrows lifted as he looked at her.

Is he accusing me of being overly emotional and unable to deal with an executive decision? The undertones of his statement hit Katy; she dug her nails into her palm. No way was she giving him the satisfaction of revealing her true feelings about the whole ordeal. She had spoken her truth yesterday and was moving on. "No, I just want to spend the holidays with my family. It's been a while." *And that's all I'm telling you.*

"Okay. Try and be available if Nancy needs you, if you don't mind."

"Sure thing." She plastered a smile on her face and stood up to shake his hand. "Happy holidays, William."

"Happy holidays to you, too."

Katy held her head high as she walked down the corridor towards her office. But before settling into her to-do lists, she swung around and landed in front of Simon's door, which was open.

"Got a minute?" she asked.

"Absolutely. Come in." He gestured to the chair in front of him. "Please, sit."

"That's okay. I'll stand. I won't be long. I wanted to let you know I'm taking a long vacation for the holidays since I haven't used any of my days. I'm leaving tomorrow for Maple Ridge and staying with Christine." She stood perfectly still, watching his reaction.

Simon rose from his seat and walked closer. Closing the door, he reached out for her hand. "I'm so sorry about this whole mess. You're right. I didn't fight for you. Maybe I should have a talk with William and see if there's something I can work out. Maybe there's still a chance for us." His eyes searched hers for an answer.

"I've made up my mind, Simon. I'll see you in the new year." She pulled her hand out of his grasp. "Happy holidays."

"Happy holidays, Katy." He stopped and stared at her. "Is that it? With us?"

"You broke up with me, Simon. Maybe you should ask yourself the same question. Talk to you later." She flew out the door.

Simon's stunned expression hung in her rear view; that brought her pleasure for some reason. But as she entered her office and sat down, she couldn't deny a pinch in her heart. She wasn't that cold-hearted. They had been together for three years, and everything had been going along fine—until it wasn't. But perhaps things had been going too smoothly. Once conflict entered their relationship, she saw his true colors. The biggest disappointment was not him getting her position but how he had stolen her ideas to get it. He would never put her first; she needed a man who would. She was tired of men who didn't appreciate her worth. *So, I guess it's time for me to put myself first—and ward off men for a while.* Maple Ridge sounded better every second.

Chapter Two

Derek pulled his truck into the back parking lot of Sweet Ridge Bakery. He was early, but the regular bakers had probably been there for hours. This might be the busiest day of the year for them. The wind blew against his face, bringing a sharp chill in the air; he welcomed the heat and delectable smells of cinnamon, vanilla, and chocolate bursting forth in his nostrils as he entered the bakery. He greeted everyone hard at work with a smile and made his way to a small office Christine had given him at the end of the summer. She'd been impressed by his ability to apply his business skills so quickly to her online affairs and had given him a raise.

As he took off his jacket, his phone rang. His mom.

"Hey, Mom. Isn't this early for you? How's Aunt Clara?"

"She's feeling much better now that we're here. And I have to admit, this Florida weather might grow on me."

He laughed. "Yeah, it's getting cold up here. No snow yet."

"Honey, I just want to make sure you're going to be alright over Thanksgiving. We can always buy you a plane ticket."

"Mom, stop worrying. I'm fine. And besides, I received an invitation to the Andersons for a Thanksgiving feast. Should be fun." He reminisced on last Thanksgiving. He was a mess back then. He had just returned from Afghanistan and mental issues were choking the life out of him. Thanks to Dr. Mark Richards, who identified the PTSD, he got the help he needed. Like Mark said, "It was a lifelong journey. It's how you ride the waves that counts."

"Okay. I'll stop worrying. Clara's physical therapist is coming today, so Dad and I can get training to help her do those exercises."

"Tell her I said hi, Mom. I've got to run. Love you."

"Love you too, dear."

Derek looked up as Christine peeked her head around the corner. "Can I talk to you a minute?"

"Sure." He pointed to the one extra chair in the office. The space was bare bones, the interior without windows, but it was his—giving him the grounding and stability he needed. Sweet Ridge Bakery had become the rock he tethered his soul upon, steadying himself through a daily routine and human interactions.

"I may need you on the floor today. I hate to tear you away from our project, but it is the holidays."

"Whatever you need, Christine. Count me in." He grinned at her.

"My cousin, Katy, is coming for the holidays and may be able to help us. In fact, she's staying for three weeks. She works for some fancy marketing firm in New York and is quite the branding wiz I've been told. She'll be here later, so I'll introduce you."

Derek would do anything Christine asked, but working with other people wasn't his forte. He preferred living life as a lone wolf—safer and less confrontational. "Send Mary Beth to get me if you need anything."

"Will do. By the way, where do we stand on the Ferguson project?"

"They're coming next week for a meeting. We might need specs on a possible space in Manhattan soon for the proposal."

"I figured. My realtor has been sending me possibilities, but I'll go look after we have the meeting. Sooner is better."

"Gotcha. I'll see what I can do." He picked up his phone, determined to take care of business for Christine. He knew if this investor would choose her to open a second Sweet Ridge Bakery in Manhattan, it would allow her the opportunity she desperately wanted to be with Sam Hastings, her boyfriend of a year. The weekend commutes to see each other weighed on them, but they weren't ready to throw in the towel. At least, not yet. That's why this business deal was crucial. It went beyond business—more a matter of the heart.

The bells on the door continuously chimed as people came and went all morning. Most were picking up pies, cakes, or whatever else they had ordered for their holiday feast the next day.

Christine turned to Mary Beth, "We might be out of our regular items soon. Would you ask Derek to join the baker's crew for a bit? I told him that might happen."

"Sure," said Mary Beth. She was eighteen and had been working full time for Christine since June. She was one of the first *Hands-On Beyond* employees, a non-profit helping to employ, and house foster and orphan kids aging out of the system. Working here had given her the chance to build a new life in the same town as her little sister, Jolene, who still resided at Fairside Manor, an orphanage on the outskirts of town. They had lost their parents six years ago in an auto accident and had no other family.

Katy pulled her car into a parking space on Main Street and exhaled a sigh of relief. The decision to take a break from both her job and boyfriend felt like the right thing to do. And now that she was here in Maple Ridge, she knew she had made the best decision for herself.

She grabbed her purse, zipped up her coat, and stepped out into the icy wind, its temperature biting her skin. As she walked into the aroma of baked goods gone overboard, she scanned the room for her cousin but didn't see her. She walked up to the counter and said, "Is Christine here? I'm Katy, her cousin."

"Oh, she's been expecting you. Let me get her," Mary Beth said.

Within seconds, Christine came barging through the swinging doors to greet her. "Katy! You're here! Yay!" She immediately squeezed Katy with both arms.

Katy stood back after the voracious hug. "I know. I don't think we've had this much time together since high school summer vacations!"

"Got that right. I'm so excited to have you. Let me show you the bakery, then I'll give you the keys to the house so you can get settled. I made an extra set for you. I don't think I can get out of here until closing at five. It's been a whirlwind all morning."

"Do you need any help? Remember your mom put me to work all those summers I visited you; I do have a skill or two that might be helpful." She winked at her cousin.

"I couldn't ask you to do that. You just drove up from the city."

"You didn't ask. I offered. And besides, an hour or two with flour and sugar could help calm the last of my ragged nerves from the fiasco I just left."

"If you say so. And we will discuss this at dinner with a glass of wine. Come on, follow me," said Christine.

As Katy entered the back, her jaw dropped. The commercial space had quadrupled in size and looked more like a warehouse than a small-town bakery. "When did you do all of this?" she asked.

"About a year ago. Jake Sanders, you remember him, right? Jim

Anderson's nephew who used to hang out with us sometimes. He helped me with a business plan and voila!" She swept her arms around to it all.

"No wonder an investment firm is looking at you. Well done."

"Let's put your stuff in my office, and I'll get you an apron."

As Katy followed her down a corridor, a door opened, and a tall man with a buffed physique and wavy brown hair hitting his collar, nearly collided with her.

"Oh, sorry. I didn't see you," he said.

"No problem."

Derek looked down at her. "Can I help you?"

Christine pivoted back to them. "I see you've met my cousin, Katy. Katy, this is Derek, my right-hand guy with everything at this point."

"Nice to meet you," she said. She noticed his dark eyes were rather mysterious in some alluring way, and his chiseled profile and broad chest seemed to hang over her with an air of confidence.

"We're going to put her stuff in my office, and then she's joining us on the floor. Can you get her set up?" Christine asked.

"Sure. I was headed there now." He shifted his gaze to Christine. "The Ferguson guys are coming on Monday for another look around and to discuss numbers."

Christine brought her hands together in front of her chest. "Terrific! Then I can scout out locations after that."

Derek smiled and nodded.

Katy moved her head from side to side watching the conversation. "What's going on here? Are you relocating?"

"Yes and no. That's what I wanted to tell you about. A potential investor has expressed interest in opening one of my bakeries in New

York. If that happens, I can finally get to spend more time with Sam to see if what we have is the real thing. With so much back and forth between here and the city, I don't know what it would be like to be living close by and have daily interactions. Things can change then, you know."

Katy looked down, her break-up a little too fresh. "Yeah, I know."

"I'll be on the floor. Come find me when you're ready," Derek said.

After he left, Katy looked at Christine. "He's quite the handsome guy. How did you find him?"

"Mark Richards, the new town doctor, and Maggy's boyfriend, suggested him for the position back in the spring. He's a veteran and had some problems holding a job when he returned from Afghanistan. PTSD kind of stuff. I gave him a chance, and now I don't think I could run this place, let alone make an expansion of this magnitude, without him. He's a good guy but kind of shy—until he gets to know you."

"Wow, I guess I've missed a lot not visiting you for some years. Did Maggy leave LA?"

"Yep. Mark was her dad's doctor, and when she came out to help last spring after his heart attack, they couldn't stop destiny from pulling them together. I've never seen Maggy so happy. She's teaching art at Fairside and opened a chic new gallery on Main Street. She still has her hand in producing, mainly documentaries, but mostly spends her time here in Maple Ridge. We might have another wedding in the future. You'll see everyone tomorrow and meet the new characters." Christine hugged her again. "I'm so happy you're here."

A comforting sensation magnified in Katy, her heart swelling with each breath. She had forgotten how tight-knit this community was and how welcoming it had always been to her during the summers she spent at her aunt's house. After her mother died when Katy was young, her father remarried and seemed happy to drop her off in the summer while he and his new wife jaunted around Europe or some other exotic place, never including her. But Christine's mom had been like a second mother to her. She was saddened when she passed five years ago and understood why Christine wanted to keep the family tradition alive and thriving.

After tossing her stuff in Christine's office, she strolled back to the prep room in search of Derek and an apron. Christmas music was already playing. Katy grinned. Christine would blast that stuff year-round if she could. Derek saw her enter and waved her over toward him.

"Ready for duty," she said.

Derek smiled. "Grab an apron. They're hanging on the hooks."

Katy reached for an apron and tied it snugly around her petite frame. She had put her hair up in a bun, out of her face, so she could maneuver around the floor better.

"How do you feel about cookies?" he said.

"I love cookies." A fluttering in her belly took off just looking at his guy. The fact that he had served their country kind of put another spin on him. It was sexy.

"Do you want to roll dough or cut out shapes?"

"I'll cut; you roll."

He nodded not saying much more. Soon they were in a rhythm of their own as another staff person was there picking up what Katy finished. Occasionally, Katy glanced over at him and noticed his strong, bulging biceps as he rolled and flipped the dough around for her. Her body was heating up as a bead of moistness trickled down her back. She couldn't believe she was having such a physical reaction to this man she'd just met. *What is going on?*

A couple of hours passed, and Christine walked up to them. "I'm closing in an hour. Thanks for helping, Katy. Why don't you quit and go home and take a bath or something? I'll be there shortly and will pick us up dinner. No more kitchen duty." She laughed. "Derek, can you make a delivery before you head home? It's to the Andersons. I know Sara will appreciate having all her pies and treats before tomorrow." Sara was Jim Anderson's long-time housekeeper. She turned to Katy. "Jim Anderson has invited us to Thanksgiving, and Sam is coming. You'll finally get to meet him."

"I can't believe we never made that happen this last year in New York on one of your visits."

"Well, you've been a busy gal."

"Yeah, it's totally my fault. I get it." Katy reflected on all the times she had canceled on Christine because of work or something else she was doing with Simon. Geez, she was a crappy friend.

"You're here now and that's what counts. Right, Derek?" She twisted her head to see his reaction.

"Yeah, I guess so. And you're pretty efficient at cutting out cookie shapes."

Is that a joke he just tried to make? "Why, thank you."

Christine shook her head. "See you all later. I've got to check on Mary Beth in the front and see if we've forgotten any orders. Thanks again. I'm anxious to close for the holiday." She scooted away at a fast clip.

Derek looked over at Katy. "Do you need a ride anywhere?"

"No, thank you. I drove. I think I remember how to get to Christine's house."

"Okay." He turned, removed his apron, and headed towards his office.

He's not very talkative but that's okay. Kind of refreshing not having to discuss anything about her personal life and be in the present moment—something she was sorely missing these days.

Chapter Three

Katy slid one more casserole dish into the back of the SUV and joined Christine in the front of the car. "Are you sure *you're* not the one hosting Thanksgiving dinner?" She tossed her curly brown hair back as she slid into the back seat.

"I can't help myself. I can't let Sara do all the work. Pies didn't seem enough." She threw her hands in the air, lifting her shoulders.

"That's why I love you." Sam leaned across the front seat, pecking her on the cheek.

Katy's heart fluttered as she watched Sam and Christine together. He had arrived last night for the weekend, and his display of affection for her cousin was non-stop. Yes, these two needed to be together on a more permanent basis. She was more than determined to help switch their situation around so that Christine could have the love she desired in her life.

Looking out the window as they drove along country roads, she ruminated on her own love life. *Will I ever find* the one? The muscles in her neck relaxed, as she took in the scenery, realizing how badly she needed this break. She ran circles around everyone at work, rarely taking time for herself. The fact that she had four weeks' vacation time accrued said it all.

"Here we are," Christine announced. She twisted her neck around to face Katy. "Did you ever come here during high school? I can't remember."

"Maybe. I think Maggy had a pool party while I was visiting you once, but this place is still blowing me away." Her eyes widened, taking in the grandeur of the mansion from the gilded age, its regal presence visible amongst the naked tree-lined road and perfectly manicured lawns.

"Let's go around to the kitchen door," said Christine. "It will be easier for Sara."

Sara was there to greet them, her cheery face beaming, and ushered all inside. "Christine, you overdid yourself," she said.

"I don't think you can overdo any amount of food on Thanksgiving." Christine laughed.

"I guess you're right," Sara said. "Everyone's in the living room." She turned to Katy. "And this must be Katy. My, you've certainly grown up from those summers you spent in Maple Ridge as a youngster."

"Yes, I have. Summers here are some of my best memories."

"Aren't they for all of us," Sara replied.

"Do you need help?"

"No, no. Join the others. I've got everything timed perfectly. We'll eat in an hour."

Katy followed Christine and Sam into the living room and watched several people scream, seeing Sam and her. A lovely woman her age with brown hair, ran over to him and hugged him. "I'm so glad you made it. I want to hear everything about New York, the show, and my friends."

Sam hugged the woman back. "Wouldn't miss this event for anything. And I will be back for the main event as well." He winked at her.

She blushed. "You better be. I'm so grateful the executive board agreed to make the Christmas special a pre-recorded event so my maid of honor could be here." She laughed thinking about her best friend, Jenny, still living and working in television in Manhattan.

Christine stepped in to make introductions. "My cousin Katy from Manhattan is staying with me for a month. This is Alison Rockwell, soon to be Alison Sanders. Hers is the wedding I was telling you about happening on Christmas Eve."

Katy extended her hand. "Nice to meet you. Congratulations."

"Thank you. My fiancée is over there." Alison pointed by the fireplace where Jake Sanders stood talking to his uncle Jim, the proprietor of the estate.

Katy's eyes fell on Jake, vaguely remembering him from her summers, but not before her gaze skimmed past the looming figure of Derek, standing next to a man she didn't know. Although she hadn't seen her in years, a woman she thought was Maggy Anderson slowly approached them.

"Katy Flanagan! Is that you?" Maggy asked. "Christine told me you were coming." She reached her arms around her in a gentle hug. "Are you happy to be out of the city?"

"Oh, yes. In more ways than one." Katy didn't want to share all the baggage in her life today and tried hard to calm her nerves from seeing people she hadn't seen in years and meeting new ones. She glanced over at Derek again. He saw her and waved. She lifted her hand, rolling her fingers in a nonchalant gesture. Why were butterflies tickling her insides?

She was about to make an excuse to find the bathroom when Maggy took her arm. "Come on. I want you to meet my fiancée, Mark. We're getting married in the spring—not to be confused with the

Sanders' wedding happening in three weeks!"

Maybe that's what was giving her angst. All this love-in-the-air stuff. Too much pressure and reflective confirmation that her love life was a disaster and nonexistent.

Maggy dragged her into an intimate circle with Mark and Derek.

"Mark, this is Katy, Christine's cousin, visiting here for a month. And you probably met Derek at the bakery, yes?"

Katy shook Mark's hand and glanced over at Derek. "Yes, we worked together a bit yesterday. Making cookies." She smiled at him, trying to be polite.

"Yeah, she's quite skilled with a cookie cutter," he said, his dimples lifting upwards.

"Wait until you see me with cake batter," Katy said. Her stomach was still skittish; she couldn't calm it down.

"What do you do in New York, Katy?" Mark asked.

"I work for a branding and marketing firm, Martin and Lewis."

"Do you like it?" Maggy asked.

"I do. I did. I guess I'm taking this little break to see if I want to continue at this company."

"Breaks are good. As I know," Maggy said, looking up at Mark with adoring eyes. "That's how I ended up back here permanently last spring, and I have no regrets, only gratitude."

Katy could feel Derek's gaze, penetrating her with a heated intensity that she was probably imagining. Maybe the rise in temperature was from her own inner desire. *Uh-oh.*

Katy held his stare. "What about you? How did you end up in Maple Ridge?"

Derek shuffled his feet, glanced down, then looked up. "I grew up in River Falls, the next town over. When I returned from Afghanistan,

I needed a job. This one appeared at the right time, and here I am." He paused. "Does anyone want a drink? I'm getting one." He fidgeted, putting his hands in his pocket.

All three declined since they already had one. Katy watched him walk away and turned to Maggy. "He's kind of shy, isn't he?" she asked.

"War will do that to a person. I don't think it's shyness but rather an uncomfortableness in social situations. I know. I went through a similar journey," Mark said.

"You're a veteran too?" Katy asked.

"Yep. I try to help veterans with PTSD and have a yoga class and support group running at the church. That's how I met Derek."

"Oh," Katy whispered, seeing a whole other side of this man she found intriguing.

Katy felt a slight tugging on her arm and looked down to see two adorable girls around ten years old gazing up at her. Mary Beth was standing behind them.

"Hi. I'm Annie, and this is Jolene. Welcome to the Andersons."

Katy bent over and shook their hands. "Hi. I'm Katy Flanagan. Christine's cousin from New York." She looked up at Mary Beth and smiled.

"Jolene is my sister," Mary Beth said.

Then two boys appeared in the group. "I'm Reggie and this is my buddy, Brandon."

Katy was surrounded by kids, which pulled her right out of her funk. "I think the party has begun!"

Sara entered the living room, ringing a small bell. "Attention everyone. Dinner is served."

Jim Anderson was the first one to reach her. "And you're taking that apron off and sitting with us. No buts." He lightly touched his hand on her shoulder.

She smiled at him. "Of course."

When everyone was seated, Katy found herself seated next to Derek with Christine on the other side of her. Place cards with their names had been previously set, and the kids had their own table in the corner.

As they passed dishes around the table, Katy smiled with each encounter she had with him. Christine was busy chatting away with Sam, so she knew she would have to start a conversation with him if there was to be one. Or she could eat in silence, which wasn't her style.

"Derek, do you like working at the bakery?" she asked. *Lame question.*

He nodded with his mouth full of food.

Okay. Stupid question while he's chewing. "I'm impressed with what Christine's accomplished with her business. I can't wait to find out more about it."

"Yeah, your cousin is awesome."

Let's try something else. "Who do all these kids belong to? Do you know?"

"Annie is Jake's daughter and lives next door in the cottage. Jolene is Mary Beth's sister and still lives at Fairside Manor, the orphanage on the outskirts of town. Reggie and his buddy live there, too; Mark has been preparing to become a foster parent to Reggie. Thus, they brought him here today."

Katy's heart felt a slight stirring at hearing about the orphanage. Christine had told her about the *Hands-On Beyond* program, which helps orphaned and foster care kids find jobs and housing after they turned eighteen. That's how Mary Beth ended up working for the bakery. She was one of the first recipients of the organization's fundraising efforts.

She nodded in response, her feelings swimming in circles. This trip was nothing like she thought it would be. But it did bring up questions. Where was she going in her life? What the hell did she want to do next? Nothing too heavy she mused.

After the meal and dessert, the ladies helped Sara clean up in the kitchen while the men and kids prepared for some fun and games in the library. Jim suggested they play charades since they would all get a chance to move around a bit after stuffing themselves.

They divided into two teams, and Katy found herself on the same team as Derek. She was curious as to how he would participate. Charades didn't seem to be his thing, based on observing his shyness or whatever it was that kept him from being a loud, social extrovert like herself. They were definitely opposites.

She settled her body into a couch, watching Dr. Mark dance around with his cues. A surge of competitiveness was bursting at the seams as she shouted her answer and took a win for the team. For the first time in a long time, she was having fun. Down to earth, belly-laughing fun. One day away from New York, she could see how she had allowed her life to become entangled entirely in her career with hardly any room for playing and amusement. Yes, she once loved her job but realized she had become imbalanced. And that was distressing to her. But she was here now in Maple Ridge and determined to dive deeper into her psyche and discover any lost dreams while she was here. Not too big a request, right? She giggled to herself.

Derek sat down next to her after he finished his turn.

"Nice job," she whispered.

"Yeah, I'm not too keen on social games but I'm giving it a try."

"Watch out. You might have fun." She grinned.

He looked over at Katy just as she was giggling to herself. "What's so funny?" he asked.

"Oh, nothing. I was thinking about something. About myself. I'm glad I took a break from my job; I'm looking forward to exploring Maple Ridge again and helping Christine."

Derek nodded.

When the games ended, everyone helped Sara clean up and pass out leftovers to those who were interested. Katy watched Derek as he wrapped things, took out trash, and helped Sara with all her needs. *My, isn't he helpful?*

Hugs and kisses were dispersed amongst the guests as they said goodbye, and Derek carried things out to Christine's car for her along with Sam. He hugged her and then turned to Katy. "See you tomorrow?"

"Yes, I'll be there. I don't know how early." She laughed and was aware of how close his body was to hers.

Derek opened his arms and gently put them around her in an innocent hug. "Happy Thanksgiving, Katy."

He released her, slowly letting go. She was totally taken by surprise. A friendly hug, yes, but the strength of his arms and the broadness of his chest seemed to stay on her body. Like they were one for an instant. "Yes, Happy Thanksgiving to you too." Moisture was forming on her forehead, her nerves betraying her. *What is happening?*

She climbed into Sam's SUV and watched Derek walk towards his truck and get in. She had to admit she might be developing a crush on this man. But men had let her down all her life, starting with her father, who was never there for her. She was a strong, independent woman ready to make a name for herself without men. *Yes, you don't need a crush now. Focus on the prize, girl.* And with that, she leaned back into the seat, observing the millions of stars shining in the dark sky outside, and prayed all would be taken care of better than she could ever imagine.

Chapter Four

Sunlight danced through the bedroom window, caressing Katy's cheeks as she opened her eyelids. Getting her bearings, she stretched her long legs under the silky sheets and sighed. Images of the previous evening swarmed her thoughts, but she kept coming back to the ones of Derek. He was a mysterious guy, no doubt. She was curious about him, but that was it.

After brushing her teeth, she went downstairs to the kitchen. She had slept in and was sure Christine had gone to the bakery early. That's what bakers do. Of course, coffee was brewed, and a note lay on the counter.

Good morning. I'm at work. Come in anytime. Remember this is your vacation too! Hope you slept well. xo Christine

Katy poured herself a cup of coffee and scoured the refrigerator for some fruit. She was still stuffed from last night. She grabbed her computer, found a comfy living room chair, and plopped down. Checking her phone, two messages popped up from Simon and two texts. Both messages said he missed her and hoped she had a great holiday. *Really?* After you broke up with me? This is the kind of stuff you're going to do? The texts asked her to call him. Maybe he was having trouble with an account. She didn't have enough caffeine ingested yet to engage with him. She put her phone down and decided to dig out the book she had brought to read from her suitcase instead of checking her email. Like before, not enough caffeine to endure New York drama at this time of day.

Once the caffeine kicked in, she checked her email, and found her assistant had a few easy questions to answer. Next, she'd walk down the country roads surrounding Christine's home, her lungs yearning for fresh air—something she sorely missed in the city. She had no desire to call Simon back and chuckled at how free she was beginning to feel.

Her legs pumped, her sneakers slapping the pavement as she inhaled the pine-scented air. Aahh, the Berkshires. Come Christmas, she'd be walking in the snow. The evergreens stood scattered amongst the woods, rolling hills still boasting traces of greenery. Suddenly, two deer appeared in front of her. Katy stilled; their eyes met in acknowledgment before the deer leaped back into the woods—an unexpected blessing. She gazed upwards, whispering, "Thank you."

As she returned to Christine's driveway, her phone pinged. She pulled it out. Simon. Again. *I better call him or else my phone will be buzzing all day.*

She grabbed a glass of water and sat on the couch, punching in his number, still on her favorites. *Need to change that.*

"Katy! Finally. I've been worried about you. At least you could have told me you arrived safely in Maple Ridge."

Really? "I'm fine, Simon. What do you want?" The sound of his voice pierced into her solar plexus causing the muscles in her neck to tighten. Rage, all over again, boiled up from her insides, trying to consume her.

"I'm sorry about how things ended with us, and I've been thinking. I'm willing to talk to William if you want me to. I don't want to lose you."

Katy shook her head. "I don't know, Simon. Maybe it's for the better. I didn't like how we ended either, especially the part where you took credit for my cause marketing idea with the Krafton account."

"We both discussed that when brainstorming. Don't you remember?" he asked.

"I remember bringing the idea to our session, with lots of implementation ideas included. You only agreed it was a good idea. Anyway, it's water under the bridge. I'm done discussing it."

"What about us, Katy?"

"What about us, Simon? There is no *us* anymore. Look, I have to go. Have a nice holiday. I'll see you in the office in the new year."

"Let's revisit this again in a week or two, alright?" he asked.

"Why? No thank you. Goodbye, Simon." And she hung up on him—couldn't help it. She grinned; that felt good.

Her phone pinged again. She let out an exasperated moan thinking it was Simon again, but it was Christine.

> Good morning! Hope you slept like a rock. Let me know when you are heading in here. Thanks.

> I'll be there in a half hour.

> No rush but great! See you then. Heart emoji.

> Thumbs up emoji.

Katy stretched her arms above her head as she stood up. A flashing image of Derek went through her brain, and a tiny shiver went up her spine, anticipating another encounter with him. She didn't even know him, so best to maintain a professional attitude, especially if she had to work with him at the bakery.

* * *

Derek bent over his desk reviewing the expansion's investment numbers. He was confident in his proposal and wasn't sure another person coming in at this point would be helpful. Christine told him that Katy would look at everything today and give her opinion on what might be missing. Whatever Christine wanted, he would do.

Sam had come in early with Christine to spend as much time together with her as possible. He needed to do some online work and had taken over her office. Christine waltzed in, put her arms around his neck while he sat typing, and kissed him on the cheek.

"Have I told you how much I love you today?" she asked.

Sam stopped typing and grabbed her hands in both of his large ones. He gently took one hand and kissed her palm. "Not as much as I love you," he said.

They heard a knock at the door and dropped their hands.

Katy pushed it open before they could say anything. "Oh, sorry. Did I interrupt you?"

Christine jumped over to her. "No, no. Come in. And thanks for coming in on your vacation day." The edges of her mouth lifted wide into her face.

"I'm reporting for duty. What do you need?"

"Let's meet with Derek. I want you to see the whole proposal, information on the investment team, and get your opinion on everything."

"I'll get out of your way," Sam said. "I want to visit Jake at the bookstore and pick up something new to read." He turned back to Christine. "Meet you for lunch?"

"Absolutely."

After he left, Katy said, "You two belong together. I'm determined to help you make this work. And besides, having my cousin closer would be a bonus. Although, I am quite fond of Maple Ridge too."

"Yes, I'll never give up my home here and would commute from time to time, but that's nothing compared to what we've been doing this past year. It hasn't been easy."

Katy could only imagine. She never had a real love worth fighting for in her life. And it certainly wasn't Simon.

"Let me get Derek. Be right back," Christine said. "We can sit at the table over here." She pointed to a small table pushed up against the wall with three chairs, big enough for them to hunker down at as they pored over material.

A few minutes later, Derek strolled in behind her, towering over them with his six-foot stature. His gaze penetrated Katy's for a fleeting moment as he greeted her and then sat down with his computer and a notebook.

"Show Katy what you have," Christine said.

Katy pulled her chair closer to him, the only way she could look at his computer screen over his shoulder. A droplet of perspiration rolled down her forehead; she wiped it away, embarrassed at her body's sudden insurrection.

She ignored the uprising and pulled herself together. *This project is for Christine.* She pulled herself up straighter, her determination building for the mission as she listened to Derek's calm, soothing voice. He had done an excellent job developing this idea and finding an investment opportunity for her cousin. And for that, she was grateful.

When he was done, he sat back in the chair awaiting her response.

"You've done your homework, and all your numbers seem to align." She paused. "But how will you set yourself apart from the other competitors? Have you thought about that?"

Christine and Derek looked at each other. They hadn't discussed that.

"We have been focused on the bottom-line financials and how the investors can make money," Derek said.

"That's important, but with a competition, I think you need to develop your brand and what makes you stand out." She stopped.

"Well, most investors only care about making money," Derek said.

"True, but where's the heart of your proposal? That's what often tilts a win in your direction."

Derek furrowed his brow.

Christine could see he was irritated, and Katy had pushed his buttons. "Why don't you think about it, Katy, and come up with some ideas to show us? Right, Derek?"

"Sure. Let me know when you're ready." He stood up. "I'll be in my office." He closed his computer, turned abruptly, and was out the door before Katy could say a word.

"What just happened?" she asked.

"I think he took your advice the wrong way. I know Derek, and he'll get over it. He'll probably be outside taking a break."

"Did I sound like a Miss Know-it-all? Or is he just an overly sensitive guy?"

"I'm not sure, Katy. But don't worry about it. Here's the print-out of our proposal. You can use this for your research and use my office for a couple hours. I'm meeting Sam for lunch."

Katy took the papers, got her computer, and spread her things on the small table. Her hands were trembling, thinking she had insulted Derek somehow. *Man, my pushy little self can't stay quiet, can I?* Katy hoped she could talk it out with him later, especially if they had to work together to help Christine.

* * *

The invigorating, cold air filled Derek's lungs as his feet hit the pavement, walking around the block. Who was this woman? Did she know anything about business? Just because she had an important job at some fancy firm in New York didn't make her an expert about investment opportunities. Katy had pushed a button, but had he misinterpreted it? She was only trying to help, but he had to admit, she was a little full of herself. Was his job threatened? No. She was only here temporarily. Did she have some skills? Yes. Then why wasn't he welcoming her into the mix? Maybe it had nothing to do with the bakery at all. He pulled his hoodie over his head, picked up the pace, and headed toward the bakery. The investors were coming Monday, and there was no longer time to mull around in his crap. *Keep your eye on the prize for Christine, man. That's all you have to do.*

He came in through the back, passing Christine's office which was closed. He found Christine on the floor and pulled her aside.

"Hey, I'm sorry if I was so abrupt earlier," he said.

Christine reached her hand out on his arm. "Don't worry about it. This little project has us both on edge with the stakes so personal for me. I think you've absorbed all my anxiety." She chuckled. "I want this to work, but not at the expense of our health. Remember that. On another note, I'll be back later. I'm meeting Sam for lunch and shopping afterward. Big sales today."

"Have fun."

"I told Katy we'd meet at the end of the day to see what she came up with. Is that okay with you?"

"Absolutely. I'll try hard to keep my emotions in check and not lash out at the spunky little woman."

She grinned at his comment. "Okay. See you later." And she left.

* * *

Katy took a break from her research, stood up, and stretched her body in the tiny office. Fresh air was calling. She grabbed her coat and walked out the back door to avoid Derek. She wasn't ready to see him yet, especially if his moodiness was still volatile. She enjoyed the competitive battle with most guys at work; she had thrived on it. She usually was the smarter one in the room and had no problem letting others know. Her arrogant self-assuredness had gotten her to the top. Until it didn't. A twinge in her heart reminded her of the recent loss. She should have had that creative director position, and Mr. Lewis knew it. *Screw him.*

She walked around Main Street briefly and returned to the bakery. She stood outside and looked at the window display glimmering with holiday decorations Mary Beth had put out in the morning. The whole street was beginning to look like a Christmas wonderland. The residents of Maple Ridge didn't waste any time getting into the holiday spirit. The bells jingled as she entered, and Mary Beth waved to her.

"The décor in front looks fantastic," Katy said.

"Thanks. I like doing that kind of thing." She filled a box with croissants for a waiting customer.

Katy walked around the counter. "Where's your little sister?"

"She's at Fairside. I took her back this morning. She was so happy to have a sleepover with me. We don't get to do that often. I was lucky my roommate went away for the holiday with her cousin in Boston."

Katy nodded. She had no siblings, but her friendship with

Christine meant the world to her. "When you have a chance, can we talk about Fairside? I would like to know more about the *Hands-On Beyond* program and how it affected you. It's for our proposal we're working on for the possible bakery expansion."

Mary Beth's eyes lifted to meet hers. "Sure. I'll come back in about fifteen minutes."

"Perfect. Thank you." Katy had an idea brewing, but it wasn't solidified yet. She needed more research and quiet time to think.

As she passed Derek's office, the door opened, and he instantly was standing over her. "Oh, hi," she said.

"Hi."

"Just went for a walk to clear my head." *Should I apologize for coming on so strong?*

"Listen ...," they chimed at the same time, which caused them both to laugh.

"Ladies first," Derek said.

"No, go right ahead," she said.

Derek straightened his six-foot frame, his body weight shifting. "I'm sorry if I was so short earlier. I know you're only trying to help." He paused. "Sorry for being a jerk."

"No, I'm sorry. I know I come on strong sometimes. Well, all the time." She grinned. "I think your plan is solid, and from a business perspective, it's tight. I have other skills that might help enhance the pitch. I hope you don't think I was trying to bulldoze you."

Derek was quiet momentarily, then tilted his head. "No worries. Let's just work together. We all want the same thing. To help Christine's business and to bring Sam and her together on a more permanent basis. I think our goals are clear, don't you?"

She found herself getting lost in his dark eyes, his wavy unkempt hair hanging above the brow, and his muscular frame inches from her.

"Yes, very clear." Why was she having difficulty speaking now? Nothing else seemed to come out. "Alright then. Back to my computer. See you later." She turned, headed towards Christine's office but all the while sensed his eyes following her. Chills flooded her nerves before she closed the door behind her.

Chapter Five

A waft of frigid air burst through the back door as Christine and Sam entered. They opened Christine's office door to find Katy hunched over her computer and papers strewn on the table.

She looked up. "Hi, guys. Don't mind my mess."

"Of course not. That means you're working hard." Christine chuckled.

"I think I'll take my computer and go back to the house to work until you ladies are finished. It's getting a little crowded in here." Sam reached for his stuff and pecked Christine on the cheek. "See you for leftovers later?"

She nodded as she squeezed his hand. "See you then."

After he left, Katy said, "Have fun?"

"Always," Christine said. "I'm so blessed that he walked into my bakery a year ago. We're both excited about my potential move to New York. There's no way he could have moved here unless he gave up being a director. I would never ask that of him. He'd be miserable doing anything else."

"You're right. Artists must pursue their passions to live a happy life." She paused. "I'm not sure I know what makes me happy anymore. I thrive on the fast pace of corporate marketing and branding, new clients, competition, and campaigns. But being here for a few days makes me question if my job truly makes me happy. The creative director position would have catapulted me to a new level where I could put my artistic skills to good use. But without it, I don't know if I want to be part of the hamster wheel, spinning around wildly to make things happen. Especially if I have to report to my ex, Simon." She ran her fingers through her hair with manicured nails sporting ruby red and sighed.

"Don't worry. That's what this vacation is for—to become still enough to hear your own thoughts and befriend your muse again."

"You're right. No more waddling in my junk." She shuffled her papers into a neat pile.

"Are you ready to meet?"

"Yep, at least for a preliminary discussion. I saw Derek earlier, and we both apologized to each other."

"Good. The two of you need to work together."

Two minutes later Derek's commanding physique spread across the doorway. "Here I am." His steadfast eyes gravitated to Katy's and held without wavering.

Her cheeks filled with heat, and she looked away. A visible tremor infiltrated her fingers as she moved the computer and made space for the two of them.

Christine spoke first. "Tell us your ideas, Katy. Did you come up with anything?"

"We know the financials are solid." She nodded towards Derek, acknowledging him. She had learned her lesson. "But if we are to stand out in the competition, I have an idea." She opened her screen. "I've experimented with cause marketing with some of my clients and have succeeded with these campaigns. Basically, we team up and give a proportion of proceeds to a chosen non-profit organization, and in doing so, both parties benefit. The business side looks good, gets a tax write-off, and the charity receives funds and recognition. It's a win-win situation for all." She waited for a response.

"How does it work with this proposal?" Derek asked. "I admit, I like the concept."

"You have a story already built into your operation with *Hands-On Beyond*. One of your star employees, Mary Beth, has a wonderful story to tell about how she got her job and what it means to her. I'd suggest teaming up with them. That's our heart of the pitch, together with all the scrumptiousness Sweet Ridge would bring to New York from a country bakery."

Christine clapped her hands together. "Alison would be thrilled with this idea. We all do what we can around here, but this would bring exposure to the program in the city where there are countless youth facing a difficult situation."

"I'm even thinking as you scout for your location this week, try to imagine a small, satellite office for the organization off the back of your kitchen somewhere. In case it takes off. That's something to discuss with Alison, but part of your rent would be a tax write-off as well."

"This is brilliant, Katy." Christine jumped up and hugged her.

"Don't thank me yet. I still have work to do for a presentation. Can one of you go with me to Fairside tomorrow? And give me Alison's number? I will need to speak to her."

"Of course. Let's call together. Jake gave her office space upstairs above Starlight Books, his bookstore. She's usually there, although she's been busy with her wedding plans."

"I can take you to Fairside tomorrow, if you like," Derek offered.

"That's your day off, Derek," Christine said.

"I don't mind. I think we must ramp up our efforts before the investors arrive on Monday.

Katy looked at Christine and then Derek. "Okay. I'd appreciate it. I want to see the source and inspiration for the organization. Can we call the director?"

"Yes, that would be Karen. Let's make those calls now."

Derek stood up. "I'm going to leave you two and go on the floor. Christine, do you mind if I box up some cookies for the veteran's home? I wanted to stop by there after work."

"Of course. Put in some of those gingerbread ones too. They're always a hit."

"Thanks." He grabbed his computer and left.

"I'm glad to see you two are getting along," Christine said.

"Yeah, I guess we both can push each other's buttons, but I think we resolved it." She grabbed her notepad for the call. "What *home* was he talking about?" Katy asked.

"On Fridays he likes to stop by this veteran's nursing home on the edge of town and drop off treats. He's a very giving man underneath that rough, quiet solitude."

"Vets? I guess he does have a heart."

"He and Dr. Mark, Maggy's fiancé, try to do as much as possible for the veterans in this part of the state." She went back to her desk and picked up her phone. "Let's make those phone calls."

Katy conjured up an image of Derek in army fatigues and saw him in another light. *What other secrets does he have?*

* * *

Karen, the director of Fairside Manor, and Alison, the director of *Hands-On Beyond*, were thrilled at the prospect of another fundraising campaign for the after-foster-care and orphanage program. They could use all the money they could get.

Katy shut down her computer and rubbed her neck with her fingers, trying to relax the tightness lodged there. Her stomach rumbled; perhaps a cookie was calling her.

She entered the bakery floor and glanced around until she saw Derek taking a tray out of the oven. Fresh chocolate chip cookies—perfect.

As she approached, Derek looked up. "Are you eyeing my cookies?"

She smiled. "Just one?"

"Help yourself. They're hot." He handed her a paper towel.

Murmurous noises came out of Katy's throat as she swooned over the heated dough and velvety chocolate oozing into her mouth.

"That good, huh?" he said. His dimples pushed into his cheeks.

She nodded. She didn't want to stop eating it to talk.

"How are you not as big as a horse working here?" she asked. "This whole thing ..." She gestured with her hand in a sweeping motion. "Would be too much for me. I have a sweet tooth that's insatiable."

"Good to know," he said, winking at her.

Did he just wink at me? Is he flirting? No, couldn't be. "Are these for your veterans?" she asked.

"Yep. Almost done." He pointed to another pink box on the counter. "Those are packed."

"Do you need help?"

"Grab another box for some of these. Thanks." He kept his head down.

She bent over the counter to where there were flat containers, pulled one out, and began to assemble it. When finished, she placed it next to him. "There you go."

"Thanks."

"Do you want company on your excursion? Christine is spending time with Sam, and I don't want to bother them." What was she doing? She didn't need to spend any more time with this man.

"Sure, if you want. The old guys always appreciate a pretty face—much better than mine."

She blushed, then stammered, "Okay then. Let me get my things."

"I can pick you up at Christine's. I have to drive past there, and I'll bring you right back. Don't worry. But I do socialize a bit, not too long."

He actually socializes? This she has to see. "Sounds like a plan. Let me give you my number, and you can text me when you leave here."

"It will be soon. Mary Beth is closing today."

Katy's phone rang, and she pulled it out of her jeans pocket. Simon. Again. She'd call back later.

Derek looked at her but didn't ask anything.

She looked at him and smiled. "I'll see you soon."

As she sat in her car, warming up the engine, she listened to Simon's voicemail.

"Hey, Katy. I do have a question about the Krafton case. Can you call me back? It's kind of important."

She tapped her fingers on the steering wheel—Simon would have to wait. She put the car in reverse and drove away.

* * *

Katy's reflection in the mirror stared back at her. What was she doing? She was on vacation. That's what she was doing. With that thought, she pulled out her cosmetics bag and touched up her make-up, combed her thick, curly hair that easily went awry, and went downstairs to wait for Derek.

Christine had left her a message. Even with a refrigerator full of leftovers, Sam had insisted on taking her out for a romantic dinner. She sighed, thinking about their relationship. Had she ever felt that kind of love with a man? No. At times, she thought Simon could be the one, but their relationship was too entwined with their careers and look where that got her.

She peeked out the curtains in the dining room just as Derek pulled up in his massive Chevy Silverado truck with a double cab. Of course, he's got a truck. What rugged, country man didn't have a truck?

She flew out the front door before he could get out, but he did manage to open the truck door for her.

"Quite the gentleman, I see," she said.

"I try." He tipped his hat towards her in a jesting manner.

He reached over and turned up the heat. "Warm enough for you?"

"Perfect."

He turned the radio up and a song from the Zac Brown band came blaring through.

"Do you mind country?"

"No, that's fine." He definitely is a considerate man. Country music suits him—a little rough around the edges and a heart of gold. She smiled to herself.

As he pulled out of the driveway he said, "What's so funny?"

"Nothing." Two could play at this game. She could keep her conversation to a minimal but truthfully, it was killing her. She wanted to ask so many questions. Being a chatty person was second nature to her and holding it in was excruciating.

He let it go and didn't speak the entire time on their way to the veteran's home. *Doesn't he want to know more about me?* She turned her head to gaze out the window, so he wouldn't see her chuckle again. Silence was a foreign entity.

As he pulled into the driveway, Katy's shoulders released. Thank God. Not being herself was causing stress. New change of plans. She was going to be as chatty as she wanted and not worry if she said something wrong or pushed his buttons. The ride had been an experiment, and she had all the results she needed. Time to be herself even if it got her into trouble.

"Here we are." He jumped out of the truck and reached into the back seat for the pink boxes. The whole cab permeated an aroma of melted chocolate and sugar.

Katy joined him on the sidewalk. "I'll follow you."

A visitor was coming out of the door as they approached and held it open for them. "Thanks," Derek said. "Let me check in with the front desk; then we'll go to the recreation room. That's where they gather most of the time."

She noticed he had an extra smaller box with him. "Who's that for?"

"You'll see," he said.

As she followed him, she looked around the facility seeing a glass vase of sweeping seasonal flowers on a table in the foyer, its fresh appeal welcoming those who entered. Nurses and other staff scurried around taking care of patients, wheeling them around or slipping their hands into the crook of a man's arm to help him walk. Men and a few women of all ages were scattered around the recreation room. Some were chatting with each other and playing cards, and a few were watching television. When the residents saw Derek, their faces lit up and soon gathered around him.

"Didn't think I'd forget you guys, did you?" Derek placed the boxes on a table next to a coffee pot, always holding fresh coffee for its residents.

One older gentleman nearing eighty patted Derek's back. "I had faith in you." And then laughed heartily.

Soon a few of the guys were standing around him chatting, and he motioned to her to come closer. "I'd like you to meet a friend of mine, Katy. She's Christine's cousin and is visiting from New York for the holidays."

She watched as one of the guys whistled and his brow lifted.

"Are you sure she's not more than a friend?" He winked at Derek and held out his hand to her. "Nice to meet you. I'm Walter. Call me Wally for short. We look forward to Derek's visits. We all have a sweet tooth." Using a cane, he hobbled over to the table to retrieve a cookie.

She scanned the room as more veterans approached the table, but some couldn't get up without assistance.

"I'm going to take a box around to the others. Can you grab some napkins?" he asked.

Katy walked behind him, offering napkins to those who took a cookie. Circling the room, they arrived back to their original spot.

"Sometimes I hang out with the guys, but let's take this box to my other friend."

Katy's heart was aflutter. Watching him be talkative and open with these veterans made her see a whole other side to this mysterious man. He was smiling, laughing, and talking with ease. Very different than in the bakery or at the Anderson's home the night before.

Derek stopped at a room down the corridor and rapped gently before he opened it. In the corner was a young man, probably early thirties, sitting up in a hospital bed. "Hey, Nick. Look what I brought you." He held up the small pink box.

The man had a goofy grin on his face and when he spoke the words were partially slurred. "Thank you."

"I brought a friend with me today. Meet Katy," he said.

"Pretty," Nick said.

She blushed but came closer. "Nice to meet you." She didn't shake hands because he had no hands, only bandaged stumps.

Derek pulled up a chair, took out a cookie, and began feeding him. Watching Nick smile, he said, "Pretty good, eh?"

Nick nodded and chewed.

Derek turned his head to see Katy standing behind him. "Pull up a chair." He pointed to one in the corner, light enough for her to move.

Compassion wrapped around her heart as she watched him feeding Nick and making jokes. Her heart was pushing against her chest, its size expanding, watching Derek's kindness.

When finished, Derek gave him sips of water through a straw. They chatted for a bit about trivial things until Derek could see he was tired. "Anything else you need, buddy?"

Nick said, "No." He reached out his arm and Derek placed his hand over the bandage and shook it where his hand used to be.

"Alright, soldier. I'll be back soon to see you. The weather's getting cold but next time I'll get you in a chair and take you for a spin. How does that sound?"

Nick's face lit up. "Good."

"See you then." Derek turned and signaled for Katy to get up. He took her chair and placed it back in the corner.

She turned to Nick. "Nice to meet you."

Nick smiled and waved his arm to her in goodbye.

She lifted her fingers, fanning them out into a wave.

Derek was quiet as they walked out towards the truck. He opened the door for her and came around to the driver's seat. He started the ignition and then turned to her. "Are you okay?"

Her stomach was queasy from witnessing the wounded men and women inside the facility. Realizing what war could do to a person made her feel slightly ashamed of her privileged life. *What am I doing to help others?* Nothing. Unless you count on helping a major corporation get more recognition, income, and status in the business world. Somehow, that didn't feel like what she had just witnessed with Derek.

"Yeah, I guess so. Seeing those veterans put me in a reflective mood, I guess." She paused. "What happened to Nick?"

"Mortar shell hit in Afghanistan. He's partially paralyzed and as you see, has no hands. He also has a traumatic brain injury which has simplified his mind somewhat. If he was with it more mentally, he'd probably be more depressed. But he's like a little kid now. Everything excites him—especially homemade cookies."

"Does he have any family?" she asked.

"Just his mom. His sister is married, has a family of her own, and lives in California. That's the sad thing. If they had money for private care, he might be able to live at home, get a motorized wheelchair and be more independent with therapy. But his mother doesn't have those means, so he'll be here for the rest of his life. At least the veteran's administration takes care of the bills."

She nodded.

"Didn't mean to bring you down. I'm used to all of this. I forget how others might feel for the first time when they experience the personal repercussions of war."

"No, it's okay. In fact, I'm glad I came with you. I'd like to do it again sometime."

He turned, holding her gaze. "Okay." He put the truck in reverse and headed for the main road. "Let's get you home."

She peered out at the trees passing by in the darkness. Something was stirring inside her heart, and she didn't know what it was or what it meant. *Do I need a change in my life?* Obviously. But how, what, and where was clear as mud. Only time will tell.

Chapter Six

Beads of sweat rolled down Derek's face as he dug out broken branches and leaves still left in the shrubbery and garden plots around Mark's house. After Mark bought the house from the previous doctor this summer, he offered the upstairs apartment to Derek.

"Hey, man. How's it going back here?" Mark asked. He strode up next to him, surveying his work. "I appreciate you helping me on your day off."

"No problem. I live here too."

"I guess you do." Mark picked up a twig and threw it into the trash container next to them. "I hear you're taking Christine's cousin to Fairside today. How's it going with the proposal? Do you think she'll be able to help?"

"I don't know. She has a good idea about cause marketing. We'll see."

"Do you two get along?"

"Now we do. We started off on the wrong foot. She pushed my buttons—flared up like an enraged bull. I got defensive but put myself back together with a walk around the block."

"Do you know why you reacted?"

"I don't like being told what to do; I took her suggestion as criticism to my plan. All on me."

"I'm impressed. I guess all those therapy sessions are paying off." Mark laughed and slapped him on the back.

"Yeah. But I did react rudely at first. We worked it out. That's all I can ask for now."

"I understand. Let's clean up. This is good enough. We don't have to look at this yard again until spring."

Mark picked up the rakes while Derek put the last of the lawn scraps into the trash.

"Maggy and I are picking up Reggie for lunch and taking him to visit a nearby art gallery."

"That's nice. Did you make a final decision to foster him?"

"I think so. He'll live here with me until Maggy and I get married. We finalize the papers after Christmas," Mark replied.

"He's a lucky guy."

"I think we are the lucky ones. He's an awesome kid."

Derek nodded and hauled the trash can closer to the garage. Taking off his work gloves, he brushed off his jacket. "I need a shower. Catch you later?"

"I'll be around." Mark paused. "And Derek, if you need to talk before group next week, don't hesitate to call me."

"Will do." He bounded up the stairs to his apartment and couldn't deny the adrenalin running through his veins at the thought of spending more time with Katy—that vibrant, confident woman with wavy brown hair, enticing chocolate eyes, long eyelashes, and a killer body. It had been over a year since he had been with a woman. His old girlfriend broke up with him about six months after his return from duty, saying he was too irritable, angry, and unable to communicate in an intimate relationship. And she was right. Eventually, he found help and was finally getting his life back on track.

And the thought of a woman in it was very appealing.

* * *

Katy twirled in front of the mirror. Her skinny jeans and soft cashmere sweater hugged her body in all the right places, and her knee-high heeled boots gave her another inch. There was no snow yet, so she could still wear them and not fall. She giggled.

When she heard Derek's truck pull up, she grabbed her purse and notebook, and flew down the stairs. Christine and Sam had left hours ago, probably both at the bakery, but she had stayed home to do research in the quietude of an empty house.

The doorbell rang, and she opened it. "Hi." *Damn, he's good-looking.*

"Hi," he said. "Ready?"

"Yep." She locked the house, and Derek held the door as she climbed into the truck, still running, so it was warm. *Very thoughtful.*

"How was your morning?" he asked.

Did he just start a conversation with me? "Good. I spent most of the morning doing research for us on different cause marketing campaigns. Do you think the investors will tell us who our competition is?"

"I don't know. We can ask."

"That would help. How many are in the running?"

"I think they are narrowing it down to two or three by the end of the week. I heard him mention one bakery in Vermont vying for the money. Others I don't know."

Katy was silent, stirring inside with ideas. "I'm looking forward to seeing Fairside and talking more with Alison. She's meeting us there."

"Okay."

Nothing more was said between them. Katy was starting to understand that he dwelled on periods of silence more than talking. In a way, it was more intimate than chatting away at meaningless conversation. Learning to be present in the silence was an attribute she wished she could acquire.

As they pulled into Fairside's driveway, her jaw dropped. It was a massive old Victorian mansion similar to the Anderson Estate, with visible additions to the side and back of the main house. The manicured grounds and surrounding trees exuded a stately feel and certainly not one of a run-down facility. At least these kids were blessed with a beautiful place to live.

"This is awesome," she said.

"I know."

Karen, the director, and Alison were there to greet them both as they entered.

"Come in out of the cold," Karen said. "Let's go in my office, then Alison will give you a tour."

"Thanks," Katy said. She glanced around at the mahogany beams and staircase leading to the second floor and the polished wood floor. Everything was sparkling clean, and the recreation room was quite lively since it was Saturday.

The four of them sat down, and Katy opened her computer. She described what a cause marketing campaign looked like and showed examples. When she finished, she caught Derek staring at her intensely. She hoped he was okay that she was taking over his project, but she didn't see any signs of annoyance. Yet.

Karen clapped her hands together. "This is genius. Right, Alison?"

"This reminds me of how I felt last year when we first concocted *Hands-On Beyond*. And Christine is okay with giving a portion of proceeds to our non-profit?" Alison asked.

"Yes. It won't be from the entire bakery but from one signature item. Most likely something with gingerbread. What do you think, Derek?"

"Yeah, gingerbread is our biggest seller, both in the store and online."

"I'm thinking, maybe we do small gingerbread items in the shape of hearts and call it the *Hearts for Hope* campaign. We need a tag line to connect it to *Hands-On Beyond* but that should be easy enough," Katy said.

"I love it!" Karen exclaimed.

"Me too," Alison said.

Katy looked at Derek. He smiled at her so that must mean he approves too. She was learning to read him.

"I have to tell Christine, but I'm pretty sure she'll be on board with everything."

"I'm sure she will," Derek said.

"I'll talk to her tonight. I'd love that tour now."

"Come on." Alison stood up and pushed in her chair. "You can meet some of the kids too."

Katy followed Alison with Derek behind her. When they entered the recreation room, a little girl with her hair in braids came rushing up to Derek.

"Hi, Derek." She hugged him.

"Hey, Jojo. What are you working on?" He had noticed construction paper, glue, glitter, and an array of craft items spread out on a table.

"Christmas decorations for the manor. Want to help?" she asked.

Derek turned to Katy. "This is Jolene, Mary Beth's sister. Remember her from Thanksgiving?"

Katy bent down coming to eye level with her. "Yes. Let's see what you're making."

All three went over to the tables and observed the festive activity.

"I think I'll hang out here with Jolene for a bit. I've seen the manor. You go ahead with Alison," Derek said. He didn't wait for an answer and took a seat next to the kids.

"We'll be back," she said. Derek was already engaged in making a snowflake and didn't respond.

Alison and Katy meandered around the house and outside on the grounds so that she could see the bungalows built for older children. Alison discussed the program Karen had started for after foster care and kids aging out of orphanages and how *Hands-On Beyond* had grown beyond her wildest expectations. "It's turning into a national program, and I'm busting out of my office space at the bookstore upstairs. Jake might have to build me my own addition." Alison laughed.

Katy's heart swelled as she watched the expressions on the children's faces, their joy, and their shyness, and on some, their sadness.

They circled around to the rec room again, and Katy stared at Derek. His laughter and full-toned voice resounded against the walls and kids were giggling all around him. *Vets and kids must bring out the best in him.*

She sat down at the table. "I guess I'll join you."

Jolene pushed some materials in front of her. "Here you go. Make anything you want."

Katy caught Derek glancing at her and smiled at him.

He held up one stellar snowflake attached to a yarn for hanging. "Not bad, huh?"

Katy grinned. "I don't know if I can top that."

"I've got to run," Alison said. "Jake and I have a tasting with the caterer this afternoon. I can't believe the wedding is three weeks away. Call me if you have questions."

"I will," Katy said.

Sitting alone with the kids and Derek, she tried to busy herself with cutting and pasting to keep the butterflies in her stomach from raging up a storm. *Chemistry is definitely brewing with the man across the table.*

After an hour, Karen appeared at their side. "I need to run an errand. Feel free to stay as long as you like." She whispered to Katy. "These kids are starving for attention."

"Okay." A sinking feeling in her stomach replaced the jitters. Looking around, she studied the faces of the kids around her. Even with an emotionally absent father and deceased mother, Katy had a secure home life. Her dad had at least seen to that. Summers in Maple Ridge with Christine made up for lonely nights and days during the school years after her mom died. And when she turned eighteen, the money was there for college and her first apartment. *I guess he did the best he could.* The fear plaguing some of these kids turning eighteen had to be overwhelming.

Derek lifted out of his chair with several snowflakes in hand. "Let's hang these up."

Kids cheered, and an assistant brought over a ladder. He walked over to a wall as directed and started hanging up ornaments with the bunch. Jolene gave him instructions, and everyone was anxious to get their piece up for display.

As Christmas music played in the background, Katy stopped and watched. She brushed a hair out of her eyes and sighed. This was fun. She was having genuine, laugh-hardy fun. She never did any volunteer work in New York—only her own work. She spent her spare time with Simon, usually for meals or an occasional show or gallery exhibit. And primarily for work projects, even on the weekends. Hanging out in Maple Ridge, she was starting to see there was more to life.

Derek climbed down from the ladder and stood to inspect the work with kids on either side of him. "Looks pretty good."

The kids clapped, and a couple of them hugged him. He reached down and tousled one boy's hair who seemed to know him.

"Can you come back and help us more?" Jolene asked. Her eyes grew wide, her fearlessness unwavering.

"I think we can arrange that." He motioned to Katy. "Are you ready to hang that up?"

"Yes." She stood up and handed him her creation.

"How about here?" He was tall enough to hang it without the ladder and gestured to an open spot on the wall.

"Perfect."

"Looking good guys. I'll be back another time. You have many walls to do yet." He laughed.

Guess that's our cue we're leaving.

The kids were redirected to snacks and juice being served in the cafeteria, so everyone quickly cleaned up. Derek swung his arm towards the front door. "Ready?"

"Yes. Let me pick up my things in Karen's office."

Derek waited for her at the door and held it open as she approached. After both climbing into the truck, he said, "What do you think?"

"I'm blown away and feel rather emotional seeing all these kids without families. And the older ones—no one to help them survive. That's tough. I'm anxious to get back to work on the proposal. Should we work tomorrow since the investors are coming on Monday?" Keep it professional. Keep those feelings penned up.

"Sure. I had planned to meet with Jake tomorrow afternoon at the bookstore. He has an MBA in business and is going to help me tweak my numbers." He turned on the ignition and pulled out of the parking lot.

"Text me a time and I'll bring my computer."

He nodded and went into silent mode. As they pulled into Christine's driveway, she turned to him. "Thank you for today. Now I have a whole other perspective on the importance of this campaign. If we pull this off, it will be a win-win for so many people including Christine."

"We'll pull it off." He lingered in her gaze.

She grinned at him and jumped out. Stopping on the porch, she twisted around and waved goodbye. Her emotions seemed to spiral, her jumbled-up feelings spinning like a whirlwind. She needed a glass of wine—and some serious introspection.

Chapter Seven

Katy tucked her cashmere scarf closer around her neck against the frigid air as she followed Christine and Sam into the church. She rarely went to church in New York. Her Sunday mornings were consumed by coffee and the New York Times with Simon. He was Jewish, not religious, and would probably never be a partner in any spiritual endeavors she might have pursued. But today, she was going to the Maple Ridge place of worship where most town residents would be. *Would Derek be here?*

She slid into a pew next to them and glanced around. Derek was sitting tall, hands in his lap, in the next aisle over. He turned as if knowing she was looking at him and smiled. She waved as a fluttering in her stomach took over. Oh my god. She *was* crushing on him.

Reverend Michael's voice rang out strong and clear, delivering a message of the importance of nurturing gratitude in the upcoming holiday season. Katy let the words sink into her soul as her body dipped into the hardness of the wooden seat, trying to deflect any other distracting messages coming into her brain. Especially ones about the man across the aisle.

When the service was over, the three of them walked out to join others mingling in the crispness of a cold morning.

Christine turned to Katy. "Sam is leaving after lunch. I'll try and join you and Derek at Starlight Books on time."

"Okay," Katy said.

"Good morning." A voice from behind resonated into Katy's ear.

She turned around and came within inches of Derek's body leaning towards her. She could smell a faint hint of musk and spice radiating from him which sent her butterflies into a tailspin.

"Hi," she said.

"Are you still coming today?" he asked.

"Yes."

Christine spoke up. "I'll be there too. Sam and I are going to brunch before he leaves for New York. We squeeze in every moment we can."

Derek chuckled. "Yeah, I know this distance thing is wearing a toll on you guys but remember—there's hope!"

Christine side-hugged him. "Yes. Thanks for the reminder."

They turned to leave, and Katy found herself standing alone with Derek again. She shifted her feet back and forth. Should she say goodbye and walk away? Her feet seemed cemented to the ground.

"Do you like pancakes?" Derek asked.

"Who doesn't like pancakes?" She laughed.

"I'm headed out to a vet canteen for breakfast. Would you like to come?"

Is this a date? Heat inched its way up her neck.

"I mean, we can talk more about our project," he added.

Phew. This is work. That's okay. "Sure. I'm starving. Food and work are two of my favorite things if you haven't noticed already." *Keep it light, girl.*

"My truck is over there." He pointed to the parking lot.

"Lead the way."

They walked without speaking, soon cruising down a winding road through pines and bare maples, their majestic branches stretching toward an azure blue sky. His country music played in the background, and Katy was more comfortable amidst his silent interludes. She took the time to admire the scenery of woods with naked trees and the last of faded greenery and looked forward to seeing a blanket of snow covering the rolling hills and mountains in the near future.

"I hope it snows soon," she said.

"You do?"

"It must be magical when it does. I didn't spend much time here during the winters, mostly in the summers."

"It can be treacherous at times, but you're right. It is a sight to behold." He steered his truck into a lot. "Here we are."

When they walked inside, she scanned the room, noticing quite a lively bunch of men and women seated at square tables flaunting red-checked tablecloths and photos of veterans in uniform from different wars lining the walls. The whiff of cooked bacon floating through the air was intoxicating.

Derek guided her to an empty table, greeting those he knew along the way. "How's this?" he asked.

"Perfect."

An older woman with a plump waistline and curly short hair approached their table. "How's it going, Derek? What can I get you two?"

"The special as usual."

"And who's this lovely lady?"

Derek introduced Katy to her. "We're working on a project together for Christine. She lives in New York."

"Nice to meet you," Katy said. "I'll take the same."

A couple of older guys came over to the table to say hello to him but were more interested in the woman sitting with Derek.

Katy shook hands, smiled, and again noticed a different side of Derek when he was in a social situation with other veterans. The camaraderie was a safe place for him where he let his defenses down and seemed to be more comfortable in his skin. She liked this side of the man.

During breakfast, her phone pinged as it sat on the table next to her. Simon. She glanced down at it.

Call me please. It's important.

Derek saw the name. "Text if you need to. No worries. I won't be offended." He grinned.

"Okay. It's probably just a work thing."

Will do later. I'm busy now.

Simon responded. **Okay.**

"Everything alright?" he asked.

"Yeah. Just work. I think."

Derek decided not to pry. "What do you think of the food?"

"Best blueberry pancakes ever. Thanks for inviting me."

"I knew Christine would be off with Sam. It's their regular routine when he's here."

"Watching them together inspires me to work even harder. We have to rewrite the ending of this love story. In truth, I'm a diehard romantic." She grinned.

"Oh yeah? Do you have someone special back in New York? I thought a woman like you would be married."

She laughed at the thought of her being married. "I'm too married to my job. At least, I have been. This break gives me some reflection on whether I want to change that trajectory. I did have a boyfriend, but we broke up right before I came here. That was him on the phone."

"Maybe he's changed his mind."

"No, it's more complicated than that." Oh well, why not blab the whole story? "We work together and were up for the same promotion. His family has a lot of potential business connections for the agency, and I think that swayed the boss to give him the position even though I was more qualified. And on top of that, he stole one of my ideas." The muscles in the back of her neck tightened, just talking about it.

"Ouch. Sorry."

"It's okay. Maybe my life needed a change. I don't know. Hopefully I'll figure it out by Christmas." She laughed.

"Is that the reason you two broke up?"

"He was told by human resources that he couldn't be involved with me if he was my boss. So, he broke up over dinner the night before I came here." She paused, tapping her fingers on the table. "I don't know if I'm going to be able to work underneath him. It might drive me crazy."

"Hopefully you'll work it out." He reached out and lightly touched her hand. "Don't worry. You've got mad marketing skills from what I can see. Any company would be lucky to have you." He gently pulled his hand away, his fingers trailing the top of her knuckles sending heat up her arm.

She was speechless, her heartrate accelerating. But warning signs were also blaring inside of her head. You can't get involved with another man so fast. You don't live here. You live in New York. *What are you doing?*

"Thanks," she murmured. His touch was still vibrating in her body.

Derek paid the check, refusing her offer to split it. "My way of saying, welcome to Maple Ridge."

Afterward, he dropped Katy off at Christine's. "See you later." He waved to her standing on the porch as he drove away.

She floated inside the house, thinking of the innocent touch and acknowledging her desire for more with this man. She was in trouble.

* * *

Derek's head hung over spreadsheets, his fingers gliding across the page as he explained the items in detail to Jake, sitting next to him.

"What do you think? Any place where I could cut costs?"

Jake bent over closer, then picked up the papers. He pointed to a column. "Here. You might be able to get a better deal on appliances. And research distributors closer to the city. You might find some cheaper items and companies that might want to be involved with your cause marketing campaign." He paused. "I think I hear the girls now."

Katy and Christine's feet thudded on the steps coming into the conference room. "Sorry we're late. I got caught up with a customer. Totally my fault," Christine said.

Katy's hair fell out of a messy bun as she took off her hat; grabbing her scrunchy, she redid it, her eyes catching Derek's staring at her.

"No problem," Jake said. "Gave us a chance to crunch some numbers."

"Yeah. Thanks. You've given me some new ideas," Derek replied.

"Let's see what you ladies have," Jake said.

Katy opened her computer sitting on the other side of Jake. She slowly went through examples of other cause marketing accounts she had done and then displayed her rough demo of the *Hearts for Hope* campaign for the non-profit, *Hands-On Beyond*, all tied into Sweet Ridge Bakery.

"Alison told me about it, but this looks fantastic. How could they say no?" Jake asked. "The one suggestion I have is to find out who your competition is and do diligent research on them. Maybe even visit their facility. Undercover, of course." He chuckled. "Then you can target how your company is different and stands out among other bakeries."

"Good idea," Katy said.

Christine's eyes pooled with tears. "Thank you so much, all of you. This would be such a blessing if we get the money. I miss Sam every time he leaves, but the thought of selling Sweet Ridge to be with him makes me sick. Expansion would be such a better solution to my dilemma."

Katy reached over and squeezed her hand. "We'll give it our best shot. Not to worry."

"We're committed to this project, Christine. We're a team," Derek said.

The edge of Christine's mouth lifted slowly. "Thank you."

"I have another idea," Katy said. "I would like to do a video of Mary Beth and possibly the boy in New York who got the first scholarships from the *Beyond* program this past June, speaking about their experience now. I saw the original one Sam did for the *Beyond* website, but I thought it might be cool if we did a follow-up one. We could put it on both of our websites. I'm sure Alison would love it. What do you think?"

"Brilliant! I'll talk to Sam tonight. He could probably film Eddie this week, and I'll talk him into coming back next weekend to shoot Mary Beth. I'm sure she will do it. She's become a different person since working at the bakery—much more open and confident."

"Anything else for me?" Jake asked. "I promised Alison I'd help her with the wedding invitations going out tomorrow. We're a little late, but everyone we know secured the date on their calendar. We're excited."

"When I get back from New York, we'll do a cake testing too," Christine added.

"That sounds like more fun than addressing envelopes." Jake laughed. "Feel free to hang around up here if you have more to discuss. The store closes at five today." Jake turned and walked back to his office to grab his coat and computer before heading home.

"I think I'm going back to my office and look at the specs my realtor sent me and set up appointments for Wednesday and Thursday." Christine stood up.

"I'm going to stay here for a bit and do more research," Katy said.

"Me too," Derek added.

"Can you give my cousin a ride home then? We drove together in my car."

"Sure, no problem." Derek brushed his hair out of his eyes and stole a glance at Katy with a slight grin.

After Christine left, Katy looked over at him. "Guess you're stuck with me again."

"Yep." He was intently working on a spreadsheet.

Silence, again. *Okay, I can deal with that.*

The two of them worked side by side until the sound of Katy's ringtone broke the silence. Derek saw the name, Simon. "Are you going to answer that?"

"I can let it go to voicemail." Aggravation was causing her cheeks to flush with heat.

"You might want to talk to the poor guy," he chuckled. "There's plenty of empty offices where you can have privacy."

She thought about it for an instant. Maybe she could get this over with. "Okay."

She hit the green button simultaneously walking out of the conference room. She went as far away as possible, out of Derek's listening range.

"Hi."

"Katy! You finally picked up."

"I've been busy, Simon."

"I just wanted to make sure you were okay and if you might be available for a conference call this week with the Krafton account. I got an email from them, and they want you there."

She consciously willed her shoulders to drop away from her ears. Wasn't she on vacation? "I'm not sure if I can. You do know I'm on vacation."

"I know. I know. But I also know how committed you are to this job, and these accounts will still be here when you return. And I know you like to keep your clients happy."

He was right about that. "Email me some possible times, and I'll get back to you."

"Great. And Katy?"

"Yes?"

"I miss you. I missed us over the holiday weekend. Maybe I should talk to William like you suggested."

"Or maybe we should let this be a break. I'm not sure getting back together is the answer. We'll talk more after Christmas."

"Okay," he said.

"Goodbye, Simon." She was ready to get off.

"Talk soon." He hung up.

Katy stared out the window at the woods in the distance. What was she doing? Yes, she loved making her clients happy but at the expense of her mental health? These last few days had stirred an intense reflective mood in her. Did she want to continue her job at Martin and Lewis? She sighed loudly and returned to the conference room.

"All okay?" Derek asked.

She soaked in his presence with dark, alluring eyes, a chiseled jaw, and a kind face. He sure was sexy. Looking at him helped ease her angst about her job and Simon—a very enticing distraction. "Yeah, I guess so. He's trying to lure me into work on my vacation. See, this is what I mean. I'm better at this job than he is, and he will soon realize it. But he'll never admit it. Anyway, enough of that!"

"I'm almost finished here. I need to do some things at home and take a break before work tomorrow. Do you mind if we leave soon?"

"Absolutely. I think I'm ready for a break too. I'm looking forward to an evening alone with Christine. I tried to give her space while Sam was here."

He nodded, put his papers in a file, and began shutting down his computer.

She did the same.

"Let's go then," he said.

"Right behind you. Thanks for the lift."

"No problem."

And the silence fell over them again but felt like a familiar, cozy blanket to her, no longer disconcerting. She was starting to see the comfort that silence could bring to one's inner spirit—and smiled.

Chapter Eight

Christine rolled over, looked at her clock reading six o'clock, and checked her phone with several texts from Derek.

Call me! Emergency.

She jumped out of bed, an electric shockwave jolting the pit of her stomach, and punched in Derek's number.

"What is it?" she asked.

"There was a leak in the pipes last night connected to our freezer and walk-in. I'm cleaning up the mess and have called a plumber who should be here any minute," he said.

Not today, God, not today. "I'll be there in ten. Just have to get dressed. I'm glad you came in early. Thanks, Derek." She hung up.

She threw on her jeans and a sweater, wrote a note to Katy, and grabbed her car keys. She flew out the door and floored her accelerator down, navigating the back roads to the bakery. Her hands were trembling as she pulled into the parking lot.

Derek stood over the floor with a mop, cleaning the last of the mess.

"How long do you think everything can keep cold? Were both the freezer and walk-in affected?" she asked.

"It looks like the freezer is okay, but there's also an electrical problem with the walk-in. We've got a few hours before things may spoil. Who's your appliance guy?"

"I'll call him. Tom Jenkins. I've known him a long time. I'll beg him to come here first on his daily appointments. Our meeting is at one, right?"

"Yes."

Her forehead wrinkled. "Let's say a prayer. This could really screw up our production today."

"I know."

"I'll be right back." Christine hung up her coat and plopped down in her chair while looking up Tom's number. *Please, please pick up.*

"Hey, Christine. This is kind of early for a call from you. What's the emergency?" he asked.

She told him the situation, and he said he'd be over in thirty minutes. She leaned back on her chair and sighed. Maybe the day could be saved.

* * *

The sunlight streamed in from the window and woke up Katy. She wiggled her toes underneath the coziness of flannel sheets New Englanders loved to use in winter. She would take a brisk walk and then tweak her presentation before going into town. Coffee was next on the agenda.

As she went downstairs, she noticed Christine's door was open, so she had probably left for work already. Coming into the kitchen she picked up the note from her. *'Plumbing emergency at the bakery. Text me later.'* Oh, no. Not today.

She poured herself a cup of coffee and texted her.

Everything okay?

She waited a few minutes until her phone pinged.

Repairman here. Fingers crossed.

Anything I can do?

No, but thank you. Derek and I are handling it.

I'll be in soon. Want to review our presentation first.

Good idea. See you then.

Good luck. Heart emoji.

Her stomach was in knots after getting the news. Hopefully, all would work out. She grabbed her coffee and computer and hunkered down at the kitchen table to work.

* * *

Derek was on his knees next to Tom, watching and learning about the fine underpinnings of a walk-in motor in case he could repair it himself next time.

Tom rocked back on his feet and said, "It needs a new part. Let me call my supply guy. Be right back."

Derek stood up and stretched his back. He looked forward to Mark's yoga class this week. He tried to do some stuff on his own but often got distracted. Wiping the sweat off his face, he turned as Katy entered the room. The engine room was small, so he could smell a rose-infused scent emanating from her body.

"How's it going?" she asked.

"It's going. Tom's on the phone with his supply guy. It needs a part."

"Yikes. It's a good thing you came in here early before any more water damage was done."

"Yeah. The bakery got a double whammy it seems." He looked away from her as Tom entered.

"My guy has the part, but I'm going to have to go get it. I'll be back in an hour," Tom said. "Christine told me this is a big day for you guys, so I'll cancel a few appointments until we get this done."

Derek reached out his hand to shake Tom's. "Thanks, man. Appreciate it."

He reached for a towel and wiped his hands. His body had been in crisis mode all morning and tension pulsed in his neck and shoulders. He needed a break.

"I need some fresh air. See you in a bit."

He brushed by Katy walking out, and she felt a chill scale her nerves as their bodies came into contact for a brief instant. She shook her head and went back to Christine's office.

She was engrossed in her computer when a tap sounded at the door. "Come in," she said.

"Do you want to go over our pitch together one more time?" Derek asked. "Tom thinks he'll finish by noon; we may avoid a disaster."

Katy's eyes locked in with his and didn't waver. The chemistry between the two, at least on her side, was growing stronger, and she didn't know what to think about it. Ignoring it was probably the best solution. "Sure."

He already had his computer, so he walked in and sat at the table beside her. "I think I should go first and do the financial part, and then you come in with the cause marketing, like the frosting on top." He chuckled at his joke and then paused, waiting for a response.

She was quiet for a moment. "We could also go back and forth, like a tag team. Giving him tidbits of each concept." She kept her gaze firmly on his.

"I disagree. I think the financials go first."

Her upper lip twitched as she tilted her head. "Okay."

Derek exhaled, his breath brushing over pursed lips. "Okay, then. Let's begin."

"Let me see if Christine can get away from the floor and listen to us. I know we did this yesterday, but in case she has any last-minute ideas or thoughts." Katy ran out to the bakery and called to her.

As soon as Christine came in, Derek and Katy demonstrated their presentation flawlessly. Twenty minutes flew by, and they all looked at each other.

"I think we're ready," Christine said.

"I think we are," Katy added.

Derek nodded. He fiddled with his pen, his knee bouncing incessantly underneath the table.

"We've done the best that we can. Now it's up to a higher force. I have faith if I'm meant to get this investment, it will happen. But I couldn't have done it without the two of you. Thank you." She hugged them both. "Let's freshen up and wait for them in the front."

Katy looked over at Derek. "Are you nervous?" She reached out her hand and placed it on his arm. "Don't worry. You're going to do great."

He looked down at her, shifted his body weight, and put his hand over hers. "Hope so." He pulled it back, grabbed his computer and headed towards his office.

She sensed a vulnerability and fear in his eyes, but he was a strong, brave man. It was kind of sexy watching his process inching towards a new confidence in his work.

* * *

The bells jingled when a man dressed in a suit and a woman carrying a computer bag entered. Christine came around the counter to greet them.

"Hi. You must be Peter Ferguson. I'm Christine Boyle." She swung her arm around with palm facing up. "Welcome to Sweet Ridge Bakery."

The man shook her hand and turned to the woman. "This is Felicia Juarez, my right-hand person for everything. I'd be lost without her." He laughed.

After introductions were made, Derek and Katy joined them.

Christine had set up the largest table in the back corner for their meeting. They wouldn't fit in her office. "Pick out something from the shelves, and I'll bring everyone coffee."

As everyone took a seat, Peter spoke. "Mr. Higgins told me you have an update for your expansion proposal. As you know, there are several other facilities under consideration. After visiting them all, we will narrow it down to two by the end of the week. Then we will look at your holiday and online sales, make a surprise visit, and announce the winner a few days before Christmas."

The three nodded.

Peter looked at Derek. "Show me what you have so far."

Katy and Christine smiled at him, silently encouraging him to speak. He surprised them both.

Derek had printed out copies of charts and diagrams, explaining the details of the financial trajectory for both the flagship store and the projected one in Manhattan. His voice was confident and strong as he spoke, explaining details and answering Peter's questions.

"This is a strong presentation, Mr. Higgins. Now, what's the other part you were excited about?"

Derek motioned to Katy who then took over. She delivered a perfect report. This was where she was most confident—no fear, no doubt, and sure of herself.

After she was finished, Peter sat back in his chair and took a sip of coffee. He said, "This is most interesting. In fact, I love it. Investors will love it. I would like to see more details of how it would work and the projected numbers. You've made a strong case for yourselves today. All of you. Email me more information this week."

"We will," Christine said.

"Now let me try this croissant." Peter's eyes rolled up and then shut as he sighed. "There's no argument that your baked goods are stellar, Miss Boyle."

The atmosphere became more relaxed as Peter asked Christine more personal questions about the history of the bakery and her family. Katy caught Derek's eyes, and they both grinned at each other. Things were going as planned. *If only we didn't have any competition.*

After the investors left, Christine turned to the two of them. "We did it!" She jumped up and down like a kid. "I know it's not a done deal and there's more work to do, but I think we made a good impression, don't you?"

"Yes," Katy said.

Derek nodded as he grinned.

Christine hugged each of them and headed back to the production floor.

"Let me know when you have more to add to the proposal, and we can crunch the numbers and send off an update to Peter," Derek said.

"Will do."

"By the way, you did an excellent job at presenting. I can tell you've been doing this a long time."

She blushed. "You weren't so bad yourself."

"Yeah. I got through it." He turned and headed for his office.

He's so talkative. She shook her head at his hot and cold behaviors. Nothing was predictable with that man. Her phone pinged. Simon.

Please call me. Important.

Everything's important to him. Must be work. She decided to call him in Christine's office. She was busy on the floor.

"Hey, Simon. What's up?" she asked.

"Listen I'm having some difficulty with the Krafton account. They are insisting that you be on the Zoom call. Is there any way you can do it? I'll let you take the lead on it."

Exasperation fueled in her gut. She had already done most of the work on the campaign. It had been a joint venture, but it was obvious she had been the lead. Now Simon was floundering without her. He expected her to run at his beck and call. Is this how it will be when she returns to New York?

"What time is it?"

"Tomorrow at eleven." He paused. "Please? I don't want to lose this account."

Suddenly she enjoyed hearing him squirm. She knew she should probably say no, but she was too controlling to let the business go to him to screw up.

"Alright. Send me the link."

"Thank you, Katy."

"You're welcome. I've got to go."

"I'm still missing you."

"You should have thought about that before you broke up with me. Talk to you later." She hung up.

A rap sounded at the door. "Come in."

Derek's broad shoulders spread across the doorway hovering close to her. "Am I interrupting you?"

"No. no. I was dealing with something at work."

"You don't look happy, but I can come back later." He turned to leave.

"No, it's okay. It's Simon. I guess he's my new boss already. I agreed to a Zoom meeting with one of our prestigious clients. I caved."

"It seems you're working a lot on your vacation. You need to do something fun." He grinned.

Now he's back to hot. "You're probably right. Got any ideas?"

He tilted his head. "How about bowling?"

She laughed. "Bowling?" Then she realized he was serious. "I haven't been bowling in years. I'm terrible as I remember."

"After work, I'm taking you bowling," he said. He stood staring at her with his hands in his front pockets and dimples spread across his cheeks.

He had hit a chord in her. She was not having enough fun in her life. Sad but true. "Okay. Bowling it is." She reached out her hand, and they shook on it.

"They have decent food there. We can grab a burger and a beer for dinner if that's alright with you."

"Perfect. I may swing back to Christine's in a bit. Do you mind picking me up? Or text me an address, and I can meet you there."

"I'll pick you up." He turned and left.

Did I just agree to a date with him? Was it a date? No, they were colleagues and friends. That's all. And that's all it could ever be. She was going back to New York after Christmas. No long-distance relationships for her. She worked too much. Bowling. She chuckled and gathered up her papers and computer.

Chapter Nine

Katy bent over, tying the worn, suede bowling shoes she had retrieved from the guy behind the counter. Derek's arm brushed her as he plopped beside her to do the same.

"Are you ready?" he asked.

"As ready as I can be. I have to warn you; I'm not very good. Gutter balls are a specialty of mine."

"Doesn't matter. You're here to have fun. Forget about work. You need a balanced life, Katy. We all do." He stood up and motioned to the lanes. "Follow me."

She grabbed her purse and followed him weaving around other players. When they came to their lane, they sat by the scorecard table since only two of them were playing.

"Ladies first." He gestured with his hand toward the lane.

She glanced at him, his eyes sparkling with a sincere kindness when he smiled. "Don't laugh."

"Wouldn't think of it."

As promised, the ball clanged against the gutter a third of the way down. Katy spun around throwing her arms up. "What did I tell you?"

"Do you want some tips? I can show you how to use your body and release the ball."

"Yes. Otherwise, this could be a very boring game."

Derek stood up, took his turn, and easily knocked down all the pins with a spare. He turned to her. "Come on. Let me show you."

Katy's knees wobbled as she approached him. Maybe this wasn't such a great idea.

After she had picked up a ball, he came behind her and placed his hand on her arm and the other hand steadied her at the hip. "See. Nice and easy, back and forth, and release gently without turning your wrist. Don't worry if there's not a lot of momentum at first. Aim for the center and we'll adjust your movement as we go."

How can I concentrate? A scent of wood pine mixed with a sugary spice permanently engrained in the threads of his shirt drifted to her senses. But the weight of his body behind her and his hand pushing on her hips ignited a flame of desire she had no control over. Her body temperature was rising, and she might regret her next action if she didn't break away from the intensity of his proximity.

She stepped forward. "Okay. Let's see what happens." Trying to focus on his instructions she released the ball and hit two pins. She jumped up and down. "I did it! I did it!" She ran back to him and threw her arms around his neck without thinking. "Thank you."

His eyes widened, then he grinned. "You're welcome."

What's come over me? She shivered as she pulled away. "Your turn."

He ambled up to the balls and nailed a strike.

"I think this game is rigged. Definitely not an even playing field."

"It's about having fun, Flanagan, not winning."

"Easier said than done, Higgins." She giggled.

She pressed her lips together as she passed him, picked up her ball, and knocked down five balls. She wiggled her hips in a happy dance.

"I'm coming for you. Watch out." She tilted her chin up with a cocky air. "Your turn."

He shook his head at her comments but couldn't suppress a smile. With a gallant force he aimed and fired. Strike. "Take that."

"You think you're a hot shot. Move over buddy." She pushed his arm playfully and took a stance. Carefully maneuvering her body as he instructed, with two throws she got her first spare. Again, the happy dance, hips moving, arms waving. She was on a roll.

"I guess you mean business," he said. He rolled his balls and another spare.

"Okay, okay. I may not win, but I will enjoy trying." Her chestnut brown eyes locked in with his dark ones without wavering.

"How about a burger and a beer? I'll flag down the waitress. She's over there."

"Yes, sustenance is needed."

As he gave the waitress their order, she sat, twiddling with the score pencil, staring out at the lane. She was having a blast. How long since that had happened?

"She'll bring it to us. Whose turn is it?" he asked.

"Mine." She sauntered up to the balls and imagined his eyes watching her from behind. *What is he thinking?*

The two of them continued bantering back and forth, then took a break when their food came.

"How long have you been bowling?" she asked.

"My dad and I used to do it when I was younger. Lately I've been using it as a relaxation technique. Knock the pins, release the stress kind of thing." He bit into his burger.

"I can see that." She wiped a dribble of ketchup trickling down her chin. "These burgers are tasty. You were right."

He offered her another napkin, nodding with his mouth full.

After finishing, she stood up. "I'm going to use the ladies' room. I'll be right back."

"I'll be here."

Katy held her hands under the tepid water, letting the soap slide off her fingers. She smoothed out her hair in the mirror, which was a complete mess by now. But she didn't care. She wasn't trying to impress anyone. Or was she?

As she walked out, a young man reeking like a brewery stepped in front of her. "Hey, good looking. What's your name?"

She could tell he was drunk and was uncomfortably close. "None of your business."

Derek looked up, and a warning surged in his gut with a vice grip. In an instant, he was by her side.

"I think the lady wants to be left alone." He stepped between them, sliding up into the guy's face.

"Oh, yeah? And who are you?"

Derek grabbed his shirt and pulled him upward. "You don't want to know."

Katy clutched Derek's shirt. "Please. Stop."

He released him and fortunately, the guy was too tipsy to do anything else. "She's a fine bitch."

Before she could do anything, Derek swung and punched the guy squarely in the nose. He was so drunk, he just fell backward, dazed, and oblivious to the situation.

By now the management had approached. "Gentlemen, I think it's time you both leave."

Katy looked in Derek's eyes. There was something there she had never seen—a wildness, an uncontrollable frenzy. "Come on. We were done anyway." She wasn't sure what to do.

His eyes rested on hers. "I'm sorry." He picked up his jacket, returned his shoes, and headed towards the truck.

Katy hurried to keep up with him. She climbed into the truck and looked over at him. His hands were visibly shaking, resting on the steering wheel.

"I'm sorry. I'll take you home."

Should she be quiet or speak her mind? She was pissed too. "By the way, I can take care of myself. No need to go all chivalrous on me."

"It wasn't about being gallant. My anger got out of control. Yes, I didn't want the guy harassing you, but when he called you a name, something snapped inside of me. And the fact I didn't control it bothers me the most. Let's get you home."

She didn't know what to say. This was heavier than just being in a stupid guy fight. She had seen that crazed look in his eyes, and it scared her.

The silence hung heavy between them until they pulled into Christine's driveway. He stared straight ahead. "Sorry I ruined our fun time." Then he looked over at her.

She couldn't stay angry. This was different. *Choose empathy instead.* She reached out her hand, placing it on his arm. "No worries. We still had fun." She paused. "And you've got a mean right hook, too." She smiled, encouraging him to lighten up.

Her comment forced a grin out of him. "Thanks. See you tomorrow?"

"Yeah, I'll be in sometime. I'll probably work at home in the morning." She opened the door. "Goodnight, Derek."

"Goodnight, Katy."

As she stood on the porch, she watched him drive away. *What other dark secrets does he have?* The night's frosty air saturated her lungs, her body settling into the stillness before going inside to find her cousin. She decided to keep the incident to herself for the time being. She didn't want Christine thinking he was a loose cannon.

* * *

Katy rubbed her hands together, waiting for the coffee to brew and playing out the scenes from the previous evening with Derek. Up to the guy getting punched, she had been having fun. Real fun. Not just the enjoyment she got from her job but the kind of fun where you belly laugh and don't give a damn what others think. But the look in Derek's eyes also scared her in the end.

Thumpity-thump was heard from the stairs as Christine dragged her suitcase to the foyer, then walked into the kitchen.

"Coffee ready?"

"Yep. Perfect timing." Katy poured her a cup. "I was going to scramble an egg. Want one?"

"That would be great. I'm going to make a quick stop at the bakery, then get on the road."

Katy pulled out the eggs, whisked them in a bowl, and grabbed some bread for toast.

Christine sat down at the island counter and sighed. "I hope I'm ready for this."

"What do you mean?"

"I woke up with this knot in my gut. What if I fail? What if I can't find the right facility? What if Sam and I never *really* get to be together?"

"Stop it right now. All these 'what if' questions will get you nowhere and will stress you out. It's perfectly normal to have these fears. This is a huge undertaking—the kind where you have to take it one day at a time." She slid a plate of eggs and toast in front of her.

"You're right. Just normal." She picked up a fork and dug into the eggs. "These are good," Christine said.

"Thanks."

"One day at a time." She nodded and continued eating.

"That's all any of us can do. Whenever I'm overwhelmed with a project, I remind myself, I'm doing the best I can, one day at a time."

Christine took a sip of coffee. "How was bowling last night? I'm surprised Derek asked you to go somewhere with him. He's usually pretty reserved and not too social unless pushed. He must feel at ease with you after working together." She lifted an eyebrow as she looked at Katy.

She blushed. "It was fun." *Until it wasn't.* "He gave me some bowling tips, and I actually hit some pins. My gutter ball days are behind me." She giggled.

Christine chuckled as she took her dirty dishes to the sink.

"Leave those. I'll get them. You need to get on the road."

"Thanks. You're right. I'll text you when I'm safely in the city. Wish me luck. My realtor has a ton of places to look at. It's going to take a few days. I'll probably be back on Friday, depending on what happens."

"I'll be here holding down the fort. I'm working at home this morning and then will pop in at the bakery in the afternoon. Let me know if you want me to do anything there."

"No, Derek has it all covered."

Christine hugged her cousin, freshened up, and headed out the door.

Katy waved to her as she drove away and climbed the steps to her bedroom. As she changed clothes and made her bed, her phone pinged. Simon. *Was this going to be a daily annoyance?*

Please call when you can.

She picked up the phone. **Okay.** She might need a second cup of coffee to deal with him today.

She sunk into the cozy living room couch with her extra coffee, computer, and notepad. Simon probably wanted to go over details for their Zoom later. She liked this more relaxed way of working where she called her own shots. *I could get used to this.* She tapped his name on her phone.

"Hi. How are you?"

"Great. Don't forget I'm supposed to be on vacation," she said.

"I know. I'm sorry I'm bugging you. I have a few questions before our Zoom." He rattled them off and conveyed concerns with other clients.

This is more like a staff meeting than just a few questions about one client. *Is he nervous to be working alone without me there?* But she was a professional and relinquished her time to help him. "Is that all?" she asked after a half hour of back-and-forth issues.

"For now. Thanks, Katy. It seems weird without you here. Any chance you're coming back before Christmas?"

"No."

"Well, have fun. See you at one."

"Will do." She hung up and took a sip of her coffee, now cold. Floating remnants of disappointment still pooled in her gut. She should have had the director position. It was obvious, based on this last phone call. When she returned, would he expect her to bail him out and do most of the work for the clients? Another sickening feeling toyed with her insides. Was that the kind of life she wanted? Definitely not. She might have to make serious changes in her life as Christine did, and that scared her.

* * *

Derek grabbed a broom and swept the bakery floor for the second time. He liked things neat, which Christine loved. And besides, he needed to keep his body busy today. Yesterday's episode had upset him. Anger had reared its ugly head, and he had succumbed to it in an unhealthy way. Bags hung heavy underneath his eyes from hardly sleeping the night before, and a tightness in his shoulders added to his stress.

Katy had appeared an hour prior, but he refrained from speaking to her. He answered a few questions and tried not to be rude. He wasn't in a good space for conversation and desperately needed his support group tonight. Mark would help him get his head straight, and he could move on. Until then, he settled into his comfortable, withdrawn state.

Near five o'clock, Mary Beth strode into the back room. She was the welcoming face in the front of the bakery now and had come into her own. The shy, withdrawn girl from Fairside had blossomed into a social butterfly, ready to spread her wings wherever they took her—a natural with their customers.

"Katy just left, and I put the closed sign on the door, Derek. Anything else before I leave?"

"No. Thanks."

She picked up her coat and purse and waved to him as she went out the door. "Have a good evening."

"You too," he said. Alone in the bakery, he glanced around, mentally ensuring everything was in order. He stopped for a moment as he trailed his fingers along the metal countertop, remembering his first day of work there. Working for Christine had been a godsend. He had needed an anchor in the dark storm that had consumed him, its gripping claws dragging him under into an abyss of fear and depression. The bakery had saved him.

After locking up, he walked home, breathing in the chilly air of the early evening already dark. Walking down the drive to his apartment, Mark pulled up beside him, so he stopped.

Mark rolled down the window. "Hey, want a ride to the meeting?"

"That would be great," Derek said. "I have to change my clothes." He motioned to the front of his jeans spattered with flour.

"I'll wait. No problem."

Five minutes later Derek hopped into Mark's car. "Thanks."

"No problem. What's new? I heard the investors paid a visit yesterday to the bakery." He paused and shrugged. "Small town, you know." He grinned.

"Yeah. We'll know by the end of the week who the two finalists are, but I think we have a good chance. Katy, Christine's cousin, came up with this idea to include a cause marketing campaign with the opening of a new store in Manhattan." His eyes fixated on the road in front of him, still keeping his emotions close to his chest.

"She seems like a nice woman from what little I spoke with her at Thanksgiving. And very pretty." Mark gazed over at Derek.

Derek caught his glance. "Yes, she is pretty but don't get any ideas. Especially when I tell you what happened last night."

"Oh, yeah? What's that?" Mark asked.

"I'll save it for the group." And then he was quiet.

Derek helped Mark set up the metal chairs in a circle in the carpeted basement room of the church. Another member was plugging in the coffee machine and placing store-bought cookies on paper plates. Even though the room had some low windows, it was dark this time of year.

As people poured in, approximately ten veterans, casual niceties were exchanged and then Mark called the meeting to order. After a prayer, he asked, "Anyone new tonight?"

One woman raised her hand and introduced herself. She had recently returned from active duty, and her irritability and frequent headaches were causing a strain on her marriage. She wasn't ready to offer details, but it was a start to at least speak in the group.

After a few other guys shared their progress and roadblocks, Mark fixed his gaze on Derek. "Anyone else?"

Derek slowly lifted his hand. His fingers on his other hand steadily tapped on the chair while one knee bounced.

"I really lost it last night. So much so, it scared me. I thought I had my anger under control." He proceeded to tell the story to the group.

"What do you think was the trigger, Derek?" Mark asked.

"It pissed me off when he made a move on Katy in a drunken state, but when he called her a bitch, I went crazy." He rubbed his hands together non-stop now.

"Why?" Mark asked again.

Derek's breath deepened, taking in the silence. "I'm not sure." The group waited. "I guess it comes from the engrained vow to protect and serve. I felt like I had to protect her—like she was in danger."

"Yes, that could be part of it. Are there any personal feelings for this woman, Derek? Be honest with yourself," Mark said.

Derek shifted his body weight against the cold, metal chair. "Maybe. We've been working together for a few days. And last night's outing was supposed to be for fun. She works all the time, and I thought she might want to get out."

"Usually when we have an incident as intense as this, there are more personal feelings involved. And by the way, you're lucky the guy was too drunk to press charges."

Derek hung his head. "Yeah, I know."

"I know personal relationships can be intense triggers for us all, but if we don't recognize them, we will never be able to have the intimacy we all so desire. Believe me, I've been there."

"Are you saying I'm not ready for a relationship with a woman?" Derek asked.

"No. If you have feelings for someone, acknowledge it and realize by investing feelings into another person, you will get triggered down the road. It's inevitable. And as I always say, it's how you handle the episodes that count. You've taken the first step by coming here today and sharing with us."

"So, if I choose to enter a relationship with someone, just know there will be triggers down the road?"

"Yes. But don't let that stop you from getting what you want, Derek. We all deserve love in our life, but you'll need courage to take chances and face whatever obstacles might appear in your path as you proceed."

Derek's eyes looked down. "I had a girlfriend when I left for Afghanistan, but when I returned, she left me after a couple of months. I was no fun to be around. I've kept to myself since then, trying to deal with all the parameters of my PTSD, but the relationship component I've closed off. It was easier, and it's been a while since I've had a reaction like this. I thought I was over it. Guess not." He pressed his hand on his knee to stop the incessant shaking.

"Remember what my mentor told me," Mark said. "PTSD is a journey. It's how you ride the waves that count." He paused. "Anything else, Derek?"

He shrugged. "I guess not. This was enough for one evening." A slight grin broke out on his face. "I've got to sit with it for a bit."

"Take all the time you need, brother."

They ended the session with the serenity prayer, and everyone helped put away the chairs before snatching up a cookie and some coffee. Mark walked over to Derek, placing his hand on his shoulder.

"Are you alright, man?"

"Yeah. I will be. I guess I might have some feelings around Katy that I didn't even realize were there."

"That can happen. Call me this week if anything comes up. I call my guy whenever I need to, and I'm your guy, Derek. Don't forget."

Derek swung around to face Mark. "Thanks."

Mark reached out his arms, pulling Derek in for a hug. "You're welcome."

"I think I'm going to walk home. Need some fresh air." Derek left early, raw feelings of uncertainty still churning in his gut. As he strolled the short distance home, he dragged his fingers through his hair. At least he'd sleep better tonight after dumping his heavy load on the group. But Katy. What was up with that? Was he developing feelings for her? He'd better shut that down as soon as possible. He wasn't ready.

Chapter Ten

Katy's feet pounded the pavement, arms pumping, and air rushing in and out of her lungs as she turned the corner on Christine's street. Although most of the leaves had fallen, the tall maples and evergreen pines stood tall, reaching into the luminous blue sky today, their majestic presence attempting to calm her racing mind. Leisurely morning runs had become a steady constant on her vacation. In New York, she was lucky to get on her treadmill during the day unless she rose hours before dawn.

Slowing down in front of the house her phone pinged. She pulled it out and both Simon and Christine had left texts and a voicemail. After her shower, she'd return their calls. She was determined to create boundaries with Simon but was finding it more and more difficult. In between their conversations about work, he was sending her funny texts, heart emojis and whatever he felt like, as if they had never broken up. Yes, I like the attention she admitted, but she needed another conversation with him about boundaries in her personal life.

After showering, she tossed a bunch of fruit, greens, and protein powder into a blender and made a smoothie for breakfast. Christine first, as she crawled up on the cushioned bar chair in the kitchen. "Hey, Christine. How's it going?"

"My brain is on overload. Brent has shown me several sites, and we've got a ton today and tomorrow on our schedule. I'll send you links later, and you can give me your opinion. There's one on the upper east side, although very pricey, that I like. We're headed to the West Village later."

"Very exciting."

"How are things at the bakery? I talk to Derek a couple of times a day but wondered what you thought. This is a good trial run to see if they can get along without me." She laughed.

"Seems fine to me. I'm going in later for lunch and want to show Derek some new stuff I found. I like working at home on our project in the morning, but my office calls me every day. Maybe I should change my number." She stirred her drink.

"Whatever it takes. Talk to you later."

She sipped her smoothie, letting the cool, tangy liquid slide down her throat as she ran her fingers over her legal pad, skimming her notes on a work project in New York that Simon wanted to discuss. Breathing in, she rolled her shoulders in a circular fashion and picked up her phone.

Simon answered immediately. "Hey, how are you?"

"I'm great. What's up?" *Keep it professional. Erect those boundaries.*

"Did you look at the Johnson file I sent you? Any ideas for their campaign? They want to tie it up before the holidays." He paused. "Any chance you can come down for a weekend, so we could hammer it out?"

"Simon, what did I tell you? I'm on vacation. Give me a day or two, I'll look it over and send you something by email. Anything else?" She tapped her fingers on the counter faster, ready to drill holes in the wood.

"I miss you."

"And?"

"Do you miss me? I think we made a mistake."

"We? As I remember it, you broke up with me." Her shoulders were tensing upwards again. What happened to her morning relaxation? *Gone.*

"Yeah, well, I was stupid. Let me talk to William. I'm sure we can work something out with him. Then we can be a team again."

Right, so you can use my ideas and take credit for them. No way. "I don't think *we* would work anymore, Simon. I've got to run. I'll send you some stuff in a couple days."

"Please, Katy. At least think about it."

"I've thought about it enough. Gotta go." She hung up.

She needed another run to get her head straight she mused. Simon—a little too late.

* * *

The bells jingled as Katy entered the bakery. She waved to Mary Beth and took a table in the corner. Derek must be in the back. She walked up to the counter. "Will you watch my things for a minute? I'm going to order lunch but first wanted to speak to Derek. Is he in the back?"

"Yep."

She went through the swinging double doors to the bakery floor and saw him at a table in the back, placing croissants on trays ready for baking. His head was down, engrossed in the movement.

When she approached, he lifted his head. "Hi."

"Hi." She shifted her weight, then brushed a hair out of her eyes. He had already returned to his job at hand with eyes down.

"I'm going to eat lunch out front and wondered if you could meet with me after I eat? I have a couple of new ideas to show you." There. Make it about work. Squash the awkwardness in the bud.

"Sure." He didn't look up.

She paused. "Did you eat lunch yet? Want to join me?"

He looked up at her. "Let me finish this batch, and I'll be out."

"Great." Was this a mistake asking him to lunch with her? Would it be a silent ordeal? For some reason, she wanted to spend more time with this mysterious man, even after their incident at the bowling alley. Initially, it had scared her, but she felt less afraid after having time to process it. He was a good guy who had served their country and returned a changed man with scars and battle wounds in his mind, not his body.

She put in an order for a turkey sandwich and cup of soup with Mary Beth and went back to her table. Sitting down, she drank her tea, feeling the heated liquid coat her throat, soothing her nerves. Her fingers rested in the grasp of the mug as she stared out into the bakery shop, observing customers float in and out with their bags full of sugary items. What was it that made this place special? If she could unravel that mystery, she might have more ammunition for their campaign.

Her thoughts were broken when Derek came around the corner holding their lunch on a tray. He removed the plates and cups, placing them on the table.

"Here you go. Be careful. Soup's hot." He turned to hand the tray to Mary Beth behind the counter.

As he slid into the chair across from her, she couldn't help but notice his tousled wavy hair and specks of flour on his shirt and cheek. Did she dare wipe it off?

She reached her hand across the table towards his face. "You've got flour on your face."

He didn't flinch.

Her fingers grazed the side of his cheek, wiping the flour away in one swell swoop. Touching him sent a ripple up her body. She wanted to linger in the touch of his skin but didn't. "There."

"Thanks. Comes with the territory." He picked up his spoon and tasted the soup. "Pretty tasty. Sylvia's a good cook. She does most of the breakfast and lunch items."

"From what I saw in your report, they provide profitable income for the bakery, yes?"

"Yep." He kept eating.

"I wonder if the other bakeries have that addition."

He shrugged.

She could see this conversation wasn't going anywhere, so she let the silence wash over her as she chewed each bite and stole occasional glances at the good-looking man in front of her. Would he address the elephant in the room?

Derek looked up at her and noticed a mustard smear next to her upper lip. He reached over with his napkin and wiped it. "Your turn." He grinned at her.

She touched the spot where he had wiped it. "I can be a messy eater."

"We all can." He leaned back in his chair, tilted his head, and locked eyes with her. "About the other night ..."

"We don't have to talk about it if you don't want to." She put down her napkin. *What are you doing? Let him speak.*

"I do. You already know I'm a veteran, but you may not know I have PTSD. I won't go into details about why or the aftermath of my tour, but one symptom is uncontrollable anger. I thought I was managing it, but when that guy bothered you, something snapped inside me, and I lost it. Thus, the punch to the face. I'm sorry for making you feel uncomfortable or embarrassing you in front of others. There were better ways I could have handled it. One without my fist." The corners of his mouth hinted at lifting.

Should she be brutally honest with him? "It did scare me a little. When I looked into your eyes, it was as if the Derek I knew had left and some wild beast had taken over your body. That's the best I can explain it." She paused. "Just so you know, I can take care of myself. Don't need to go all Captain America on me."

He laughed. "I'm still dealing with some ugly stuff, Katy. That's why I am a loner. It works out best for me."

Was he warning her to stay away from him beyond their new friendship? Probably. "Good to know."

He pushed his chair back and started taking dishes back to the kitchen.

She watched him for an instant. *Guess this conversation is over.* She picked up her dishes and followed him.

After cleaning up, he turned to her. "Did you have something you wanted to show me?"

"Yes. Let's meet in Christine's office. Did you see the specs on some of the buildings she sent us?"

"Yeah, pretty awesome. Be right there."

As she gathered her things from the front of the store, she couldn't help but think about what he had said about PTSD. What happened in Afghanistan? It was none of her business, but curiosity tortured her imagination, and she couldn't let it go.

She headed down the hallway to Christine's office as Derek came out of his. "After you," he said. He swept his arm in a directional fashion towards the next office.

Katy threw her coat and purse on a table behind Christine's desk, grabbed her computer, and sat beside him. The closeness in the small room made her stomach quiver—nothing she could do about it. Katy opened her laptop and started talking, which she was good at. She had more information about the *Hearts for Hope* campaign and needed him to crunch some different numbers for her. "Can you do it?"

"No problem. Give me until tomorrow," he said. "Anything else?"

She looked away from his haunting eyes drilling into her. Her heart rate was accelerating; she needed fresh air. Something about this guy struck her to the very core and threatened the stability and assuredness she usually felt about herself. *What was it?*

"No, that's it. Thanks." She shuffled papers and began packing up. A bead of sweat was rolling down her back. She could feel it.

"Thanks for understanding about what we talked about earlier." He stood up.

"Yeah, sure." She couldn't look at him. Too intense. "See you tomorrow?" she asked.

"I'll be here." And he walked out.

As soon as he was gone, she collapsed limply into the chair. *I can't be attracted to Derek. I just can't.* You heard him. He's a loner. Let him be.

She swiftly put her hat and coat on, grasped her computer bag and purse, and went out the back door. Right now, she needed to avoid the man and get a grip on herself. An evening in front of the fire with a book and a glass of wine sounded like the best solution.

Chapter Eleven

Katy sat at the kitchen counter, slurping her smoothie when her ringtone sounded. Christine.

"Hi!" she answered.

"Wanted to let you know I'm on my way home. Sam is with me and will shoot the remaining part of our video with Mary Beth tomorrow. He'll take the train home on Sunday."

"Fantastic."

"How's it going with you? Are you getting any rest and relaxation? Derek updated me on the proposal."

"Not rushing into my office every morning is relaxing, don't worry. I like working and I'm determined to polish this up before next week. Jake offered us his social media queen, Liza, for some volunteer hours. This town is rooting for you."

"I know. Makes it hard to leave; I'll always keep my home there. But I've found true love with Sam, and I don't want to let it go."

"You won't. I'll make sure of it."

"From your lips to God's ears, girl." She giggled. "See you in a couple of hours. We'll drop off our bags at the house, and you can ride with us into town if you like."

"Perfect. Will give me some time to work here where it's peaceful and quiet."

"See you then," Christine said.

A subtle twinge pinched Katy's gut as she swirled her straw in the thick fruity nectar of the glass in front of her. Could she pull this off for her cousin? The work she did with Derek had to be seamless. She pulled her hair tie from her wrist, scooped her messy locks in a bun, and retreated to the living room with her computer.

* * *

Derek was on the floor helping the other staff with Christmas cookies since it was Friday, and he always took some to the veteran's home. As he pulled a tray out of the oven, he heard lively voices from the rear of the store—most likely Christine and the crew. She had texted earlier. He glanced up as they waltzed into the room, laughing, and joking. Seeing Katy, his stomach tensed into a knot. His growing attraction to her made him nervous, and he struggled to maintain a balance of his emotions mixed with professionalism.

"Did you miss me?" asked Christine. She walked up to Derek, placing her hand on his shoulder.

"Every day, boss," he said.

Sam was already sampling the wares and tossed a nod towards Derek.

Katy waved, and Derek nodded back towards her.

"Listen, when you're done, can the three of us meet in my office? I want to discuss what I found and see your updates with Katy," Christine said.

"Sure." Derek gave instructions to his fellow workers, took off his apron, and followed them to the office.

Sam leaned over and kissed Christine. "I'm going to head over to

Starlight Books to see Jake. Be back later."

"Okay," she said.

As Derek sat down, his leg grazed Katy's. He glanced at her. "Sorry. Tight fit."

"No problem." She readjusted her position to make space for him.

Christine displayed the listings she liked the best on her computer, and they discussed the pros and cons of each one. Real estate prices in Manhattan were ten times higher than in Maple Ridge, but the investors already knew that. They were looking at the online sales, which had been booming for two years. In New York, they would need a warehouse for production, separate from the storefront. Christine didn't like that part, but there was nothing they could do. The bakery required foot traffic in a busier area, and the warehouse space would be in another part of the city.

"Do you think you can make some new projections for the warehouse space, Derek?"

"Yes. I think I want to show this to Jake. I'll call him later."

The ringtone on Christine's phone interrupted them. She looked down. "It's them!"

"Pick up," Katy exclaimed.

Derek squeezed his pencil hard as his knee began to bounce under the table. *Would they make the finals?*

"Yes. Yes. That's wonderful news." She nodded her head, giving the thumbs up sign to the others while they waited for her to get off the phone. "Can you tell me the name of the other store?" She paused. "Thank you so much, Mr. Ferguson. We will be ready for another visit, and we have some property suggestions we'll be sending you next week as well." She listened a minute more. "Goodbye and have a great weekend."

Christine leaped out of her chair, jumping up and down. "We made it! It's down to two of us now. Oh my god, I'm sweating up a storm."

Katy stood up and hugged her cousin. "See. We can do this. The three of us."

"Come on, Derek. Get in here." She motioned for him to stand in a three-way hug.

He slowly rose and agreed to a short embrace. "There. Feel better?" he asked.

"Yes," Christine said.

"Who's the competition? Would they tell you?"

"Yes. It's in Vermont and called *Frosty Mountain Bakeshop*, about two to three hours from here."

Katy was already googling it as she sat down. "They have a nice website. Let me dig a little deeper."

"Supposedly, people come from all over New England to sample their cupcakes with frostings of a hundred flavors. In addition to their online presence, soft chocolate chip and oatmeal raisin cookies are also a hit." Christine peered over Katy's shoulder.

Derek had it pulled up on his screen as well. "Wish we could see their financials."

"Wouldn't that be helpful?" Christine chuckled, then became serious. "I have an idea but will need both of you to help."

"Sure," they both chimed in at once.

"I want the two of you to drive up there on Monday and check it out. Be my little spies. Bring some samples back, talk to the staff, and get a feel of what we're up against. What do you say?"

Derek knew there was nothing to say but yes. But the thought of being alone with Katy on a road trip made his stomach queasy. He didn't know how he would handle it. Yes, you like to be alone, but some day you've got to get over that to have intimacy again. No way around the muck, only through it. *Man up, soldier.* "Of course." His eyes met Katy's. What was she thinking?

Katy fidgeted in her seat. "Sure."

Christine clapped her hands together. "Wonderful. You guys are the best. I can't wait to see what you think."

Katy's phone went off. Simon.

Derek saw the name too. "At lease he's consistent." A grin broke out across his face. "Maybe you should give the poor guy a chance."

"Ha, ha. Very funny." Katy pursed her lips together as she deleted the call.

Christine sat down at her desk. "I have a ton of emails to answer. We can talk later." She looked at her watch. "Closing shop in an hour."

Derek nodded, stood up with his computer and left.

When they were alone, Christine turned to her. "Are you really okay with this?"

"Absolutely. What's the harm in a little road trip? And besides, the idea of becoming a spy intrigues me." She laughed, tossing back her curly hair.

"I know Derek can be moody at times, but he's a good guy. And he's really stepped up to the plate since I hired him."

"I think we're becoming friends. But I have to admit, he is an attractive man."

"Katy Flanagan! Do you have a crush on him?"

"No, no. Just stating the facts." Heat was rising in her neck, forcing her to undo the top button of her shirt. "I'm going to take a walk. See you later."

What just happened? Did she have a crush on the lone wolf? Yikes. She did.

As she walked through the bakery, Derek was in the corner wrapping up pink boxes for his weekly run to the veteran's home. She approached him. It was like some invisible magnet kept drawing her to him. So much for the walk outside, she mused.

"Are you leaving soon?" she asked.

"In about fifteen minutes." He kept placing the cookies between sheets of parchment paper, arranging them neatly in rows.

"Can I come again? I'd like to help. I don't do enough volunteer work in New York. Well, none for that matter. Always too busy."

"Sure. Can you grab a smaller box for Nick? He always gets his own. Over there." He pointed to a shelf. "Put it together, then pack it like these."

Katy obeyed and fell into working next to him until they were ready to go.

"I'll go heat up the truck," he said.

"Let me grab my coat and things. Can you drop me off at Christine's afterward? I didn't drive today."

"No problem." He picked up the box and left.

* * *

Hardly a word was spoken as they drove the short distance to the facility. She was getting used to silence with him—a calming veil spread over her without resistance. She held the door for him as they entered, greeting familiar faces.

Derek placed the box on a table next to the coffee machine, its tempting aroma drawing residents to gather around him. She watched as he morphed into a different person. His smile broadened across his face, his laughter rang out effortlessly, and his kindness exuded a quality she found very charming. This was the man she was attracted to, but this man wasn't always available.

"I'll take a box around to those seated, okay?"

"That would be great."

She made the rounds, stopping and chatting with those who were alone. One lady asked, "Is that your husband, dear?" She pointed to Derek.

"Oh, no. He's a friend."

"Why not? He was looking at you with that look, you know, as you walked over here. I may be old, but I know when a guy has the hots for a woman. I've been around."

She stopped and stared at this petite woman with white hair and a twinkle in her eye sitting in a wheelchair. *Is Derek crushing on me as well?*

"Well, we're new friends. Maybe he's watching me to make sure I don't screw up."

"How can you screw up giving out cookies? Take my word for it. I know." The older woman reached in the box and took out a chocolate chip cookie. "My name is Alice. Would you be a dear and get me a cup of coffee? Black."

"Sure." Katy walked away, her knees wobbling, trying to maintain an even gait. In her gut, Alice had spoken a truth she didn't want to see. She and Derek had chemistry. Period. But nothing could evolve from it. She lived in New York, and he was very clear, he wanted no part of a relationship. *Just enjoy the crush.* How often does that happen? And it will keep your mind off Simon.

"I see you met Alice," Derek said.

Katy filled up the cup and grinned at him. "Yes, I did. She's quite the pistol, isn't she?"

"Yep." He turned to his conversation with another older gentleman swapping war stories.

Katy brought the coffee to Alice and finished making her rounds around the recreation room, making sure everyone had what they wanted. She returned with an empty box to Derek, still gabbing away. Unbelievable. He couldn't shut up.

When he saw her, he put down his cup of coffee. "Ready to visit, Nick?"

"Yes." She held up her empty box. "Cookies are quite the hit around here."

"Yep." He grinned and picked up the smaller box. "Follow me."

As they proceeded down the hall towards the room, a woman possibly in her late fifties, or sixty, was coming out. Katy noticed her face was flushed as she wiped a tear from her cheek before looking up at them.

"Derek! So good to see you." She hugged him.

He held up the box. "His Friday special." He forced a limp smile and turned to Katy.

"This is my friend, Katy. We're working on a project together for the bakery. This is Mrs. Johnson. Nick's mother."

Katy extended her hand.

"Nice to meet you. Thank you both for visiting him. Butch and Ricky were here yesterday. Drove over from Boston. I know he gets lonely. I wish I could care for him at home, but I just can't. His father died a few years ago, and he's too heavy for me to lift and maneuver. But I never miss a day visiting him."

Katy noticed the bags under her eyes and the hunched shoulders. "I'm sure he appreciates it."

Mrs. Johnson patted Derek on the arm. "Enjoy your visit." She walked away.

They both paused before entering.

"That must be tough," she said.

"You can't even imagine." Derek knocked on the door, then opened it. "Surprise!"

Nick laughed when he saw the pink box and Derek. "About time," he said. His speech was slurred but intelligible enough.

Derek walked over, fist-bumped him on his bandaged hand, and navigated his bed to a better sitting position for eating. He opened the box. "An assortment today. Which one?"

"Brownie," Nick said.

Derek obliged by putting it on a napkin and cutting it into bite size pieces for him. "Good choice, soldier." That made him smile again.

Derek started talking to him about Butch and Ricky, and then switched to sports.

Katy pulled up a chair next to Derek after saying hello. Did he know Nick before he had been wounded?

Nick motioned his head towards her and said, "Pretty."

Katy blushed. "Thank you."

Derek looked at her, then looked at Nick. "Yes, she is."

He thinks I'm pretty? "How's the brownie?" she asked.

"Good," Nick said. She sat quietly as the two men conversed in short sentences filled with inside jokes and jesting. Her eyes roamed around the room until they rested on a photo by the window of three soldiers with their arms around each other. She squinted to see better. One of them was Derek. He knew this man before his injuries. Now it all made sense.

A nurse walked in with some medications. "I see you have more company. You're quite the popular guy." She grinned at Nick.

Nick nodded and motioned his head to Derek towards the young nurse. "Pretty."

Derek laughed. "Yes, you're surrounded by beautiful women. Way to go, soldier."

That made him smile.

"We were just leaving. See you soon, buddy." Derek fist bumped with Nick and turned to Katy. "Let's go."

As they walked out of the room, she noticed his demeanor changed immediately. Zipping up his coat, she swore his eyes were misty.

He held the truck door for her, but the silence was thick with unsaid thoughts and feelings.

Katy turned towards him. "Thanks for bringing me with you today."

He nodded.

"Can I ask you something personal?"

"Depends," he said.

"You knew Nick before his injuries, right?"

"Yes."

"I saw the photo of you guys on the window shelf. Was he in your platoon?"

"Yes."

For some reason she wanted to know his story. She wanted him to open up to her. She yearned for a more intimate relationship with this man, be it friend or more. "What happened over there?"

Derek tightened the grip on his steering wheel and stared straight ahead as he drove.

Oops. Did I cross a boundary? This was therapy kind of stuff not casual conversation.

He cleared his throat—then more silence.

"I'm sorry. Maybe that was too personal. Forget it," she said.

Derek guided his truck into Christine's driveway and turned off the ignition. He turned his head to meet Katy's eyes.

"Nick and I were in the same platoon and were on our second tour in Afghanistan. We all had shifts of night patrol. I had a bad twenty-four-hour stomach flu, so Nick traded nights with me. That evening a mortar shell hit the guys, and the rest is history. That should be me in the hospital bed, not him."

Katy reached out, placing her hand over his. "Oh, Derek. There was nothing you could have done. It wasn't your fault. Circumstances change all the time. It was out of your control. Don't blame yourself. Please, don't."

He locked in with her consoling eyes and took a hold of her hand resting on his. He squeezed it. "Easier said than done. It tears me up inside seeing him, but I vowed to always be there for him however I can. Even if it's just cookies. When the weather is nicer, I take him outside." He didn't let go of her hand.

A heated sensation was radiating up her arm from his touch. She didn't want to let go so she didn't. She let her hand sink into his firm grasp and laid her head back against the seat. She ached to support him more, but just sitting with him was all she could think of to do.

After a couple of minutes, Derek gently pulled his hand away. "Thanks for coming. It's nice having a friend go with me."

Did he just call her a friend? She'd take it. "Going with you is a gift. It helps me get out of my self-absorbed world which I frequently find myself in these last few years. See you tomorrow."

He waved to her as she hopped onto the front porch and then took off.

Christine and Sam were out to dinner, so Katy climbed the stairs to her bedroom. She was looking forward to a hot bath and some emotional decompressing. Derek had finally opened up which made her like him more. *Uh-oh. I'm losing control.* Not good. But what else lurked behind his dark past?

Chapter Twelve

Sam erected light stands and discussed best shots in the bakery with Mary Beth on Saturday afternoon. Christine, Alison, and Katy stood to the side, watching it unfold, and Derek agreed to work the counter while they were filming. Alison would ask her questions as they had done a year ago when launching the non-profit, *Hands-On Beyond,* for after-foster-care kids and orphans turning eighteen who needed jobs and housing. Now they would focus on the organization's *Hearts for Hope* campaign. Sweet Ridge Bakery would sponsor it as they sold small, heart-shaped gingerbread cakes with significant proceeds going to *Hands-On Beyond*—a perfect cause marketing plan for launching a new store in Manhattan.

Sam set up the camera, and Alison invited Mary Beth to sit beside her at a table.

"I can't believe a whole year has passed since we first told you of your job offer here at Sweet Ridge Bakery. Can you?" Alison smiled.

The corners of Mary Beth's mouth lifted spontaneously. "No. Time has flown by."

"Tell me what your experience has been working here and how it's affected you," Alison said.

"At first, I was nervous, but Christine, the owner, is a kind and considerate person; she eased me into taking more and more responsibility at my job. I was in a pretty dark space when my parents died, and my sister and I landed at Fairside Orphanage. I was stressed about what would happen to me when I turned eighteen and had no other relatives to take care of me. I couldn't leave Maple Ridge since Jolene would still live at Fairside. That day you announced I was receiving the first *Hands-On Beyond* scholarship was the happiest day of my life."

Alison reached over, gently placing her hand on Mary Beth's shoulder as a wetness began pooling in her eyes.

Mary Beth wiped the tear before it fell. "*Hands-On Beyond* gave me the best gift I could ever imagine. A chance to start a life as a young, competent woman. A chance to become financially viable, so I can bring Jolene home to live with me next year. And a chance to come out of my shell and begin living my life again after tragedy. Thank you." Mary Beth leaned over and hugged Alison.

Alison turned to the camera. "There you have it. The miracles of *Hands-On Beyond* and what this special *Hearts for Hope* campaign can do to help other young people like Mary Beth find their way. Please buy gingerbread cakes now, visit our website, and donate generously. Happy holidays!"

"Cut," Sam said. He shook his head. "Wow, what a difference from a year ago. Mary Beth, you have grown into an outgoing, confident woman."

Mary Beth blushed. "Thank you, Sam."

Sam directed everyone to the front counter where he picked up shots for B-roll of her serving customers and conversing with them. People didn't mind the commotion in the store. The Maple Ridge community always pulled together for anything related to Fairside Manor and *Hands-On Beyond*.

"And that's a wrap," Sam called. Those in the store cheered and clapped their hands.

Alison put her arm around Mary Beth. "Thank you. You've gotten quite skilled at being filmed." She grinned.

"I'm a different person than the one you met a year ago—thanks to you and everyone who helped me along the way." Her gaze zeroed in on Christine who had offered the job without hesitation.

Sam turned to Christine and Katy. "I'll work on this footage today and show you what I got from Eddie. He was a natural in front of the camera and was stoked to be included."

"You can use my office if you like," Christine said.

Derek overheard them. "Katy, you can use my office if you want. I'll be on the floor most of the day."

He seemed in a good mood today. "Yes, if you don't mind. It might be too crowded in Christine's."

"No problem. It's all yours." He grinned at her and walked away.

Katy's gaze fixated on him from behind, noticing his broad shoulders filling out his flannel shirt and his long strides taken to the other side of the room.

"Katy." No response. "Katy!" Christine said emphatically. "What are you daydreaming about?"

Katy snapped her head around. "Sorry. Just thinking. Did you need something?"

"A few of us are going to dinner tonight. Would you care to join us? Just Sam, me, Alison, Jake, Maggy and Mark."

All couples. *Great. I'll be the third wheel.* But what else did she have going on? "Sure. Thanks." She bent over to pick up her notepad which had fallen on the floor. "I'll be in Derek's office if you need me."

Christine gave her a thumbs up. "You know where to find me."

She smiled.

An hour later, a tap sounded on Katy's door.

"Hey, didn't mean to bother you, but I need something in my desk," Derek said.

"No problem." She leaned back as he bent over pulling out a drawer. His arm grazed hers and she stared at his hands, strong and firm, as it took out the file he needed. *What would those hands feel like on my body?* She shook her head. *Stop it. None of these thoughts, girl!*

With the door still open, Mary Beth peered around the entrance. "Derek, there's some woman here to see you. Said her name was Sophie. She's out front."

Katy watched as the expression on his face transformed into a frown. "A friend?" she asked.

"You could say that." His lips pressed together as he closed the drawer, tossed the file on his desk, and walked away.

She saw the tension wash over him. *Who is this woman?* Should she dare go peek out front and spy? *Of course, I should.* She put down her pen, stood up, and casually strolled toward the front. The doors had glass windows, so if she stood at the right angle, she could look without him seeing her.

Derek was sitting in the corner with a woman with shoulder-length blond hair and blue eyes that sparkled with adoration for this man. Derek didn't look happy, but she was talking, smiling, and reaching her hand out to his every few minutes. He didn't grasp it. *Good.* Must be someone from his past, most likely. Maybe an old girlfriend.

"What are you looking at?"

Startled, Katy jumped and twisted her head to see Christine staring at her.

"Uh, nothing."

Christine peeked through the window. "Derek, huh?"

Katy shook her head. *Busted.* "No, no. Just wanted to see how many customers you have today."

"You're such a liar." Christine grinned. "You like him, don't you?"

"What? Me? No, no." *Oh, stop it girl. This is your cousin. She's like your sister.* "I was curious. This girl seemed to stop by out of the blue, and he didn't seem happy when he found out."

"I'll find out. Wait here." Christine swooshed through the doors, grabbed the coffee pot to refill this mysterious woman's cup, and marched right over to their table.

"Need a refill?" she asked.

Derek looked up. "I'm fine. Sophie?"

"I would love some." She held out her cup.

"Christine, this is Sophie, an old friend of mine. Christine, the owner." He waved his hand toward her.

Sophie put her hand over his again. "Yes, we were more than just friends." She winked at Derek.

Derek pulled his hand back and looked up at Christine. "I'll be there in a minute."

"No worries. Take your time." She grinned.

After placing the coffeepot back in its place, she found Katy still standing behind the door.

Christine pulled her aside. "Definitely an old girlfriend. Probably the one who broke up with him after he returned."

Katy nodded. That would make sense. He had to have had a girlfriend. He was too hot not to have one.

Her head raised up as the doors swung open and Derek marched in with a scowl on his face. Obviously, he didn't like surprises. He nodded to the women and went straight to his office.

Christine looked at Katy with a lifted eyebrow.

Katy shrugged and went back to his office as well.

The door was left ajar, so she quietly stepped in and sat at the small table where her computer was still open. Derek was just sitting, running his fingers through his hair, staring at the wall in front of him.

"I can give you some privacy if you want. I was almost done." She waited for a response.

"Whatever works for you," he said. Still not moving, just staring.

"Did you have a nice visit with your friend?" *What are you doing? Leave him alone. Can't you see he's processing something heavy? Don't be a pushy woman.*

"It was okay. Her name is Sophie. She was an old girlfriend." He glanced up at her. "It didn't work out after I came home, and I haven't seen her since. She saw my mom who told her I worked here." He paused. "Kind of a shock." He looked at his watch. "It's almost quitting time. I'm going out front." As he stood up, Christine appeared in the doorway.

"Derek, what are you doing tonight?" she asked.

"Not much."

"A group of us are going to dinner at Vinny's. Come with us. It will be fun. We've all been working way too hard." She put her hand on his arm. "No buts about it."

He looked over at Katy. "Are you going?"

"How can I say no to this woman?" She pointed at her cousin.

"Alright. What time?"

"Six-thirty."

"I'll be there," he said. "I'm going to help clean up before closing.

See you ladies later."

After he left, Katy glared at Christine. "What are you doing?"

"He's our friend first. I'm not matchmaking." She chuckled. "But if sparks fly ..." She threw up her palms facing out.

"I live in New York, and he's a loner. Two big obstacles with red flags flying."

"God works in miraculous ways my dear. Look at me." She tossed her shoulders and left Katy with her jaw open.

* * *

Katy slipped gold hoop earrings into her ears and stepped back to inspect her appearance before going downstairs. Not bad. Years of New York living had given her a style she wasn't afraid to flaunt. If she was honest, there was more to this dress-up thing than just dinner with her cousin. A certain man was causing her to think twice about her appearance and what to wear.

Putting on her leather high-heeled boots, she looked down at her phone as it pinged. Another text from Simon. She received them daily and had decided to take the weekend off from any engagement with him. She needed to set boundaries.

A man's whistle sounded as she descended the stairs. Sam stood grinning at her with his arm around Christine. "How did I get so lucky to escort two beautiful women to dinner?"

Katy couldn't resist the smile spreading across her cheeks. "Guess it's your lucky day." She laughed.

"Come on. Let's go have some fun!" Christine threaded her arm through Katy's after putting on her coat.

The ride to Vinny's was short, and as they walked in, Katy saw everyone was there including Derek. He waved when he saw her.

"Saved you a seat," he said. Derek pointed to the empty chair next to him.

Katy greeted everyone around the table.

Derek leaned over to her. "You look radiant tonight."

Her long eyelashes lifted as she met his gaze. "Thank you. You dress up nice yourself." His hair was still damp from a shower smelling of musk and a woodsy odor, and his muscular chest filled out the clean dress shirt he was wearing. *Yes, he's a hunk.*

The group ordered a couple of bottles of wine, and the conversation turned to Alison and Jake's wedding, the plans, things still on the to-do list, and the venue. Alison and Jake had rented a space at Brookhurst Farms, a barn on the outskirts of town that often did weddings where the events planner could whip up her magic and create a whimsical setting exploding with love and everything Christmas.

Derek turned to Katy. "Are you going to the wedding?"

"Alison mentioned something about it. I didn't get a formal invitation because I just got here and didn't know her. I think I'll still be here."

He nodded.

"Are you?"

"Wouldn't miss it. Jake's become a good friend, and my parents will still be in Florida."

She nodded. Was he going to ask her to be his plus one? No, she was imagining things. Then she noticed his facial expression changed. She followed his gaze to a woman sitting at the bar. The same woman she had seen at the bakery. His old girlfriend. She was alone, saw Derek, and waved to him.

"Isn't that your friend?" asked Katy. His distraction was obvious.

He picked up his napkin, wiping a cold sweat breaking out on his neck. "Yeah."

"Maybe you should go say hi." Katy couldn't keep her mouth shut.

He stood up. "Excuse me, everyone. I see a friend at the bar. Be right back."

Her eyes stayed focused on him as he maneuvered through the restaurant to the bar. Sophie's face lit up as he approached and quickly touched his arm, motioning for him to sit next to her.

Christine leaned over to Katy. "What do you think she's saying to him?"

Katy swiftly stopped her glare. "I don't know. It's none of my business."

"Uh-huh." Christine's voice teased in a suggestive manner. "Interesting how she showed up here tonight. I wonder if it was more than a coincidence."

"How would she have even known?"

"The heart wants what the heart wants and will do anything to get it." Christine glanced over their way. "He's coming back."

Derek strolled to his chair, sat down, and gulped down a large swallow of his cabernet sitting in front of him. He wiped the dampness on his forehead and stared straight ahead.

"Funny coincidence, huh? Your friend showing up at this restaurant," Katy said.

"Yeah. She's waiting for someone from some dating website." He picked up his fork and started jabbing at his salad.

Should I push? "How do you feel about that? She is your old girlfriend, right?"

Derek dropped his fork on his plate and looked at her.

"It's none of my business."

Sorry I asked. This was a bad idea.

He reached out his hand and placed it on hers for a moment. "No. It's okay. I need to deal with this crap and all the feelings that get stuck inside of me. She knew I was coming here. She had texted earlier. She's doing this on purpose—to flaunt another man in front of me. She knows how to press my buttons." He squeezed her hand and went back to eating.

Katy sat still for a second, lingering in the tingling of his touch and fantasizing about having more skin contact with this dreamy guy. "If you ever want to talk about it, I'm here. I know we don't know each other that well, but I've told you about my hot mess in New York with work and a man. I won't judge."

He grinned. "Alright. Good to know."

Katy glanced over at Sophie as a tall, well-built man in a suit sidled up beside her, kissing her on the cheek. Yuk, on a first date? He had balls.

Derek viewed the scenario and tightened his grip on his knife while cutting a steak.

Katy saw the whites of his knuckles bulging as she glanced over at him. *He must be dealing with a shit storm inside.*

"I'm going to get some fresh air. Be right back," he said.

She nodded and continued watching the little show Sophie displayed. *What is this woman doing?* With Derek's background, this seemed a cruel way to get your boyfriend back. A gentler approach would work better with him. And the fact that she knew that was revealing.

"Should I go talk to him?" Katy asked Christine.

"No, leave him alone. I find his little walks turn him around."

Katy was feeling protective of him. She wanted to punch this girl in the face like he had done for her earlier in the week. She grinned at the thought as he returned to the table.

As he settled into his chair, she put her hand on his arm in full view of the woman across the way. "Feel better?"

"Always. What are you grinning about?"

"I have an idea. Two can play at this game. Put your arm around me."

His eyebrows lifted, and then he got it. His dimples slowly raised into his cheeks as he gently placed his arm around her shoulders. Casually, but as if they'd been doing this forever.

"Good. Now look at me and pretend to laugh at something I say."

"I don't have to pretend, Flanagan. You are hysterical."

They both laughed while the others at the table caught on. And for the next hour, Derek pretended to act as if Katy was his date, and he was totally into her. And she loved it.

When Sophie left, she waved to him. He barely waved and then immediately turned his face close to hers. "She's finally leaving. I think she got the message."

"Yeah. Don't mess with us." Katy laughed but was having a difficult time when his mouth was so close to hers. His breath was tickling her lips with desire.

"I think she's gone."

Slowly she unwrapped herself from the caress of his rock-solid body against hers, although she was reluctant to end their make-believe performance. "Yep." What had she done? She'd created an unreal situation that left her feeling empty. She didn't want it to end. She wanted more of this man sitting next to her.

"Thanks for being a friend," he said.

"Anytime." Yes, that's all it was. A display of friendship with a little humor.

As the group divided up the check into couples, Derek grabbed hers. "My treat. That little stunt you did with me calmed some dark stuff about to explode inside. Thanks."

Kindness poured out of his eyes, enveloping her with a sweet tenderness. "And thanks for dinner."

"Do you need a ride home?"

"No, I'm going with Christine and Sam." She needed some space from him.

"Let's talk tomorrow about this trip to Vermont, okay?"

"Sounds good."

Derek said his goodbyes and left the restaurant.

Christine put her arm around her as they walked out to the car. "Are you okay?"

"Yeah. I don't know what came over me, but I couldn't stand how Sophie was trying to get him back. She must have no clue as to what PTSD does to a person."

"And when did you become such an expert?" Christine asked.

"When you told me about Derek, I did my own research, but being around him more, visiting the veterans, and hearing part of his story, I have a whole new understanding about his situation."

Christine nodded, then squeezed her. "You're the best. Hope you know it."

"Thanks. Back at ya."

They climbed into the SUV, and Katy dropped her head back contemplating the evening's events. She liked Derek. Maybe more than she should.

Chapter Thirteen

Katy and Christine hopped out of the SUV in the back parking lot of the bakery. They had dropped off Sam at the train station after church and were now in work mode. The special heart-shaped pans had arrived yesterday, and they were going to make the first batch of gingerbread cakes as a test drive for the campaign.

During church, Katy saw Derek but didn't interact much, just a wave. She was dealing with an emotional whirlwind of her own after the little pretend escapade she had instigated at the restaurant. He may feel lighter, but the whole thing left her feeling a bit off-center. She didn't want to admit her attraction to him was growing—*oy vey*.

Christine threw her coat on a hook and purse in the drawer. "Why don't you help us on the floor? Jake and Alison are coming later for their cake testing too, but that's all handled. The samples were done yesterday and are in the walk-in."

More time with Derek. "Sure. Sounds like fun." She followed her out.

Derek was already on the floor, mixing batter as he followed Christine's recipe. Christine looked at Katy and pointed in his direction. "Why don't you help him?"

She nodded and grabbed an apron. Tying it around her waist, she sauntered up to Derek. His hair fell over one eye, and his bulging bicep exuded strength in manipulating the industrial blender. She stared for a moment, her heart fluttering as she watched him.

His eyes locked with hers. "Why don't you get the pans over there? It will take two of us to spoon the batter inside."

She spun around, hand over her belly to calm her nerves, and returned with the trays. "Here you go." She watched as he poured the batter into a large bowl, making it easier to scoop into the pans. *He's just so darn sexy whatever he does.*

"Come stand over here. We can both spoon in the mix with the bowl between us."

Thank god the bowl was between them. The scent of his woodsy cologne mixed with sugar and spice baking in the oven was making her light-headed.

He demonstrated how much to put in the pans and picked up a spoon for her. As he handed it to her, their fingers touched. Oh dear, was she sweating too? Not good.

They quickly fell into a mixing, scooping, baking, and repeating rhythm. After the first batch cooled, Christine joined them.

"Now, the question is, what do we do with the top? Leave them plain or put some type of topping or frosting on them?" She furrowed her forehead, inspecting one in her hand.

"Let's try a few different ways and see which one we like best," Derek said.

"Good idea. Let's try a dollop of whipped cream, make some pink and red frosting, and make designs of some sort, or whatever you guys come up with. This will be fun." She clapped her hands together.

Derek and Christine pulled out the ingredients, and the three started experimenting. Derek stood next to Katy as she made a whipped cream sample. He looked over and saw she had a small glob on her cheek. He reached his hand out, wiped it off with his finger, and placed it in his mouth with a grin. "That's good."

He's flirting with me. She swung her towel and slapped it on his arm. "Stop that. I was saving it for later." She laughed and playfully put her finger in the whipped cream and spread it across his face.

"Oh, that's how you want to play?" He put his finger in his frosting and smeared it across her cheek. He stepped back before she could hit him again with the towel.

She wiped the frosting off her face and licked her fingers. "Hmm. Good."

"Okay, you two. Back to work," Christine said. She shook her head.

"Truce?" Derek asked.

"Truce," Katy said. A wide grin was plastered to her face; she couldn't remove it.

Christine had designed boxes, briefly describing the *Hands-On Beyond* program benefitting from the *Hearts for Hope* campaign on the lids. Katy had designed the logo, and a local printer had done the boxes. By the time they finished, they had decided a simple, yet fancy outline of pink frosting was the winner and would endure shipping better.

Christine looked at them. "Let's taste test now." She handed one to each of them, and they all bit in at the same time.

A giddy noise escaped Katy's mouth as she swooned over her first bite. "Oh, my god. This is delicious."

Derek popped the whole thing in his mouth after the first bite and nodded.

Christine held up one box. "And they're so cute!"

"Hey, anybody home?" Jake and Alison came through the front doors, ready for their taste-testing.

"Oh, my gosh. Time got away from us. I have everything in the walk-in, but first come sample the gingerbread cakes for the campaign!" Christine said.

Alison and Jake walked over, and Derek gave each one their own little heart.

"These are amazing," Alison said. She picked up one of the boxes and read the inscription for *Hands-On Beyond.* Her eyes became wet as she held back the tears. "I'm so touched you came up with this idea."

Derek pointed to Katy. "Thank her. She's the brain behind the campaign." He watched her blush as he mentioned her name.

"It was a team effort. Still is," Katy said.

Alison hugged Katy. "Yes, I know. It takes a village to do the work we do."

"Can you two clean up in here while I do my professional tasting?" Christine laughed.

"No problem," they both chimed.

After the last bunch was taken from the oven, Derek began to wash up while Katy put the finishing touches on the cakes. When finished, she turned to him. "This was fun today."

"I'm glad you could help." He paused. "We should talk about tomorrow. I heard that they might get some snow so be sure and bring an emergency bag of extra clothes and toiletries in case we get stuck somewhere."

Did he just ask me to pack an overnight bag? "Really?"

"You probably won't need it, but I like to be prepared. Army thing."

"Okay. What time are we leaving?"

"I'll pick you up around ten. We'll get there around one. We can have lunch, do our snooping, and return home by five or six."

"Sounds like a plan."

"I'm headed out. Do you need a ride home? Christine might be here for a while."

"Yeah, that would be great. Let me get my things and tell her."

Katy interrupted the tasting to let Christine know she would catch a ride with Derek.

Christine looked at Jake and Alison. "Derek and Katy are doing a little recon trip for me tomorrow to scope out our competition in Vermont."

Jake nodded with a grin. "You two are becoming quite the team."

Katy felt heat spreading across her cheeks again. "We're both committed to helping my cousin here." She fondly tapped Christine's shoulder. "I'll see you at home." She said goodbye and joined Derek at the back door.

He opened the door for her and slid into the front seat. "Hope you don't mind making this trip in my truck, but she's solid in any bad weather."

"Good to know." She fiddled her hands in her lap as she thought about tomorrow—all day with this man and nowhere to hide. She'd better get it together—and quick.

* * *

As Derek rooted through his closet for a small duffel bag that evening, he heard heavy footsteps bounding up the stairs and a knock on the door. Opening it, he grinned, seeing Mark standing there.

"Hey. I just got back from dropping off Reggie at Fairside, saw your light on, and thought I'd stop by," he said.

"Yeah, come on in. Don't mind the mess. It's been kind of a crazy week. Can I get you something to drink? Beer? Water?"

"No, nothing, thanks. It's getting late. I wanted to see how you were doing after that little fiasco at the restaurant last night. That was Sophie, wasn't it?"

"Yeah. I never dreamed she'd show up there. She had stopped by at the bakery earlier, then texted me to see if I wanted to get a drink with her. I told her I had dinner plans with friends at Vinny's, and the rest is history. She arranged a date in front of me to make me jealous, most likely. She thought she could slide in on the dinner plans when she was leaving. But Katy threw a wrench in that plan." He laughed.

"Yeah, it was kind of comical on our end. Seems like you're making friends with Katy." Mark tilted his head, awaiting his response.

"At first, she pushed my buttons, but we talked about that in group. Now we seem to have this bond forming because we're on the same mission—to win this competition for Christine."

"And how's that going?" Mark asked.

"Good. We're driving up to Vermont tomorrow for our little recon spy mission." He chuckled. "I'll be spending a lot of time with her and have to admit I'm attracted to her as a woman." *Yes, her perfect curves, soft, curly hair, large brown eyes, and pink lips have caught my attention.*

"Yes, she is a vibrant, striking woman. What's her relationship status?"

"She just went through a break-up in New York. Seems her boyfriend got her coveted position at the office, stole one of her ideas, and broke up with her because of the company's policy with bosses and employees."

"Ouch. That must have hurt."

"I don't know if she's let herself feel the pain. I think she's in the anger stage still."

"So wise, brother."

"It's all those therapy sessions with Dr. McPherson." He laughed.

"What are you going to do about Sophie?"

Straight to the point. That's what Derek liked about Mark. "I'm not sure." His phone pinged. He looked down to see a message from Sophie.

Can we talk? Let's meet for dinner this week. Smiley emoji.

"Who is it?" Mark asked.

"Sophie. I'll text her later."

"You know my experience with Sandra, my girlfriend before deployment. I couldn't move on until I asked for her forgiveness. She had forgiven me a long time ago, but I needed to forgive myself. You might have some unresolved issues there, my friend." Mark's eyes bared down on him with laser intensity.

Derek fidgeted with his hands, cracking his knuckles. "You're probably right. When I get back, I'll deal with it."

Mark stood up and placed his hand on Derek's shoulder. "I have no doubt you will. Have a good trip tomorrow. Watch the weather. I heard we're supposed to get some snow."

"I will."

The two hugged and Mark left. Derek picked up his phone and texted Sophie.

I'll call you midweek. Have been busy with a project.

She wrote back immediately.

Okay. Kissy emoji.

Derek shook his head. Yes, he was going to have deal with this. She wasn't going away.

Chapter Fourteen

Katy packed toiletries and a few things in her emergency bag, a small tote, just in case. She doubted she would need them but was willing to follow Derek's suggestion. Her stomach had been in a knot all morning, preparing for the short trip to Vermont. Her hand rubbed her tummy, trying to soothe the tension lodged there. *Deep breaths, girl. He's just a friend.*

Peeking out the dining room window, she saw his truck pull up. She took one last look in the mirror, applied some lip gloss, and opened the door when he knocked.

"Hi. I'm ready. I'm bringing my computer in case we want to look up anything." His dark eyes seemed to scan her body up and down, giving her a chill.

"Sure." He reached down to pick up her bag for her while she handled her computer bag and purse. He held it up. "Emergency stuff?" he asked.

"Yep. Hopefully Army approved." His grin wrapped around her like a soft blanket. She was sunk.

As she climbed into the front seat, he held up another bag from the bakery. "Christine insisted we take a goodie bag when I left the bakery."

"For emergencies?"

"I think we're covered now." He laughed, started the ignition, and pulled out of the driveway.

She eased herself into the leather seat and watched as the forests of pine trees, naked maples, and oaks whooshed by her. The knot in her stomach was unwinding. Being with him in person was more manageable than all the mind projections she seemed to create for herself. *He's just a guy. You work with plenty of men in New York and never have a problem. But don't fool yourself. This guy is different.* Something about him pulled her in, stirring a desire she had suppressed.

"Country music okay with you?" he asked.

"Sure."

"I didn't know if a New Yorker was into that kind of music."

"I am a New Yorker, but I can do country. I'm a versatile woman."

"Yes, I'm starting to see that."

Is he flirting with me? This could be a long trip.

"On a serious note, I wanted to thank you for stepping in the other night. I admit, it was fun."

"When I saw she was torturing you on purpose, it pissed me off. And besides, I like fun and games." She lifted her eyebrow at him.

He laughed. "I'll remember that."

Oh god, now she was flirting with him—unbelievable. "Did she call you yesterday?"

"She texted. I do need to talk to her, though. I've been avoiding it, but after that incident, I realized I needed to resolve some issues from our break-up last year. I was a different person—not so nice to be around."

She nodded. She was beginning to understand how the darkness of PTSD might still haunt him. She reached her hand out and touched his arm. "From what I see now, you're a kind- hearted guy. Your work with the veterans is inspiring."

"My work with veterans is a necessity. I'll do it until the day I die."

She let her hand slip down but had an uncontrollable urge to cuddle up into this man. She wanted to take his pain away, consoling any hurt left inside.

As the GPS guided them off the main highway a couple of hours later, they found themselves in the thick of northern hardwoods, sugar maples, and beech extending their naked branches over the hills. The country road twisted and turned around banks of hemlock and red oaks in the lower elevation; after crossing a quaint covered bridge, a *Welcome to Wheaton, Vermont* sign popped up to greet them.

"This is beautiful!" Katy exclaimed. "No wonder the investment firm was captivated by its charm."

Like Maple Ridge, boutique stores, a coffee shop, a hardware store, a couple of restaurants, and a few art galleries, were scattered along Main Street, their uniqueness inviting tourists to stop and browse.

Derek pulled into an empty parking space. "Frosty Mountain Bakeshop should be at the end of the street according to my directions. They also serve lunch, so we can sit and observe the customers without being noticed."

"I'm ready."

Derek took their personal belongings and her computer bag, securing them in the back of the trunk under lock and key. He placed his hand on her shoulder. "I'm enjoying this."

Me too. In more ways than one. "Yes, being on a spy mission with you is a change from my habitual life in New York." She tossed her hair to one side as she pulled on her fuzzy hat. She reached her hand out letting several snowflakes fall onto her palm. "It's snowing. How magical is that?"

Derek pulled his baseball hat over his head as she spoke, and grinned, watching her excitement. "Just flurries for now. Let's hope it stays that way. Come on, let's go." He placed his hand on her back guiding her towards the shop.

His touch warmed her body for an instant, and she let it. She was tired of fighting with herself.

Standing on the sidewalk, Katy pulled out her phone camera when they were close. She tried to take as many pictures as possible without being noticed. The shop was in an old Victorian home, like the ones in Maple Ridge. Since it was located at the end of the street, she noticed a dirt road reaching back to a grassy field, now brown, with a large red barn placed at the end. Five or six cars were parked in the lot, and a van advertising the shop's logo was in plain sight.

"I bet that's part of their baking facility. This house would be too small to produce the items for their online store. Maybe we can sneak down there after lunch and take some pictures."

"Or maybe we can say we're really into baking and would love a tour of the facility." He lifted his eyebrow to her.

"That could work too. But the spy stuff kind of thrills me."

"We don't want to get arrested while we're here, Flanagan."

"Okay. You win." She grinned, her mischievous spirit soaring.

Derek held the door for her as they walked into the sound of bells jingling, just like Sweet Ridge Bakery. He pointed to a table in the corner, and she followed.

"Looks like we order at the counter, and they bring it to us. Tell me what you want, and I'll get it," he said.

She studied the menu and noticed they had paper ones on the counter. "Derek, can you get one of those menus, please? For reference." She winked at him. "I'll take a chicken salad sandwich and a cup of vegetable soup. Thanks."

In front of the counter, he gave his order, and stared at the baked goods inside of the shelves. Everything looked delicious, and he saw the famous Frosty cupcakes with notable choices for frosting flavors. He would love to see their spreadsheets but knew that was impossible. Maybe if they got a tour, he could ask questions. He looked back at Katy and watched her taking indoor pictures trying to be nonchalant. *She is adorable.*

"Getting what you need?" He slid onto his chair across from her.

"I'm sending pics to Christine. She keeps asking me questions."

"Tell her we'll call her when we're done. I definitely want to see their facility."

"Me too."

One of the staff brought out their lunch, and they ate, chatting about the shop and comparing it to Christine's. When they were finished, they both walked over to the baked goods to load up on several boxes to take back to Maple Ridge.

The kind woman behind the counter selected some of her favorites for them, and Derek had no problem picking out items he wanted to eat. "My you two must be having a party or else have a very large family." She laughed as she secured five boxes of assorted goods for them.

"Oh, I'm totally into baking. I love trying new things. Where do these get made?" Katy asked.

"Out back you'll see a barn. That's our production facility. Makes it easy."

"Do you think there's any chance we could see it? I would love to know what goes into the underpinnings of a store like this. Maybe I can open one someday."

"I have to go down there in a few minutes. If you don't mind waiting you could come with me. I'm sure the owner wouldn't mind. They're out of town and will be back later tonight if the storm doesn't hit us first," the woman said.

"That would be great. Thank you." Katy tried hard to refrain from jumping up and down. She looked over at Derek, whose lips pursed, holding his dimples from flying wide, trying to hide his amusement at her overzealous nature.

When they sat down again, Derek couldn't help but smile. "You are in your element you know. Detective work could be a second career."

She laughed. "I know. Hopefully we'll have a successful recon."

"I'm sure we will."

Soon the woman came over to them. "My name is Nancy, by the way. Follow me. You can leave your packages behind the counter until you come back."

As they walked outside, snow was falling more than a few flurries. "I think the storm is coming. Are you two staying in town tonight?" Nancy asked.

Katy looked at Derek.

"Not sure yet," he said.

"After your tour, watch the local news on your phone. I heard there might be an ice storm. They'll close the road getting into town if that happens."

"Okay, thanks." He looked at Katy and shrugged. They both knew that could happen.

"Here we are." Nancy walked around to a side door and swung it open. The intense scent of cinnamon, sugar, chocolate, and bread baking all mixed together bombarded their olfactory glands, nearly knocking them over as they stepped inside.

Katy's mouth dropped. It was bigger than Christine's and had a massive assembly line running with people busy doing individual jobs. "Wow."

"This is enormous. Is this mostly for your online business?" he asked.

"Yes, we bake fresh daily but our online business with Frosty cupcakes and cookies is sold everywhere. We have quite a few grocery store accounts in Vermont and other parts of New England. That makes up for most of the business. Our boss wants to expand into New York City and is working on some kind of investment project. Let me give you a tour."

Nancy showed them all the stations and preparation essentials to mass produce. When she wasn't looking, Katy grabbed a few pictures.

When they were finished, Nancy turned to her. "So, do you think you'd want to open a store someday?"

"I don't know. This is a major undertaking. I may stick to my kitchen baking for friends and family." Katy laughed.

"Yes, this is a vocation not a hobby anymore. Mr. and Mrs. Stiles love it. They grew up here, so they're never leaving. I have to stay down here but when you go back to the shop, walk across Main Street, and ask Bobby about the local weather report. He owns the hardware store and knows everything about it. Trust me."

Derek reached out his hand to her. "Thank you so much for the tour. It was enlightening."

"Yes, thank you," Katy said.

When they opened the door to the driveway a strong wind nearly knocked Katy over. A winter storm had landed in Wheaton and was getting worse by the minute. She pulled her scarf tighter around her neck as the flakes were falling at a faster clip than before.

Derek grabbed her arm as they walked back to the bakery, steadying her in the wet snow accumulating on her not-so weatherproof boots. "Let's pick up the boxes and find this Bobby guy. If we need to stay here overnight, no problem. That's what our emergency bags are for, right?"

His words soothed her nerves which were exploding like firecrackers on the fourth of July. "Right." She slipped on the sidewalk, but he caught her with both hands before she went down and pulled her closer to him. "Thanks," she said.

"No problem." They made it to the truck, tossed the boxes in the back, and turned to walk across the street. The snow was piling up fast.

As they opened the front door, Derek guided her toward the cash register. She could feel this other side of him, probably the soldier one, where he was taking charge now. He was on a mission. *To protect her at all costs?* Certainly felt like it.

"Is Bobby here?" he asked.

"Yeah, in the back," said the young clerk. "It's really coming down out there, isn't it?"

"Got that right," Derek said. He grabbed Katy's hand and pulled her alongside with him.

A stocky man with a broad chest and white hair was in the back helping a customer. "Are you, Bobby?" Derek asked.

He looked up. "Sure am. What can I do for you?"

"Nancy at the bakery told us you were the best one to decipher the weather patterns coming through here. Should we drive south or stay put?"

"Stay put. There's an ice storm raging south of us, and they're closing the bridge coming into town from the west. You'd be safer. By morning the salt trucks will be out, and it looks like a sunny day and colder."

"Can you suggest a hotel?" he asked.

"I'd stay at Lola's Bed and Breakfast at the edge of Main Street. The roads are getting icy out towards the highway where you would find more hotels. Don't take the risk."

"Okay, thanks."

"Yeah. Welcome to Wheaton where the weather changes on a dime." He chuckled and went back to helping his customer.

Derek turned to Katy, lifting his shoulders and eyebrows at the same time. "Well?"

This was a no-brainer. "Let's go."

As they walked towards the truck, Derek's arm squeezed around her shoulders, making sure she didn't fall. Katy surrendered. Something was letting go inside. Not sure of what it was, but it felt damn good.

They drove the three blocks to the inn and got out. "Fingers crossed they have rooms," Katy said.

Approaching the front desk, a petite woman with curly grey hair, bright green eyes, and a smile as big as Texas greeted them. "Come in! Get out of that cold and mess!" she said.

"Do you have a couple of rooms available for tonight?" Derek asked.

"I have one room left, but that should be alright for you two, right?" Her eyes darted back and forth between Katy and Derek.

Derek looked at Katy to decide.

She nodded. This wasn't part of the emergency plan.

He whispered in her ear. "We'll figure it out. I can sleep on the floor. Remember I am Army trained in survival skills." He grinned.

The woman came around to the front of the entrance. "My name is Lola. Follow me." She proceeded up the stairs with the two of them following. Derek took both overnight bags. When they came to the end of the hall, she opened the door. "Voila! One of our larger rooms so you should be fine. We have dinner at six if you'd like to eat here and a buffet breakfast in the morning. Would you like a reservation for tonight? I need a head count."

Derek looked at Katy.

"Sure. Then we don't have to go out in the storm again."

"Smart choice," Lola said. "Just call the front desk if you need anything—extra towels, linens, anything. Here's your keys." She handed the keys to Katy and left.

The two stood in the middle of the room and stared at each other. Then they both busted up laughing at the same time.

"Well, who could predict this?" Derek asked.

"Not me," she said. She hoped she survived the next twenty-four hours and plopped down on the end of the bed. "Let's call Christine."

He nodded and pulled up a chair next to her.

Christine picked up right away. "Katy, Derek! Are you okay? I never should have sent you two knowing the weather might get bad. I watched the news and route eighty-seven is an icy mess. Where are you?"

"You can relax. We decided to stay here in town for the night. Tomorrow is supposed to be much better for traveling."

"Oh, thank God. Where are you staying?"

"At a charming little bed and breakfast near the bake shop. We're fine. Don't worry."

"The pictures you sent were awesome. I can't believe you got into their facility. Nice job," Christine said.

"Yeah, we make a pretty good team," Derek said, eyes glued to Katy's.

Katy held his glance, her insides trembling with anticipation of their evening together. "We'll text you tomorrow when we're on the road."

"At least enjoy the inn and the snow. Remember, you are on vacation." Christine laughed.

"This vacation has become quite an adventure," Katy said.

"The best kind. See you tomorrow, guys. Love you." And she hung up.

Derek stood up. "I'm going to find Lola and get an extra blanket and sheet. I'll just tell her you get cold." He laughed.

"Ha, ha. Blame it on me, huh?"

"Why not?"

Katy picked up a pillow from the bed and threw it at him.

"Is that how you want to play?" He threw it back at her, hitting her squarely in the head.

"Okay, okay. I'll stop. You're a better aim for sure. Not an even playing field." *What am I doing?* An uncontrollable urge to tease this man? What was that about?

Derek strode out the door, leaving her to sit with her feelings, but she suddenly found everything comical. Here she was, being forced into tight quarters with a hot, irresistible man for the next twelve hours. *What could go wrong?*

When he came back, Katy was at the desk with her computer,

looking over their campaign. Keeping busy, maybe she could handle this unexpected situation.

He tossed the bedding on the floor in the corner and walked over to her. "Whatcha looking at?"

"Just reviewing our campaign." She looked at the pile on the floor. "Maybe we could get a roll-away bed."

"I asked. They're all taken. Don't worry about me. I'll be fine. I've learned to sleep anywhere."

"Pull up that other chair and let's look at everything again. See if we're missing something, since we've seen the inside operation of Frosty Mountain Bakeshop." She scooted over to make room for him.

He pulled up a chair, got his notebook out, and the two of them remained focused on work until dinner.

Chapter Fifteen

Holiday music drifted in the background, and evergreen swag and garlands were strung along mantels, tables, and walls. A cinnamon scent emanated from lit votives, and a well-garnished Christmas tree was poised in the corner. There were about a dozen tables set up in two rooms with candlelight centerpieces on each of them. "This is magical," Katy said. *And very romantic.*

"I guess not such a bad place to be stuck, right?" Derek asked.

Lola came to greet them. "I saved you two a table in the corner."

"Thank you," Katy said. She felt like she was on a weekend getaway with her lover, not a business trip. *Get a grip, girl. He's not relationship material, and you're too busy for love in your life. You need to figure out what you're doing next.*

Derek held her chair for her as she sat down. "Quite the gentleman, I see," she said.

"Trained well."

She looked across the table at him. "Thank you for the emergency bag suggestion. At least I had a clean shirt to put on." She giggled.

"Yeah, me too." He put his napkin on his lap, took a sip of water, and picked up the wine menu. "Care for a drink?" he asked.

"Yes, please. I think we deserve one, don't you?"

"Most definitely, Flanagan. How about a cabernet? I'll order a half bottle."

"Excellent." As she gazed around the room, the Christmas spirit wrapped around her, landing in her heart, giving her hope for a miracle in her life—both personally and professionally. Derek's voice brought her back to reality.

"So, Miss Flanagan, why the branding and marketing career? What inspired you to take that path?"

"Curious about me, huh, Higgins?" She grinned. "I always had an artistic side and couldn't figure out how to apply my talents. In college, I took this marketing course by fluke when the class I wanted wasn't available. We did this project for a fictitious corporation, and I got an A plus. My ability to draw and connect with people's visions came together and voila, here I am!"

"Do you like working at a big firm?"

"Yes and no. Yes, it's given me plenty of opportunities to grow and learn, and the money's good. But lately, I'm stifled by the recent roadblocks placed before me and disheartened about working under Simon. Wasn't part of my plan." She took a huge sip of her cabernet.

"Do you miss him?"

My, he's getting personal. Well, this night is anything but ordinary. Bring it on. "I don't know. I was so angry when I left, and rightly so. It was more about his taking credit for my ideas to win the director position that infuriated me. We've been good working partners in the last few years, and it overflowed into our personal life. I never questioned it. Being here in Maple Ridge has brought up many questions for me."

"Yeah? Like what?"

His eyes penetrated hers with a determined earnestness she couldn't ignore. "I'm not sure I can work at Martin and Lewis anymore. And that scares me." She took another gulp of wine.

"What about it scares you?" he asked.

She grinned. "When did you become a therapist?"

"Let's just say, lots of personal experience working through my PTSD symptoms. So, what are you afraid of?" He didn't back down.

"Starting over at the bottom rung in a new firm. Getting used to different company policies and people. Even though I didn't get the position, I'm still respected at the office and most know my skills." Droplets of moisture were forming along her hairline; she brushed them away.

"So, being recognized is important to you?"

"What do you mean?" She squirmed in her chair as an irritable twinge pinched her gut.

"I'm not criticizing. Everyone wants to be acknowledged for their skills, but have you ever considered that you're putting up roadblocks for yourself?"

She looked down, rubbing the neck of her wineglass with her fingers, stalling for an answer. *Is my ego that big?*

Derek reached his hand out, touch hers. "Hey, I'm sorry if I went too deep here. Perhaps I'm out of line. Sorry."

She inhaled, still not looking at him, and exhaled slowly. "No. It's alright." She raised her eyes to meet his. "I guess I do have this thing of wanting to be recognized for being the smartest person in the room, the most talented, and above all, the most valuable." She started laughing. "Oh, dear god. Can I be fixed?"

Now he laughed. "We can only do our best, Katy. And from where I'm sitting, you're doing just that. We're lucky to have you in our corner." He released his hand on hers and picked up the dinner menu. "Let's order. I'm starved. We can come back to your inner probing another time."

"Ha, ha. Very funny." But Derek was right on about her. She was always trying to prove herself to someone, some boss, some company, or some boyfriend, her entire life. When would she be enough as she was? She shook her head and decided to let it go.

After ordering, they kept the conversation light, although Katy was dying to ask him more questions about his military life. She figured she'd have another chance later.

When the waitress brought their check, he was quick to grab it.

"Come on, let's split it," she said.

"No. Christine and I discussed this. You're our guest and have been working long hours as a volunteer. It's the least we can do. This is a company expense with one of your new clients." He winked at her.

She surrendered and watched as he took out a credit card. Looking out the window, the snow was still falling. "I wish I had my winter boots with me. I'd love to go for a walk."

He turned his head towards the picturesque view outside. "Don't worry. I'm sure there will be another opportunity in Maple Ridge for a snowy outing. You're staying through Christmas, right?"

"Yes." A tiny pang in her heart fluttered, thinking about her departure. *You still have plenty of time with this man. Don't get all sentimental quite yet.* That she was thinking about him this way jolted her into a reality check. *Not relationship material. Remember that.*

"Good. We'll make that happen."

Did he say we? *Uh-oh. Sliding into dangerous territory.* She smiled at him.

Derek opened the door to their room and motioned to the bathroom. "Ladies, first."

"I might take a shower. Do you need to use it before I do?"

"Nah, go ahead. I'll do the same after you."

She fumbled through her bag for her pajamas and toiletries. Her hands were trembling, thinking of the intimacy they were sharing, even if there was no sex involved. Sex. It had been a while. She needed a shower to wash away all these agonizing thoughts she was having about the man in the room with her.

When she came out, she saw that he had made a bed for himself on the floor. "Are you sure you're okay with this? I feel bad I get the bed."

"You forget I've slept on rocks in the mountains of Afghanistan. Warmth, cozy blankets, and peace are all I need." He walked past her into the bathroom.

Katy checked her emails, noting one long one from Simon about a potential new client he thought would be perfect for cause marketing. He wanted to Zoom with her on Wednesday since some deadline was involved. She ignored his request, sent a note to Christine, and shut down her computer.

Derek walked out of the bathroom wearing a T-shirt and sweats. Thank god, he got dressed and wasn't wearing just a towel. That would have put her over the edge.

"Time for bed, young lady. Stop working."

"Just an email or two." She threw up her hands placing the computer on the desk. "See? All done." She climbed into bed, as he did the same.

"Goodnight, Katy," he said.

"Goodnight, Derek. Thanks for an unusually fun day," she said.

"We're an unusually good team, Flanagan."

With a smile on her lips, she rolled over and turned out the lights.

* * *

Sounds of moaning awoke Katy in the middle of the night. Where was it coming from? Once she acclimated to where she was in the hotel room, she realized it was coming from Derek. He was mumbling something in his sleep. Should she wake him up or shake him gently?

In the pitch dark, a faint light shone through the curtains from the street below. She crawled out of bed as the moans got louder and turned into words filled with anguish and fright.

"Help! Nick! Get out of here. Get out!"

She bent down beside him just as he flew up sitting, shouting. "Run!"

She watched as his eyes widened, sweat poured down his face, and his hands visibly trembled.

"Derek?" Her voice was almost a whisper.

Panting with rapid breaths, he looked towards the voice and saw her kneeling next to him.

"Are you alright?" She hesitated from touching him. She imagined he was having a nightmare caused by PTSD but didn't know what to do. Sit with him? Go back to bed?

He sat up straighter, his body shaking. "Yeah. Was I screaming?"

"Kind of," she said.

"Sorry about that."

"Can I get you anything?" she asked.

"No. I'll get up in a minute and get some water." He stared straight ahead letting his breathing return to normal. They sat together, no words spoken, while he regained control of himself.

She felt an urge to touch him. Is it safe now? She placed her hand on his shoulder and could see a wetness spreading behind his eyes. She remained silent, something she was getting used to doing with this man.

He slowly reached for her hand and grabbed it, bringing it down to his lap and drawing her closer. She heard his breath regulating as heat radiated from him, teasing her skin beneath her silk top. As her eyes acclimated to the darkness, he turned his head inches from hers. She wanted him to kiss her. She wanted him and could see the same desire in his eyes. They had been dancing around it for too long.

She didn't know what to say. "Do you want a hug?" She pulled her hands from his grasp and wrapped them around him, her intention consoling the shaken man. After a moment, she leaned back, looking at him without wavering.

In slow motion, his head lowered, his breath tickling her cheek. She raised her lips to meet his mouth, inching closer to him, pressing her chest against his shirt. His hand slid behind her head, grasping her hair, and pulled her into him— diving into the kiss with a fierceness long suppressed. She couldn't stop the pleasure noises emanating from her throat, her desire floating like music into the room.

As they separated, he gazed into her eyes. "I'm sorry if I crossed a line." He waited for her response.

She placed her hand on his cheek. "I think we both have been wanting to do that for a while."

He grinned. "Got that right." He noticed she was shivering and opened his blanket. "Here. Get under. You're cold. I promise no funny business."

All she wanted to do was crawl under that blanket with this man. Just a few moments, that's all. "Okay."

She eased down next to him as he wrapped her up in his blanket and held her in his arms, letting her head fall on his chest. She couldn't move, nor did she want to. *What am I doing?*

Her head moved up and down on his chest with the rhythm of

his breathing. His fingers automatically threaded her hair, stroking her gently. They lay in silence enveloping her with a fulfilled satisfaction she didn't know she needed. She didn't want to think of all the impossibilities of why a relationship would never work with him. Not right now.

After about fifteen minutes, her body jerked, falling asleep. She lifted her head to see his eyes closed, almost snoring. She needed to get to her bed. She slowly inched her way out from under the blanket and tiptoed back, sliding onto her mattress, and pulling the duvet over her body.

Lying in the stillness she could still taste the fierceness of his lips, his toughened hands in her hair, and his rock, solid body against hers in the dark. A fire had been ignited, but how long would it burn? Did she have any control over it? Probably not.

* * *

The sunlight poured through the window as Katy opened her eyes, trying to remember where she was. And then it hit her, as images from the middle of the night with Derek flashed in front of her. What had she done? She had fully allowed herself to open to him on some intimate level that she knew she couldn't commit to. She needed to talk to him later. She was a New Yorker through and through, not a country gal. She needed to let him know. And she didn't do casual.

She peeked around the room and saw Derek's blanket and sheets neatly folded on the chair with him nowhere in sight. Did he go to breakfast without her? She padded over to the bathroom, brushed her teeth, washed her face, and got dressed. When she opened the door, he was standing there with two coffees in his hand.

He lifted one towards her. "Good morning."

She took it and smiled. "Good morning."

"Sleep well?" he asked. His smile broadened across his face.

A mischievous sparkle was in his eyes this morning. "Yes, I did." *Are we going to talk about last night?*

He sat down in the chair after throwing his blanket on the bed.

She sat in the other chair waiting for the conversation to begin.

"About last night," he started. "I'm sorry about waking you up." He paused. "But I'm not sorry about kissing you."

Her eyes locked in with his, and she couldn't stop the grin from stretching across her face. Oh, no. She was sinking fast. "I'm not sorry either." She paused. "But ..."

"But it's not a smart thing since we're working together, right?"

"Probably. And Derek ..."

"Yes?" he asked.

"I live in New York. I'm a city girl." She paused. "And I don't do casual flings."

"I figured. I'll try to keep my testosterone in check in the future, okay?"

"Okay." What was she doing? She didn't want him to stop the fire. She wanted him to stoke it.

"But I have to say, you've got some luscious lips, woman."

"Now you're teasing me. No fair." *Oh, God, help me.*

He threw his hands up in the air, palms facing out. "Alright, alright. Got me." He pantomimed his fingers across his lips, closing them shut tight.

Back to business. That's what you have to do. Build a wall and keep it there. "I'm hungry. Let's take our notebooks downstairs and discuss next steps for us while we eat breakfast." She buried her head in her computer bag, pulling out a notepad and pen, then grabbing her purse. She ended the intimate chat, her head still swimming, and tried to move on.

"They've got quite the spread down there," he said.

He was still grinning at her. If she was honest, all she wanted to do was toss her arms around him and kiss again. The yearning wasn't stopping, only escalating.

"Good." Maybe she could eat her way out of this predicament. Stuff everything down. *Yes, that's a possible solution. Not healthy but who cares at this point?*

He opened the door, swinging his arms out in front. "After you."

No matter how hard she tried, she couldn't ignore an electrical current pulling her towards him. Three hours in the car were going to do her in for sure.

Chapter Sixteen

The sunlight's rays flickered on the fallen snow, reflecting like diamonds and mesmerizing Katy as they drove home. After breakfast, they had stopped at the bake shop and gathered more samples for Christine and the crew back in Maple Ridge. They never met the owners, who also got stuck in the bad weather on their way home the night before.

She glanced at him, taking in the day-old stubble on his face, his worn Army hat cocked to the side, and rugged hands gripping the steering wheel. Just looking at him, butterflies flew rampant across her belly. Would it ever stop?

Thoughts were interrupted by her phone's ringtone. Simon.

"Take it if you need to. No problem."

He had already texted her twice this morning. "Hi, Simon."

"Katy, I've been trying to reach you."

"Yes, I know, but I did tell you I was going on a side trip. I'm still not home. Can it wait?"

"Not really. Krafton's people have questions I can't answer, and that new client called again wanting to know if we had anything yet to show them."

"Send me the Krafton questions; I haven't looked at the new client stuff. Have you come up with anything yet?"

He paused. "No. I've been so busy trying to learn all the responsibilities of this new position I haven't. Maybe we can brainstorm together like old times. What do you say?"

Right. Not happening. "I can't talk now, Simon. I'll call you later." She hung up.

Derek turned his head. "Everything alright?"

Dealing with Simon, irritation hung over her like a thick, heavy cloud. His sweet talking her into assisting him—him taking credit. Same old, same old pattern.

"Not really. Just Simon being Simon. I think it's time I stop helping him."

"He seems to ruffle your feathers from what you've told me."

"Are we going to have another therapy session now?"

"If you want to," he chuckled.

"Maybe I need one. Why do I let him get under my skin, and why do I keep working for a company that doesn't value me?"

"I don't know. Why?"

She laughed. "You're supposed to answer that question."

"I think you're the only one who can."

"You're a slick therapist, you know that, right?"

"I'll take that as a compliment."

Katy sighed and plopped her head back on the seat behind her to catch the ivory wonderland fleeting by outside her window, its towering pines tickling the blue sky, covered in feathery white powder. "I'll figure it out. Eventually." She rolled her head back in his direction and grinned.

Another ringtone sounded. She looked down and saw Sophie's name on Derek's phone laying on the seat. "Want to take it?" she asked.

"No, I'll call her later. I need to resolve some issues I have with her."

"Care to elaborate? I can be a good listener too, you know."

"Thanks, but I can handle it. I just have to make time to do so."

She realized that he was going to be tight-lipped about this one. But she was dying of curiosity. *Does he still have feelings for her?* A pang of jealousy teased her psyche. *Why do you care? You're going back to your life in the city. Your soldier man stays here.*

Derek pulled off the highway and entered the back roads of the Berkshires, where the snow lay scattered on the ground and tall firs. "Looks like they got the same storm."

She smiled, gazing out at the winter spectacle. Holiday wreaths were hung on front doors, and outdoor decorations adorned homes both inside and out. "I bet the lights around here at night are awesome."

"Yeah. Mark and I got ours up before I left. Everyone is quite serious about Christmas in Maple Ridge. There are tons of activities. Saturday, we take trees to Fairside Manor and host a tree decorating party. Do you want to come?"

"Yes! I'd love to."

"Okay, consider it a date." He paused. "You know what I mean."

"Yes." Just an outing with a friend. That's all it was. A small pang of sadness reverberated in her heart.

"Here we are." Derek pulled into the back of the bakery. "I'm sorry. I forgot to ask if you wanted to go home instead of here."

"Are you kidding? I can't wait to show Christine our pictures and baked goods. You can't get rid of me yet."

"I'll take you home whenever you want to go," he replied.

"Thanks."

They both barged in through the back door and found Christine in her office.

"We're back!" Katy yelled.

Derek walked behind her. "We made it."

"You two had quite the adventure. I can't wait to hear all about it. Put your things down, then let's meet in here."

Derek went to his office and Katy took off her coat, throwing it on the hook behind Christine's door.

"I want to hear everything about your expedition," Christine said.

"I know what you're thinking. I'll tell you the personal stuff when we get home. Right now, I have to keep it all business, so I don't fall apart."

Christine could see a wetness forming behind Katy's eyes and put her arms around her. "Oh, honey. I didn't mean to upset you. We could go talk somewhere else if you want."

Katy wiped the wetness away, shocked at her sudden emotion. "I don't know what's wrong with me. I guess this trip triggered more than I realized. Between work and our handsome male partner, I'm questioning choices I've made in my life and my future. Nothing too heavy, huh?" She giggled, pushing the emotions away for now. "Let's stay focused on the prize. Sweet Ridge Bakery in Manhattan." She squeezed Christine's hand.

"Alright. But I have a bottle of pinot that has our name on it at home."

"Can't wait."

Derek knocked at the door a few minutes later. "Ready," he said. He sat down, and the two women joined him, both anxious to delve into the material about their competition.

* * *

Katy curled her feet under her, sitting on the couch before the fire, its flames leaping amongst the logs. Her fingers traced the rim of a wine glass filled with the burgundy liquid, her thoughts drifting into a daydream of Derek and their kiss.

"Hey, earth to space. What's going on in the that little mind of yours?" Christine dropped down on the other end of the couch, placing an assorted charcuterie tray on the table in front of them.

A subtle smile lifted across Katy's face. "Just thinking."

"About what?"

"Derek." She turned her head towards Christine. "I have a confession."

"Let's hear it."

"Last night at the inn he had a nightmare. I got out of bed to see if he was okay and sat with him while he calmed down. The moment became very intimate unexpectedly, and before I knew it, we kissed." There she had said it.

"And?" Christine asked.

"And that's it. I'm a New Yorker; he lives here. We both agreed a relationship couldn't work for us. I'm a workaholic with no time for a relationship unless they're right in front of me every day—like Simon was."

"I've heard this story before. I'm not buying it. Do you like him?"

"Yes. We've become friends. And yes, I am attracted to him. We do have chemistry. But is that enough to start a relationship? I don't think so."

Christine shook her head. "Katy, Katy, Katy."

"What?" Was there something she wasn't seeing in this picture?

"How long has it been since you've allowed yourself to open to love? Really open?"

Katy sighed. "Probably never. I thought I had with Simon, but in retrospect, I don't think it was the real deal after everything that happened. It was more out of convenience. And it worked. Until it didn't."

"Do you deserve love, Katy?"

"Of course. Doesn't everyone?"

"You don't act like it. Why don't you see if this goes anywhere with Derek? I watch him observing you when you're not looking. He's smitten but would never admit it. He keeps things close to his chest if you haven't noticed."

Katy sipped her wine. "Do you think so?"

"I know so. Listen, do what you want, but I think a little introspection on why you think you don't deserve love is what's needed here." She paused. "Does it have anything to do with your father's behaviors over the years?"

The thought pinched Katy's heart as she closed her eyes. Her dad always left her during the summer holidays and barely had time to do things with her during the school year. His job entailed a lot of traveling. After he remarried, the distance between them grew even more until she stopped trying to get together with him. They lived in Florida now, and she was a grown woman busy with her life. She flew down once a year to get out of the winter weather in New York but only for a few days.

Christine reached her hand out placing it on Katy's leg. "Are you okay?"

Katy slowly opened her eyes. "Yeah. I think you might have hit the nail on the head. Am I afraid of being abandoned again by a man if I open to love?"

"Yeah, you might be. At least you're getting clear what your fears are. That's a good first step. You don't have to figure it all out tonight."

"Yeah, you're right." She gulped down the rest of her wine as her phone pinged. Simon.

"What's he saying?" Christine asked.

"Wants me to call him. Another emergency. He has no boundaries, night or day. I think he's freaking out without me there—finally seeing my worth." Katy giggled.

"Good. Let him sweat it out." Christine reached over for a slice of cheese and downed her drink. "Listen. I'm going into the city for just one night if you want to ride with me and go to your office. Maybe a few hours there will stop him from harassing you on your vacation. Just a thought."

Katy nodded. "I'll think about it. Thanks."

Christine stretched. "I'm beat and I'm sure you are too. My bed is calling. See ya in the morning." She squeezed Katy's hand.

"Thanks for our little talk. I needed it."

"Remember, no decisions need to be made. Let everything percolate until you're ready. 'Night."

"Goodnight." Katy leaned back, her eyes mesmerized by the flames in the fire, and prayed. *Dear God, please guide me. Help me overcome my fears. Let me believe in love again. Let me be happy.*

Satisfied she had given up her worries to a higher power, or at least tried, she floated off to her bedroom and the company of a worthy novel. Reading would calm her nerves—she hoped.

* * *

Derek jumped out of the shower and was toweling his wet locks when his phone rang. Sophie's name appeared, and he texted her back.

Just got out of the shower. Call you in five.

She sent a thumbs up emoji back to him.

He had decided to plan an outing with her to get everything off his chest. Apologize for his actions and ask her for forgiveness. It had worked for Mark, and he hoped it would work for him. They both had returned from the battlefield with invisible scars on their innermost self and had lashed out at the ones they cared about most. Derek knew he had been an asshole with Sophie; he was stronger now and understood his emotional challenges with better insight.

After dressing, he punched in her number. "Hey," he said.

"Hi. I didn't think you'd ever call me again," she said.

"I've been busy, but I appreciate that you reached out to me." He paused. "I have to head out to a meeting in a few, but I wondered if you were free Saturday night for dinner? I need to explain my past actions to you now that I understand them myself more clearly."

"Of course."

"I'll text you a place and time—probably Vinny's on Main Street, where I saw you, around six. Okay?"

"Perfect. Thanks, Derek for reaching out. I appreciate it."

"See you then." He hung up. His chest expanded with a breath, then he exhaled with relief. One thing checked off his to-do list on the road to recovery.

His phone pinged again. Mark.

Want a ride to group? Leaving in five.

Be right down. Thanks.

He grabbed his coat, put on his boots, and pulled a cap over his head. Group is what he needed now. Being with Katy for twenty-four hours and kissing her lush, sensual lips had stirred his soul all day.

* * *

Derek lowered his body onto the metal chair, now cushioned, an improvement Dr. Mark had made to upgrade the room. He nodded, greeting others as they came in. The group was still small since Mark had started it in the spring, but that gave everyone time to share if they chose to do so.

Mark led the serenity prayer and opened it to the floor for sharing. Derek sat still and listened to some of the recently returned guys who were having difficulty acclimating to their home surroundings again. Mark gave solid advice on dealing with their issues, and then his eyes landed on Derek. He lifted his eyebrow without saying a thing.

Derek grinned at the push and raised his hand. "I had an interesting experience last night." He told the group about his trip to Vermont and his closeness to Katy for twenty-four hours. He described the nightmare, Katy's compassion during the middle of the night, and his desire for her. And the kiss.

"It was the first time since returning from Afghanistan I've felt comfortable enough to kiss a woman without the withdrawal behaviors PTSD caused in the past. I know this woman is unavailable for a relationship, living in New York, and married to her job, but I like her. It felt damn good to break through the barriers I've put up before. Can't say those barriers won't pop up again, probably will, but I think I had a breakthrough." He laughed as the group clapped for him.

"And what about the woman? Are you going to ask her out on a date?" Mark asked.

"We work together, so we decided that wouldn't be a good idea." He paused. "But I can't say I'll hold back on kissing her again." The group laughed. "The woman I was practically engaged to before leaving contacted me again. We broke up soon after I returned due to my miserable behavior and lashing out at her due to PTSD. Talking to Mark, I think I need to have a serious conversation with her and ask for her forgiveness."

"One step at a time," Mark said. "How about the dark moods descending on you? Have any of these lately?"

"I get them on an average once a week. But I'm learning how to deal with them." Derek didn't want to talk about that today. One breakthrough was all he could handle.

Mark moved on and listened to a woman talk about the disconnect she was having with her teenage daughter and the fights it was causing with her husband. Mark delved into the causes and outlined a plan she could try for the next week.

After the meeting, Derek grabbed a coffee and donut with the others and helped Mark clean up before they left.

Pulling up to their driveway, Mark turned towards Derek. "Thanks for sharing tonight. Be kind to yourself. Getting back into the intimacy game isn't always as easy as just one kiss. There are deeper waters you have to tread, and I'm here if you want to talk before next group."

"Thanks, man. Appreciate it." He hopped out of the truck. "See ya tomorrow."

"Yep. Goodnight."

Derek climbed the steps to his apartment, opened the door, kicked off his shoes, and threw his keys on the kitchen counter. Walking into his bedroom, he sat on the edge of his bed and fell back onto the duvet, staring at the ceiling. *What am I doing with my life?* Katy was beautiful but had a thriving life outside of Maple Ridge. No way she'd give that up. He saw how addicted she was to her job and how she was scaling the heights of success. A wave of defeat circled him, pressing into his chest, tempting him down a dark hole. *Not going there.* A good night's rest was all he needed. Tomorrow was a new day.

Chapter Seventeen

Katy sipped her coffee, scrolled through countless emails on her computer, and admired the view out the living room window of the wintery scene in the back of Christine's house. She had agreed to a Zoom with Simon but was more interested in researching Christine's competition in Vermont. She had read almost everything about the shop's history and how it went back four generations. That's a feat in itself. She wished she hadn't liked their staff so much and their baked goods. When they returned from the trip, she could see the worry in Christine's eyes as she perused the photos and sampled the treats. There was no denying they had significant competition with Frosty Mountain.

Her alarm pinged reminding her it was time for the Zoom. Simon's face came on the screen, charming as ever, but the attraction stopped there. "Hi," she said.

"Hi. Thanks for doing this, Katy. They were insisting to talk to you as well. They'll be on in ten minutes. How are you?"

"I'm great. It's beautiful here."

"Any chance you're coming back to the city before Christmas?" he asked.

"I might ride in with Christine on Monday morning and stay for one night."

"Can you come into the office? That would be awesome." He paused. "I know you're on vacation, but I also know how much your clients mean to you. And I've missed you. I'm still questioning whether we made the right decision to end things."

Are you kidding me? He's being passive-aggressive to make me feel guilty about my clients and come to work. And he realizes he can't do his job without me. "You did break up with me, not the other way around. Remember?"

"I know. I know. But let's have dinner Monday night. We can talk about it again. Please?"

She had to admit that she liked to see him squirm and beg. Gave her some evil satisfaction. "I'll come to the office Monday afternoon for a bit but no promises. I was hoping to do Christmas shopping while I'm in the city. I did none before I left."

"Alright. I'm letting the Krafton team into our meeting now. Thanks."

Katy shut down her computer after the Zoom finished. She put on an extra layer of clothing, pulled her winter boots out, and bundled up for a stroll down the snow-covered country road. She needed to clear her head of business, Simon, and Derek. Derek. She wished she could do casual. Hanging with him could be fun, but her heart would get involved, and then she'd be sunk. *Is my heart already involved?* Unfortunately, she knew the answer. Derek had touched her heart, and she didn't want it to stop. But she needed to keep her distance. Today she was staying away from Sweet Ridge Bakery. She couldn't fall in love with the guy if she wasn't around him. She would pamper herself and get a massage at that little spa place she saw on the outskirts of town.

She pulled out her phone to let Christine know.

Decided I'm getting a massage this afternoon. No bakery visits. Is that okay with you?

She waited. Her response came.

No problem. Enjoy! You've done enough already. See you at dinner.

Katy sent back a heart emoji which was quickly reciprocated. Perfect. She was taking care of herself and her heart today. Space away from Derek would hopefully give her the perspective she needed.

* * *

Derek lifted the box from the shelf and put it down with a thud on one of the stainless-steel tables in the working room of the bakery. He was used to the staff calling on him when something was too heavy for them to maneuver—always made him feel useful.

It was after lunch, and he hadn't seen Katy yet. Christine rushed into the room and nearly collided with him. "Whoa there. Slow down. What's the hurry?"

"I'm so nervous. Our surprise visit could be anytime. I want to make sure everything is in tip-top shape out front and in here," she said. "Do you think we have enough Christmas decorations up?"

"Yes, we do, and yes, we're ready. You'll throw yourself a gasket if you keep this up. Here. Have a cookie." He held up a tray of freshly baked ones out of the oven. "Eat your stress away. Works for me."

She reached for one, chuckling. "You're right. Everything is in order. I need to calm down." She looked up at him. "But it's hard."

"Yeah, I know." He put the tray down. "Is Katy coming in today?"

"No. She's having a spa day. Why? Do you need her?"

"No. Just curious." A small pang clipped his heart. *Am I missing her?*

"I'm going to my office if you need me," Christine said.

"Me too. I want to recalculate our numbers. Just to be sure." He followed her down the hallway.

About an hour later, a scream jolted Derek out of his seat. What was that? He raced out of the room, but it was coming from the parking lot. As he opened the back door, he gasped seeing Christine sprawled out in the parking lot. He ran down to help her.

"Christine! What happened?"

Christine rocked back and forth, visibly in pain and holding her arm. "Stupid me. I fell on the ice."

"We're going to the hospital. Let me get you in my truck, and I'll grab my keys."

Derek slowly lifted her, then helped her maneuver in the truck, which wasn't easy since it was high off the ground.

"Get my purse too. It's in my office."

"I'll let Mary Beth know she's in charge," Derek said.

"Oh, no. What if the investors come while we're gone?"

"Don't worry about that. Everything will run smoothly in that bakery without us for a bit. You need an X-ray. Surrender."

She looked down at her arm resting in her lap, still wincing. "Okay."

* * *

Derek scrolled through his phone sitting on the hard, plastic chair in the emergency room cubicle bay waiting for Christine to come back from radiology. From what he'd seen on the battlefield, he was pretty sure she had broken her wrist or arm. Not good.

He looked up as the orderly rolled her in, displaying a fresh, new cast on her wrist and a frown on her face.

"Can you believe this?" she asked.

Derek shook his head. "I'm so sorry. That ice can be nasty."

"How could I be so careless? I've lived enough winters in the Berkshires to know better."

"Too much stress?"

"You're probably right. You warned me to slow down." She attempted to lift her arm, now in a sling for support but cringed at the pain. "And now this."

He stood up and took the handles of the wheelchair. "Come on. I'm taking you home. No more work. It's almost closing time, and Mary Beth texted to say no unfamiliar faces came in so not to worry. Our day will be tomorrow or Friday for the visit. She said she could close, no worries."

"What would I do without you guys?" she asked. "Did you text Katy about my little debacle?"

"No. I didn't want to worry her. You can show her yourself." He grinned.

"Alright. Home, James." Christine pressed her lips together, forcing a smile.

*   *   *

Katy peeked out the window when she heard someone pull into the driveway. Oh, no. Derek's truck. What was he doing here? But then she saw Christine in the front seat. Car trouble? Derek walked around and was visibly helping her get out and walk. *Uh, oh. What happened?*

She flew to the door, swinging it wide open and stepping onto the porch. "Christine! Are you alright?"

Derek grabbed hold of her other arm, guiding her gingerly up the path to the house.

"Broke my wrist," she yelled out. "Fell on the ice in the parking lot behind the bakery. Stupid." By then she was climbing the steps to the porch.

Katy glanced up, catching Derek's eyes, and a tingling surged through her body, not from the cold air but from the man standing in front of her. "Come in and get out of the cold. Both of you."

Derek helped Christine get her coat off and turned to Katy. "We picked up a prescription for a higher dosage Ibuprofen, so the pain should ease up soon."

His gaze held steadfast on her until she looked down. *Oh, God, no. I'm in my sweatpants, rattiest T-shirt, no make-up, and did I comb my hair after the massage?* "Oh, good. Come on. Let me help you."

"Smells good in here. Did you cook?" Christine asked.

"I made chili. No promises of how it will taste, though." She giggled.

Christine looked at Derek. "Can you stay for dinner? You were my knight in shining armor, you know."

Katy felt his gaze on her. *Please, please say, no.*

"Thanks, but I promised Mark I'd help him tonight with something. Another night?" His eyes questioned Katy directly.

"Yes, another night," she said. "Thanks again for helping."

"No problem. I'm glad I heard her." He turned to Christine. "See you tomorrow?"

"I'll be there. Don't know how much use I'll be."

"Don't worry." He gently touched her shoulder. "We'll figure it out."

"Thanks, Derek. Appreciate it."

After closing the door, the two women went into the kitchen. Christine's eyes pooled with tears. "What am I going to do? I need both of my hands in the bakery. Especially these weeks before the competition ends and Alison and Jake's wedding." A tear dripped down her face.

Katy grabbed a tissue. "Here. Not to fret. I'm here, Christine. I'll work in the bakery for you. Your mom showed me things, remember? And you can tell me what to do. And we get to be together. What's better than that?"

The tears were flooding down her face and nose. "But it's your vacation! I can't ask you to work the entire time." She blew her nose.

"You didn't ask. I offered. And besides it's the holiday season and time for giving. It will do my soul good." Katy hugged her cousin, being careful not to disturb her arm. "Now, what do you say about some chili and a glass of wine?"

Christine wiped her face with another tissue. "You're the best, Katy. I'm so glad you're here."

"So am I," she said. But her stomach squeezed, fraught with tension, at the thought of working with Derek closely every day until Christmas. No way around it with Christine's injury. It was all hands-on deck now. *Dear God, help me.*

* * *

Katy swept a hair out of her eyes as she focused on frosting the outline of a gingerbread heart. On her feet all day, she didn't know how

Christine did it. Tomorrow she was wearing her running shoes.

"Looking good." A voice resounded over her shoulder from Derek.

She could feel the heat of his body radiating against her back and smelled his scent of mixed pine with a hint of musk. She had tried her best to ignore him most of the day, but in such closeness, it was impossible.

"Thanks. I'm trying." *Don't look at him. Breathe.*

"Would you mind taking the next batch out of the oven? I have to make a phone call. The timer will ding."

"Sure, no problem."

"Thanks. Mary Beth and our new hire are crazy busy up front."

His footsteps shuffling on the cement floor signaled he had left. She turned around to glimpse his flannel shirt from the back and his tight jeans outlining his perfect body as he headed towards his office. *Still hot.*

About twenty minutes later, the timer went off. Katy wiped her hands clean on a towel, then grabbed an oven mitt. As she opened the door to the industrial oven, she reached inside for a tray, but unfamiliar with the weight of it, she bumped into one of the racks, burning her wrist.

"Owww." Leaving the door open, she ran over to a sink and held her arm under the faucet, letting the cold water rush over the burn.

Derek came around the corner, saw the open door, and Katy at the sink. "Are you okay?" He quickly took out the trays and came to her side. "Did you burn yourself?"

She nodded, staring at the wetness pouring over her wrist.

"Keep it there while I get the first aid kit." He hurriedly went to a nearby cabinet, pulled out a box and returned.

"I feel so stupid," she said.

"Don't worry. This stuff happens all the time. You should have seen me the first month I worked here. Burns and cuts everywhere. You get used to it."

"Yeah, but this isn't my first time. I spent hours in here when I was younger." She paused. "I guess I'm out of practice."

"Here. Let me bandage it."

Might as well surrender. The universe keeps putting him directly in my path every day. There must be a reason.

Derek took her hand and dried it with a towel, gently patting it. Next, he applied antiseptic salve to the wound, dotting it with his finger around the burnt area. His fingers moved gently, and she closed her eyes imagining what his fingers might feel like on other parts of her body. Would he be this tender with her? Her body jerked at the thought.

"You okay?" he asked.

"Yes." *Just having a little fantasy over here.*

"Does it still hurt?"

"Yes."

He put the bandage over the area, being careful not to press too hard. "I'll get you an Ibuprofen. Should do the trick."

When Christine came into the room, she immediately joined them. "What happened over here? Another injury? Are we cursed?"

"No, no. Just a silly burn. I'm fine to resume duties. I wasn't thinking. Won't happen again."

Christine put her arm around her. "Oh, honey. I'm sorry."

Mary Beth burst into the room. "They're here! The investors."

Derek quickly cleaned up the counter, then joined Katy at the baker's table, pulling out the rest of the cakes while she resumed frosting them. Christine scurried to the front to greet their guests.

"Hi. Welcome back to Sweet Ridge Bakery," she said. Shaking their hands with her good hand, she offered coffee and treats which they gladly accepted and sat down at a table in the corner.

"What happened to your hand, Christine?" Peter asked.

"Silly accident. I slipped on the ice. But it hasn't slowed down our production. We have great staff."

"Sorry to hear that. Yes, these icy winters can be dangerous," he said.

She swiftly changed the subject. "I want you to know that we are launching a video this afternoon on our website about our *Hearts for Hope* campaign benefiting the *Hands-On Beyond* program we discussed. Katy sent you a detailed email about it, I'm sure."

"Yes, we've read all about it. Stellar idea," Mr. Ferguson said. "What's the video about?" He sipped his coffee while his assistant happily ate a croissant.

"We interviewed two program graduates, Mary Beth, who works here, and Eddie, who works in New York. They tell their story about *Hands-On Beyond's* importance for them in dealing with life without any other support when they turned eighteen. Mary Beth has proved invaluable to our store, and her confidence level has sky-rocketed way beyond my expectations. You'll see more on the video." She smiled at them both. "When you're finished, let's go in the back, and I'll give you a sample of the gingerbread fresh out of the oven."

"Thank you. Although this investment is not doing any wonders for my waistline. But my wife loves gingerbread, so I'll save it for her."

"You can have two, Mr. Ferguson. No problem."

They all laughed and followed her to the back when they finished their coffee.

As they entered, Derek and Katy were side by side, frosting the petite cakes and placing them into specialty boxes with an assortment of red and pink ribbons. Thank goodness, the boxes had arrived yesterday from the printer and were beautiful.

Mr. Ferguson picked up a box, examining it top and bottom. "Clever," he said.

Christine and Katy looked at each other, reading each other's minds, hoping he meant it.

Christine selected two boxes for him and one for his assistant. "Let me put these in a bag for you." She looked around, grateful none of her other staff had called in sick today. The place was bustling with Christmas music playing and holiday décor dangling from the ceiling and aligned along the walls. It was a festive sight at Sweet Ridge Bakery—no denying it.

Mr. Ferguson and his assistant walked around, chatting with the staff while Christine watched, trying hard not to bite her nails but stood fidgeting, her feet shifting from one side to the other. She would jump into frosting hearts if she could, but she had hurt her dominant right hand and didn't trust her left hand to apply the edging on the cake skillfully.

"You have a wonderful operation here, Christine," said Mr. Ferguson. "We'll be making our final decision a few days before Christmas. Send me updates for your proposal as you make them."

"We'll send you the link for our campaign video this afternoon. It will go live tomorrow," she added.

"And thanks for the treats." He smiled, and his assistant followed him out the door.

Christine sighed and looked at Katy and Derek. "What do you think?"

"I think it went well. No worries," Derek said. He patted her shoulder.

"Yes. We're doing the best we can. We can keep adding to the campaign and details for a site in New York and tweaking our numbers, but in the end, it comes down to the magic of Sweet Ridge coming across the pages. Hopefully, they will feel that and pick us," Katy said.

"Well said. I have to remember the magic."

"Don't we all," Katy said. Her eyes caught Derek's staring at her. His look unveiling a window to his soul touched her heart, and that scared her more than she cared to admit.

Chapter Eighteen

Katy rubbed her neck with one hand, sitting on a stool at the end of a worktable. She couldn't believe it was Friday; the week had flown by.

"Tight neck?" Derek's voice questioned from behind.

"Yeah. From bending over so much, probably. I don't know how you guys do this all day long, day after day." Her body temperature began to rise as he stepped closer.

"Here, let me do that. I've got stronger hands," he said.

Oh, dear god, don't you think I know that? "I won't turn down a massage." She grinned, but when his hands touched her skin, her imagination portal flew open, flooding her thoughts with scenes of his hands moving across other parts of her body. *Should I stop him?* No. *This feels too good.* She deserved a break and a free massage from a stud like Derek.

"Am I working you too hard?" Christine approached them.

"No, but I couldn't resist him working out the kinks in my neck." Her head hung down, not moving from Derek's fingers kneading and gliding across her shoulders.

"I don't mean to interrupt, but I just got off the phone with Mr. Ferguson. He saw the video and was very impressed." She clapped her hands together awaiting their response.

Derek stopped, and Katy looked up. "That's fantastic," she said.

"He said he didn't realize the desperate situation many foster kids and orphans face when they turn eighteen. And how *Hands-On Beyond* can change the trajectory of a child's life. He was moved."

"And hopefully, that will be the magic of our proposal to win the competition," Katy said.

Derek nodded. "I'm going to check on our numbers again and get payroll ready as well. Can't fall apart here." He grinned and left.

When he was gone, Christine turned to Katy. "How's it going? You know, working so closely with him every day? I know you wanted to keep some distance, but that's not happening, is it?" She lifted her wrist, still in a cast but no longer painful.

"It's fine. I surrendered. Whatever the universe has in store for me, I'm trying to be open to all possibilities."

"Spoken like a true warrior. I was starting to feel guilty that I had put you in an uncomfortable situation."

Katy slung her arm around Christine. "Let go of those silly thoughts right now. I'm here because I want to be here. In retrospect, coming to Maple Ridge was one of the best decisions I've ever made."

Christine squeezed her hand. "I think so, too."

Near the end of the day, Katy took off her apron and bumped into Derek coming around the corner. "Oops, sorry. Didn't see you coming." She smiled.

"Have to pack up my Friday goodies," he said.

"For the vets?" she asked.

"Yep." He reached for a couple of boxes and started filling them with cookies and goodies. He had made a deal with Christine that he would cover the costs for all of them each week. "I think I'll take a gingerbread heart for Nick. What do you think?"

"Yes. Can I come with you?"

"You sure you don't want to go home, take a bath, and put your feet up?"

"Yes, but I can do all of that afterward. I like going with you."

"I like your company." He grinned. "I'm leaving in ten minutes."

"Can you drop me off at home afterward? I rode in with Christine today. She was able to navigate driving the car, no problem."

"It would be my pleasure." He pantomimed tipping a hat towards her as his dimples rose higher.

Katy giggled and went to retrieve her belongings in Christine's office. She shook her head. Derek was a funny guy. Sometimes, he was charming and amusing—other times, moody, dark, and silent—and occasionally, open, vulnerable, and sensual. She wanted more of the latter but knew she was playing with fire. *I could get hurt.*

Derek guided his truck into the parking lot at the veterans' home, and Katy helped him with the boxes. As they entered, she greeted a few people she knew now, and followed him to the recreation room. The regulars soon swarmed Derek, anxious to bite into whatever he had brought them. Katy took a box and made her way around the area to those who were less mobile.

When she came to Betty, the army veteran who was a nurse in the Viet Nam war, she pulled up a chair next to her. "Hello, Betty. Care to sample something?"

"You know I do, dear," she said. She reached into the box pulling out a powdered sugar covered Russian tea cookie. "My favorite."

"I like those too," Katy said.

"I see you're still with that cute Derek. Are you two officially dating now?"

Katy touched her cheek, her face getting hotter. "No, no. We're just friends. We work together, remember? And I live in New York."

"That doesn't mean anything. I see the way he looks at you. There's more there. What are you afraid of?" Betty asked.

Katy was taken aback by the woman's straightforwardness. "It would never work. And long-distance relationships usually fall apart. Besides, I work too many hours at my job."

"Why do you work so much?"

Katy paused. *Why do I work so much?* "I don't know. I've always been like that ever since I left home and went to college."

"I don't mean to be blunt, dear, but what are you getting out of it?" Her arthritis-crippled fingers patted Katy on the knee. "I've lived longer than you and know a thing or two about love. If you have a chance for real love, go for it. Forget about the other stuff. It will sort itself out. Always does."

Katy stared down into the box she held on her lap. "Okay, Betty. I'll give your advice some thought." She looked up and smiled at the older woman, but her comments hung on the edge of a hole in her heart she had been avoiding.

Derek walked over to them. "Hello, ladies. Enjoying your cookies, Betty?" he asked.

"You know it," she said. "You're a good man, Derek." She turned to Katy and winked.

"Glad to hear it. Katy, I'm going to Nick's room if you want to come with me."

"Sure. Anymore cookies, Betty?" She held out the box.

"No, thank you. Two was enough. Think about what I said, alright?"

"I will," Katy said.

As they walked, Derek turned to her. "What were you two talking about?"

"Oh, nothing. Girl stuff." She lightly socked him in the arm. "And none of your business." She giggled.

He nodded and waved to Nick's mother walking down the hall.

"Hi, Mrs. Johnson. How's Nick today?" he asked.

"He's not feeling so great. I think he's coming down with something. But they're monitoring him regularly. He'll appreciate seeing you."

"Sorry to hear that." Derek didn't like to hear his buddy might be sick.

They walked in, and Nick still had a smile on his face seeing the two of them. He sneezed, and Derek was quick to help him with a tissue since he couldn't himself.

"Man, sounds like a nasty cold coming on, soldier," Derek said.

"Yeah," he said. Nick nodded at Katy. "Pretty."

"Yes, she is pretty," Derek replied.

"Keep her," Nick said.

"We're just friends. Remember?"

"Bull crap."

Derek laughed. "You always were straight to the point. Like that about you."

The three of them chatted about trivial stuff, but Derek could see Nick was tired. He gave him his little cake and told him about the campaign. Nick didn't feel like eating so Derek put it on his tray. The fact that he didn't want to eat troubled Derek.

"Hey, man, I'm going to let you get some sleep. That always makes me feel better when I'm sick. I'll stop by in a few days. Then you can give me your opinion on the gingerbread, alright?"

Nick nodded, and fist-bumped him with his bandaged hand as they left.

Derek turned at the door to wave again. "See you, buddy."

Nick smiled and nodded.

Walking down the hallway, Derek stopped at the nurse's station. "Hey, I wanted to let you know, Nick's sick and will need help blowing his nose and drinking more fluids." His facial expression tensed, and his lips tightened after he spoke.

"Yes, we know. I have someone going in every ten to fifteen minutes to help him. Don't worry, Mr. Higgins. We'll take good care of him."

"Thank you." He glanced at Katy. "Come on. Let's go."

Derek's whole demeanor changed. She could see he was distraught.

She lightly touched his shoulder. "Don't worry. They'll take good care of him. You'll see."

"Being in a place like this, people don't always get the care they deserve."

He was right. People say they will do something, but often promises are overlooked or forgotten. Nursing staff were overworked.

They rode home in silence. Katy knew his moods now and respected them. Pulling up in Christine's driveway, she turned to him. "Thanks for letting me tag along. I like visiting with your veteran friends. It makes me feel like I'm doing more than just thinking about myself all the time. I need more of this."

"Sorry, I'm not much for talking now. Do you still want to go to Fairside tomorrow for the tree decorating party?"

"I'd love too."

"I'll pick you up at one."

He turned and reached his hand out to hold hers. "Thanks for coming." He held it for a moment longer.

She let him hold it as long as he wanted to. The warmth radiated up her arm making its way to her heart thumping against her chest. The connection they were forming was real. Maybe Betty was right.

Slowly he released her hand. "See you tomorrow."

"Yep." She hopped out of the truck and floated up the steps to the front porch. She turned and waved once more, then went inside for the evening.

* * *

The hot water soothed her sore muscles as she sunk into the bubbles of her evening bath. Katy closed her eyes, leaning back against the porcelain tub, her hair's ringlets skimming the water's surface. A lit candle flickered by her side on a shelf while her phone caressed the room with meditation music, tempting her to relax. Thoughts of Derek kept forcing their way into her head, and she intentionally pushed them away. So much for her plan to stay away from him this week. That didn't happen. But her conversation with Betty was the primary source of her confusion. *Would I be able to recognize true love when it came to me?*

She didn't know. Simon didn't appear to be the one, nor any of the other men she had dated since high school. Was her heart open to love? That was the main question. A web of fear had woven its way around her heart and remained there, affecting how she handled her relationships and preventing a chance for real intimacy. Perhaps she'd be ready for love if she could untangle this fear. Maybe.

Chapter Nineteen

Wearing a red sweater and jeans, Katy stood in front of the mirror, checking herself out again. She selected a pair of fun holiday earrings she had brought, dangling snowflakes with fake diamonds, making them glitter as she walked. The corners of her mouth lifted as she peeked out the window, hearing Derek's truck pull into the driveway.

She opened the door before he could ring the bell. "Ready?" he asked.

"Yes, let me get my coat."

As they drove along the winding roads to Fairside, she stared out the window. The white blanket of snow was stunning, still covering the ground and mountains in the distance—magic frozen in time. "It's so beautiful outside. I hope it stays like this the whole time I'm here," she said.

"We'll probably get more snow before Christmas. We usually do."

Her phone rang. She pulled it out of her purse and a tiny gasp leaked from her throat. Her father. He rarely called her. Usually just an email or a text.

"Go ahead and pick up if you want."

She slowly hit the answer button. "Hi, Dad."

"Hi, honey. I thought I'd check in. How are you?"

"I'm ... fine," she stammered. "How are you?"

"Good. Marge and I are coming to New York over the holidays for a few days. She wants to see a couple of shows on Broadway, and I thought we could see you. What do you say?"

Okay. This makes more sense. They're coming because *Marge* wants to, not because he wants to see me. "I'm actually in Maple Ridge and plan to stay here through Christmas. I took a bunch of vacation days I had accumulated, and I'm helping Christine with a big project. It depends on when you come if I'll be around."

"Let me talk to her and see what she wants to do. Nice chatting with you. I'll keep you posted."

"Okay," she said. A tightening in her gut squeezed hard as a wave of nausea rushed over her, making her want to puke. If she didn't talk to him too much, she couldn't be reminded of how he had always placed others above her, especially Marge. He didn't even ask anything about her life. He didn't know she had lost out on a big promotion or that she had broken up with her boyfriend. Or what Christine was doing with the bakery. Did he really love her? It never felt like it.

"Are you okay?" Derek asked.

"Yeah." She lapsed into silence. This was a big one for her, and she wasn't ready to spill her guts about it to Derek.

"You don't look okay."

"I guess I'm not. I have this strained relationship with my dad, mostly on my end. He probably thinks everything is fine between us, but it isn't. Ever since he got remarried when I was in junior high school, I feel like I've taken a back seat to his love and caring. Saying it out loud sounds silly. I guess I felt abandoned by him, and it continues to this day."

"That's tough." He reached his hand out, placing it on top of hers.

They rode in silence the rest of the way. Pulling up to the manor,

Katy gazed out to see multiple cars and a large truck from a nearby tree farm.

"How many trees are we decorating?"

"Probably five or six. That's why they needed volunteers."

"This is just what I need. To get out of my head and into my heart. Come on, let's go!" She jumped out of the truck before he had a chance to respond.

Katy saw Alison and waved. Jake was helping the guys carry the trees inside, and Maggy and Mark were also there. She turned to Alison. "This must be a family affair. All of you are here." She laughed.

"Yep. Come in and I'll give you your assignment. I put you and Derek overseeing the tree in the cafeteria. You'll have plenty of little ones helping you; they have assignments too. When it's finished, we'll bring treats for everyone."

"Sounds like fun," Katy said. "Which way to the cafeteria?"

Alison pointed her in the right direction and when Katy walked in, Derek was already there securing the tree in the holder. A bunch of kids were around him, some he knew, anxious to put on the ornaments.

He waved her over. "Will you help me put the lights on first?"

Thoughts of her dad faded away, and the atmosphere of Christmas lifted her spirit. Derek's eyes and kindness reassured her heart and enticed her to relax and enjoy the festivities.

He bent down from the ladder and handed her a string of lights to loop around the back of the tree. His fingers brushed her skin, sending ripples of energy everywhere, but she was getting used to these reactions to him and welcomed them. *Would Derek be different in a relationship than other men I've been with?* Lost in her daydream, she dropped the lights.

"Hey, butterfingers," he teased.

"Ha, ha. Very funny. Just got distracted for a minute."

She pulled herself together, falling into a rhythm of adjusting lights and winding them around the tree. Mary Beth's sister, Jolene, waited patiently until she was done and then led a group in putting up their handmade ornaments. She and Derek stood back as the kids overtook their job and filled the tree.

Jolene looked up at Katy. "Did you bring an ornament for the tree? You can make one if you like. We have plenty of supplies over there." She pointed to a table in the corner.

"I guess I could make one. I didn't think to bring one." Her brain had been so tied up with work that she sometimes forgot it was almost Christmas.

Derek overheard Jolene; he tapped Katy's arm. "Come on. I'll make one too."

The two of them sat with some other kids, immersing themselves in glitter and glue. Soon Katy held up a shimmering yellow star, ready to join the other dazzling adornments on the tree. She laughed when she saw Derek's snowman out of construction paper.

"You may have found your true calling, soldier," she said.

"Don't laugh. My talents are teeming with surprises. You better watch out."

She giggled, forgetting all her anguish for the day, and followed him to put their ornaments on the tree. The Douglas fir stood tall, its branches adorned with handmade crafts and kids squealing at their creations standing around it.

"Turn on the lights!" Jolene yelled.

"Yes, yes!" kids shouted.

Derek reached down and grabbed the plug. "Five, four, three, two, one!"

The tree lit up, captivating the young hearts that swarmed around it, clapping madly for their work of art.

As the kids screamed in delight, Katy caught Derek's gaze washing over her, unwavering, secretly inviting her into what could be possible. No words had been spoken about the two of them since their kiss, but in the silence, Katy imagined what he might say to her—if she gave him a chance.

Alison's announcement for snacks and drinks interrupted her thoughts. She bent over to clean up while the kids sprinted towards the tables being set up with cookies and beverages. Derek joined her.

"I think that was successful, don't you?" he said.

"Very, but I'm ready for a cookie. How about you?"

"I never turn down a cookie."

They joined the rest of the crew and adults until Karen, Fairside's director, announced it was time to clean-up. Katy and Derek pitched in, chatted with Alison and Jake a bit, then got their coats.

Katy placed her hand on her chest; she was going to make a move. "Hey, Derek. Do you have plans tonight?"

"Yeah, I do. I'm meeting Sophie for dinner."

Ouch. A sharp pain landed in her heart. "Oh, nice." That was all she could say.

"I need to resolve some issues with her—from the past. I've been putting it off way too long."

"I see." She paused. "Good luck. Maybe the two of you can work things out."

"I don't know about that, but I have some things I need to get off my chest." He reached out for her hand. "Another time? I like spending time with you."

She swept her eyes over him with a wave of longing. She knew they had chemistry, but she couldn't do a darn thing about Sophie. They had history. Who knows what might happen? She couldn't dwell on it now. She wanted to keep this tender, fuzzy feeling in her heart from the afternoon at Fairside. She'd settle for another hot bath and a good book by the fireplace at Christine's.

"Yeah, me too." She kept her hand in his and walked out to the truck with him after saying goodbye to everyone.

She climbed into the front seat. "Thanks for inviting me today. I needed this," she said.

"I think we all crave an outlet to give. Thanks for coming." His hand slid across the seat, grasping her palm against his. He stayed like that the entire ride home.

* * *

Derek adjusted his collar while glimpsing in the mirror, ran a comb through his hair, and grabbed his truck keys. Sophie was meeting him at Vinny's, the favorite Italian restaurant in town. He glanced at the red neon sign lit up across the storefront window as he pulled up, ignoring the whitened knuckles gripping the steering wheel. *Why am I so nervous?* He had known Sophie since high school but was a different man now. Different from before and after Afghanistan. He was finally healing and needed this conversation for that reason. And that reason only.

As he walked into the restaurant, Sophie waved from the bar. Her long, flowing blonde hair and bright blue eyes caught his breath for a minute. He flashbacked to her as a cheerleader their senior year and him as a star football player by her side. Everyone thought they would marry and have a slew of kids. That didn't happen.

"Hey, Sophie. Sorry, I'm a few minutes late. I was at Fairside Manor today helping with the Christmas trees." He climbed up on the seat next to her. "Do you want to get a table?"

"Yes, might be more private."

After being seated in a corner table that looked out onto the street, they each ordered a drink. "Thanks for meeting me here."

"Are you kidding? I've been wanting to spend quality time with you ever since your mother told me you were on the mend. I didn't like how we ended things last year." She reached out and touched his arm.

"Yeah, I didn't either." He paused. "I might as well jump into it. Sophie, I'm sorry I was such a jerk to you when I returned from overseas. I couldn't handle any relationship when I got back. I was out of sorts—angry, tired, and irritable. I didn't want to be around anyone. I still don't sometimes. PTSD is a silent predator that can overtake you when you least expect it, suffocating your best intentions."

She rubbed his arm. "Yeah, I finally figured it out that it wasn't about me but what you had brought back from Afghanistan. I had to leave. It was unhealthy for me and too much pressure for you."

Her silky eyelashes batted at him, urging him to feel the chemistry again. His gut was twisting inside, unable to respond to her desires the way he used to before the Army. He pulled his arm away, gulping his beer. "Can you forgive me, Sophie? Forgive me for not being able to follow through with all our plans and dreams?"

Her hand covered his, squeezing it gently. "Of course. I love you, Derek. Always have and always will. I'm willing to give you all the time in the world that you need. Maybe we could try again but take it slow and easy. What do you say?"

The twisting in his stomach tightened into a vice grip; he pulled his sweaty hand away from her, placing it on his trembling knee under the table. "I don't know, Sophie. I'm just starting to feel normal again. I don't think I'm ready for a relationship yet. Hope you understand." How was he going to make it through dinner if she kept pushing?

"Okay. I understand. I'll back off for now, but not forever." Her smile spread across her face.

She was trying. He could see that. "Okay. Friends for now." He picked up the menu. "I'm starved. How about you?"

She nodded, but her lips were pressed together.

Glancing up from the menu, Derek's eyes widened when he saw Katy get out of her parked car on the street and enter the restaurant. She must be picking up take-out. He watched as she stood by the maître-de, giving her name. While waiting she scanned the restaurant and caught Derek's eyes. She waved to him.

"I'll be right back, Sophie. Katy just walked in for take-out. I'm going to say hi."

"Okay," she said. Her lips drooped in a pouty face, but he didn't see.

Katy kept her head down, slightly mortified that she had selected the same restaurant as Derek's date.

"Hey, there," he said. "Getting take-out?"

His dark eyes penetrated hers as she held her own with him. "Yes. Christine and I didn't feel like cooking. Popular place, huh?"

"Great food, but you know that since we came here after Thanksgiving." He couldn't take his eyes off her.

The waiter appeared with her food, and she took the bag. "Have fun with Sophie. Thanks for coming over."

He reached his hand out, lightly touching her arm. "Enjoy."

"Oh, we will." She laughed and left.

Sophie's face did not look happy as he sat down. "Sorry about that. I didn't want to be rude."

"That's Christine's cousin, right?"

"Yeah. Katy. We've been working on this project together. Did you decide what you want?" In the past, Sophie had a jealous streak that would emerge around other women when he was in high school. He could tell she still had it.

"Yes. So, when is Katy going back to New York? That's where she lives, right?"

She wasn't letting up. "I don't know. After Christmas I think." The thought of Katy's impending departure did not sit well with him. A twinge in his heart reminded him they had an expiration date on their time together. He gulped down his beer again, pushing away that thought.

As they ate dinner, Sophie playfully talked about events in their past. They laughed, thinking of things they had done together and the mischief they had gotten into. When they finished, Derek picked up the check, ready to leave.

"Thank you, Derek, for asking me out tonight. I'm glad we got to catch up. Maybe I can make you dinner soon. What do you say?"

His foot started tapping on the floor. Man, he still couldn't take any pressure from this woman. "Maybe. But not until after Christmas. I'm too busy." Not really, but he could only take so much probing with his ex.

"Okay," she said.

They walked outside into the chilly evening as flurries swirled in front of them, landing on the street and cars. "I'll walk you to your car," he said.

"I'm down that side street. Not too far." She threaded her arm through his, and they walked in silence.

When they got in front of the car, Sophie pulled herself closer to him, trying to bring her face within inches of his. She stretched on her tip-toes to kiss him on the cheek but let her lips slide closer to his mouth, trying to tempt him with a real kiss.

Derek wasn't into it. He pulled away and pecked her on the cheek. "Thanks for coming tonight and thank you for your forgiveness. It means a lot to me."

"I forgive you, Derek. I already did a long time ago. Don't be a stranger." She opened her door, got in, and waved as she slowly drove away.

As Derek returned to his truck, his mind mulled over his interactions with both women. Katy excited him. Sophie's desires stressed him out. Katy made his heart feel safe. Sophie's ulterior motives troubled him. But Katy lived in New York, and Sophie lived here. Two different women. Two different scenarios. At least he had accomplished what he had wanted tonight. Forgiveness was crucial for moving on with his healing. Was he ready for a relationship? Maybe—maybe not.

Chapter Twenty

As the Sunday service ended the next morning, Katy leaned over to Christine. "I think I'm going to sit here for a moment."

"I'll be over at the Community Center getting coffee." Christine rose, joining the other parishioners in socializing next door.

In the empty stillness afterward, Katy slid her body down, kneeling on the padded platform below her. She threaded her fingers together in prayer and bowed her head. *Dear God, I need guidance. I'm conflicted about my job and confused about my love life. Help me know what to do. Help me sort out my feelings and know what is best for me. Please, give me a sign. Thank you, thank you, thank you.*

She remained like that for a while, her body melting into the tranquility, then glided back onto the pew to sit. She slowly opened her eyes, gazing around the place of worship with its stained-glass windows, holiday wreaths adorned with sparkling red bows strung on the mantles and windowsills, and the massive cathedral ceilings. She loved it here. She loved the church, the town, and all its people. *What would it be like to live here?* She sure hoped her prayers would be answered, and soon. Nothing like impatience when it comes to the unknown. She chuckled. She didn't think prayers worked like that. Her mother had taught her that prayer and trust go hand in hand. She guessed that's what she needed more than anything. Trust. Trust all would work out for her in the best way possible.

She let out a muffled sigh, conscious of the few people left in the dwelling. She slipped her arm into her coat, picked up her purse, and headed toward the Center. As she walked in, she waved to Christine and went to the refreshment table to grab a coffee. A woman's voice sounded behind her as she spooned sugar into her cup.

"This is a lovely church, don't you think?"

Katy turned around and came face to face with Sophie. "Oh, hi. Yes, I agree. And the Reverend is always inspiring."

"Derek told me about it, and I think I'm going to start coming here. I like the vibe better than my church in River Falls." She smiled at her.

Katy nodded. She didn't have anything else to say to this woman.

"How was your take-out?"

"Delicious. And your dinner?"

"Same. I love that place. That's where Derek and I had our first date. It's sad he's in no condition to explore a relationship again."

"Is that what he told you?"

"Oh, yes. We had a long talk about it. But I think with time, he'll come around. After all, we've known each other since we were sixteen."

Is this woman claiming her property? Katy sensed hidden motives beneath her words. "I'm sure you'll work it out." Katy was finding it hard to breathe as her stomach constricted into a knot. Did Derek not want a relationship with any woman? Or just Sophie? "Nice to see you, but my ride might leave soon."

"Sure," Sophie said.

Katy joined Christine who was talking to Maggy and Alison.

"There you are," Christine said. "I know we said we'd take the train into the city tonight, but these guys have a car taking them too.

They said they have plenty of room."

"We're spending the day tomorrow taking care of last-minute wedding prep," Alison said. "I have to pick up Annie's dress and do some shopping."

"That would be great. What time?" Katy asked.

"Around four? We can pick you two up, no problem," Maggy said. "This will be fun. Girls' night out in the city! Let's do dinner together too."

"Sounds like a plan," Christine said. She turned to Katy. "Let's talk to Derek. I want to make sure he's okay running things for a couple of days."

Katy followed her to where Derek stood next to Mark and Jake. Christine motioned to him to come join the two of them.

"We're catching a ride later today with Alison and Maggy to the city. We'll be back on Tuesday and might need a ride from the train station. I think Alison and Maggy are staying until Wednesday."

"No problem, anything you need."

Katy locked her gaze with him. "I'm going to look at two properties with Christine in the morning and will stop by my office most likely in the afternoon. They keep bugging me, but I'm not staying long."

Derek grinned at her. "Remember you are on vacation."

"Yes, thank you for the reminder." She wanted to reach out and touch him, pull herself into his arms and feel his lips on her mouth, wet and soft. Her heart raced thinking about it, but she couldn't. Not here or ever. The pent-up energy propelled her arms around him, settling for a hug goodbye. "See you, Tuesday."

He squeezed her hard and lingered in her arms longer than his hug with Christine. "Yeah, text me if you need a ride."

Katy glanced over and saw Sophie waiting for them to leave and would most likely make a beeline for him. She didn't want them to get back together. *What's wrong with me? Where are these jealous demons coming from?* She was usually in control of relationships with men. This feeling was oddly different, and she didn't know if she liked it. She smiled and followed Christine to the car. She needed to go home, pack an overnight bag, and gather her wits about her job and this man she was leaving in Maple Ridge.

* * *

Katy's legs stretched underneath the soft, silky covers as her alarm went off. She opened her eyes, peering out from the blanket, seeing her clothes scattered on her apartment floor and books arrayed on the dresser as she had left them. She had been in a hurry leaving for Maple Ridge that day before Thanksgiving. It seemed so long ago.

Coffee. Next on the agenda. Christine had stayed with Sam, but they were meeting up at nine with the realtor who would take them to re-look at two properties; he had another one that just came on the market. Katy's stomach fluttered at the thought of this competition ending. She prayed that Christine would get the happily-ever-after she so deserved. Love and a successful business all in one. She sighed. Love and a successful business. *Is that what I want too?*

Simon texted and called repeatedly, never letting up. Her phone pinged again.

> Good morning. What time will I see you?
> Smiley emoji.

> Late afternoon depending
> on my outing with Christine.

> Dinner tonight?

I don't know.

She wasn't making any promises.

After getting dressed, she met Christine at the realtor's office, and they spent the morning looking at properties. Katy was impressed with all of them, but one stood out in the West Village with the right vibe. There was another industrial space close by in the Meat Packing District they could use for overflow and the online business. Christine and she agreed they would select that one if they won the competition.

They grabbed a late lunch together, then Katy headed for her office. Christine was joining Alison and Maggy for some pre-wedding activities and would call her later.

In the cab ride over to Martin and Lewis agency, her stomach was in a knot. *Why am I so nervous?* She had walked into this office a thousand times before. But things were different now. She had been running on a hamster wheel for years, working up to becoming creative director. That didn't happen. And how would it feel to be under the watchful eye of Simon every day? *Yuk.*

You're still on vacation. You don't need to stay long or have dinner with Simon. You have the power here. The knot started to subside as she reined in her courage. She could do this. As she gazed out the window at people bustling in the streets with their packages, holiday lights strung on store windows, and remnants of snow scattered on the sidewalk, she thought of Derek. She thought of him often and wondered what he was doing. She pulled out her phone and texted him.

How's it going? Miss us?

She waited until she saw the bubbles forming on the screen.

No worries. I'm holding down the fort. How's it going with you guys?

Saw the properties. Loved one in particular. On my way to my office now. Wish me luck.

I'm sure you'll be fine. You're a powerhouse. Don't forget.

An inkling of confidence wrapped around her heart. Derek did that to her.

Thanks. Smiley emoji.

Call me if you need to talk later.

Okay.

What was she doing? Derek was her friend, and she wanted to share things with him. That's all. The cab pulled up to the building.

Katy pulled her coat collar close to her chin to keep the wind out and hopped out of the taxi. Riding the elevator to the tenth floor, she stared straight ahead amongst the people around her, their shoulders almost touching in the tight space. She had done this a hundred times before, but somehow it all felt foreign. So much had happened in the last several weeks.

Walking into reception, she was greeted by familiar faces and her assistant hugged her. Hearing the commotion, Simon came out of his office and was quick to hug her as well.

"We missed you around here!" Simon said.

Katy hung back for a second, her emotions fraught with confusion. *Do I belong here anymore?* She smiled. "Nice to see you all," she said.

"Come into my office, Katy. I have the files I mentioned and some questions if you wouldn't mind."

"Sure." She followed him, passing William's closed office down the hall.

When she entered, he asked her to shut the door behind her. She sensed he wanted privacy with her. She sat in front of his desk, which would have been *her* desk if things had worked out the way they were supposed to for her. She deserved that desk. Thinking about it and seeing it shining before her eyes were two different things. Ripples of agitation resurfaced as she sat there.

"Let's talk about the Krafton project once more." Simon said.

Katy fidgeted with her pen, listening to him ramble on about their clients, and answered each question curtly, with little creative contribution, her patience wavering. *It's stuffy in here. I need air.* She looked at her watch. *Maybe this was a mistake.*

When he had finished, Simon stood up, walking around the desk to be closer to her. "Listen, Katy. I've had much time to think about us and this job. I miss you, and I miss us. What would you say if I asked William to reassign this position as two co-directors? We'd each have our clients yet help each other when one of us needed it. Then we could get our relationship back on track." He reached out and took her hand lying on her lap. "I'm sorry if I wasn't sensitive to your needs. But I love the way we work together. We make a dynamic team, and I miss that."

You mean you miss me doing all the work. That's what this is all about. She saw so clearly. Katy slowly rose out of her chair and turned to face him. "I don't think I can trust you, Simon. Not after what happened."

He reached up, brushing a loose hair from her face. "I still love you, Katy. Please give me another chance." Without warning he leaned down and pressed his lips against hers.

She gently pushed him away. "No. This is not happening, I'm done with our relationship, Simon. I wish you all the best." She picked up her coat and headed towards the door.

He grabbed her hand once more. "Please. I'm sorry. I thought maybe you'd remember what we had if I kissed you."

She pulled her hand away. "What we had is broken, unrepairable, at least on my end. Let's keep our business professional, that's it. If you'll excuse me, I am on vacation, and I need to go." She looked at his shocked face.

"No dinner tonight?" he asked.

"No. But thank you."

"There's one more thing. We have a potential new client who is in a rush for a cause marketing plan. I was hoping to get your input before we show them something tomorrow."

"It might be time for you to take the lead on this one." She placed her hand on the doorknob. "Happy holidays, Simon. See you in the new year." She walked out, leaving him staring at her as she left.

Her swift gait was interrupted by William exiting his office. At six feet one, he towered over her. "Katy! I heard you might be stopping by. How are you?"

"Fine, Mr. Lewis. And you?" Her getaway derailed.

"Fine. Busy. Come in for a minute." He pointed towards his office.

"Sure." What else could she say?

He closed the door, walked to his desk, and pointed to the chair in front of it. "Please."

As she sat down, she rubbed her sweaty palms on her pants, then wiped the moistness along her hairline with the back of her hand.

"Simon tells me you've been consulting on your clients while away. Are you coming back sooner?"

"No, sir. I had something I needed to do with my cousin in the city. I'm returning to Maple Ridge tomorrow."

"I hope you aren't harboring any grudges about our decision about the directorship position. There were other factors besides skill that went into the selection." He leaned back into his leather chair, tapping his fingers on the armrest.

"No. But you know how I feel about it. I already told you."

"See, that's just it. I can hear resentment in your voice as we speak. I can have none of that attitude here in the office." He paused. "Do you understand?"

"Yes." *Did he just reprimand me?*

"Can I count on you to be the team player you've always been while here?" he asked.

"Yes." Her throat was constricting. *I'm suffocating. I need to get out.* "If you'll excuse me, I have an appointment with my cousin. I'll see you in the new year."

"Yes. And I hope you can give Simon some good ideas for this new client. It's time sensitive."

She nodded, then stood up. No way was she bailing Simon out again on a new project. "Happy holidays, Mr. Lewis."

"Same to you, Miss Flanagan."

Katy practically ran to the elevator. So many emotions bursting inside of her. Yes, she was still angry, and she didn't know when she would get over it. And now, the passive-aggressive pressure her boss had slung at her—what was that about? She hoped Christine was up for a glass of wine and sisterly conversation. She needed to sort out these emotions before they consumed her. She was drowning in uncertainty and that scared her the most.

Chapter Twenty-One

Katy scrolled through her phone, listening to the announcement of her train. The weight on her shoulders had lifted, and Maple Ridge beckoned with alluring promise. Last night she had flushed out things with Christine and concluded to do nothing. Nothing, no decisions about her life until after Christmas. Enjoy the holidays. She loved her cousin—always such wise advice.

Christine would stay an extra day and ride back with Alison and Maggy. Katy couldn't wait to leave the city and return to her vacation cocoon. Derek had offered to pick her up at the train station, which made her smile. She had been thinking about him quite a bit.

The train chugged along, rocking Katy until her eyes closed. Dozing into a dream, she saw herself walking in a field toward someone, her body tingling with anticipation. As she came closer, she saw Derek. She ran to him and jumped into his arms, her face snuggling into his neck. He swung her around, legs flying in the air, then gently placed her feet back on the ground. Holding her shoulders, he bent over, bringing his lips to hers. She welcomed him as he grasped her head, running his fingers through her hair, not relenting on the kiss. She lost herself in the touch of his skin and mouths pressing together. He caressed her body with his hands until they collapsed onto the grass below, bodies enfolding in unison.

A train whistle blew, and Katy jerked open her eyes, grasping onto the seat beneath her. Where was she? What happened? She stretched her arm up to dab the perspiration forming on her forehead, gathering herself. *Whoa, that was some dream.* Now she was going to arrive at the station all hot and bothered. *Great.*

Katy sat up, repacked her computer bag, and waited until the train stopped. Her mind kept flipping to the images of her dream. It seemed so real, and now she had to face the man in the flesh. Hopefully, she would act normal with him.

As she stepped down, she saw him right away. Standing tall in his winter field coat, tattered jeans, and worn cable-knit sweater underneath, his hair fell below his eyebrow as he waved to her. The ruggedness of his stature turned her on; she filled her lungs with air, gaining composure.

"Hey, there," he said. He grabbed her suitcase. "Good trip?"

If you only knew. "Yes, yes. The train ride was ... delightful." She chuckled.

"What's so funny?"

"Oh, nothing. Thanks for picking me up."

"No problem. Mary Beth and the crew work seamlessly on target without us. How was New York? Miss it?"

"Not really. I had fun with the girls, but my office experience was challenging."

"Oh, yeah? How so?"

"I guess the attitude of them expecting me to work no matter what, even if I'm on vacation. I guess it's my fault. I created this mess. Whatever they ask of me, I do it. I should have turned my phone off for three weeks." She laughed. "And my boss threatened me to change my attitude about not getting the creative director position. Said I need to be a team player."

"Want me to take care of him?" Derek grinned, lifting a fist into the air.

She laughed. "The thought of you socking Mr. Lewis in the jaw is enough to lift my spirits."

"I think you're one of the best team players I know. Maybe you can enjoy these last days in Maple Ridge and get the rest you deserve." He put his arm around her shoulders, side-hugging her before he put her bags into the truck.

Days? *Is that all I have left in Maple Ridge?* And with Derek? Her stomach lurched at the thought. "I hope so."

"Would you mind stopping at the veterans' home with me to visit Nick? He was sick all weekend, and I want to check on him."

"Sure. You know I love going there. Got any treats?"

"In the back."

"You're always prepared, soldier. Aren't you?" She grinned.

"I try, Flanagan. I try."

As they strolled into the foyer of the facility, Derek turned to her. "I think I want to see Nick first. Make sure he's okay."

"I'll go with you."

When they approached Nick's room, they noticed the door was open, but when they entered, Derek's jaw dropped. It was empty. "Where is he?"

"Let's ask at the nurse's station. Maybe they just changed rooms." She could see he was distraught, his eyes emanating a silent fear.

He walked over to Nick's regular nurse when he saw her writing in a chart. "Hey, where's Nick?"

By this time, Katy could see his hands trembling, anticipating the worse she presumed.

The nurse stopped what she was doing and came around the

counter, standing in front of Derek. She placed her hand on his shoulder. "Mr. Higgins, I'm so sorry. He passed away last night. He got an infection and couldn't fight it any longer. We did everything we could. His mother was with him, so he wasn't alone."

Derek froze.

Katy could see pools of tears building up behind his eyes, his shoulders shaking on the verge of a volatile eruption. "Let's sit down over there." She pointed to some chairs in an alcove by a window. She took a hold of his arm and guided him there.

When he sat down, he collapsed over with his hands holding his head, shuddering as the tears rushed out. Katy placed her hand on his back, gently rubbing it back and forth. She had no words.

Through his sobs he mumbled. "I should have been here. I should have been here."

"You didn't know." Katy's eyes filled with tears, and she wiped one away with her other hand as it trickled down her cheek. She barely knew Nick, but she could feel Derek's pain wrenching her heart, its pressure squeezing with a powerful force.

A nurse brought over a box of tissues, but Derek didn't even look up. Katy took them, mouthing a thank you to her.

They sat like that for fifteen minutes until Derek lifted himself to a seated position and grasped one of the tissues Katy had in her hand. Wiping his eyes, he stared straight ahead. "It's not fair. He was so young. It should have been me."

Katy was careful of her words. "I don't think we have control over life and death stuff, Derek. The fact that you always visited him was enough. His mother was with him, and I'm sure he was consoled by that."

Derek sat, shaking his head until his phone rang. He pulled it out of his jeans pocket and saw Nick's mother's name. He picked up right away. "Mrs. Johnson, I'm here at the home. I just found out."

He listened to her talk, telling him details of the last few days regarding Nick's health decline. "There was nothing any of us could have done, Derek. It was his time." Her voice cracked as she spoke.

"Did you eat anything? Can I bring you dinner?" he asked.

"No, dear. I already have a month's supply of casseroles. News travels fast. Why don't you stop by tomorrow? Maybe you can help me with the funeral arrangements."

"I'll be there."

Katy could see a change in his demeanor. Helping Nick's mother would give him purpose and hopefully prevent him from sinking into a depression which was a genuine possibility she knew from her research on PTSD.

After he hung up, he turned to Katy. "I need to go home. Ready?"

"Yes. I'll drop off the cookies to the rec room and meet you in the truck." She knew he needed space, and quick.

"Thanks."

When both were settled in the truck, Derek cranked up the heat and pulled out of the parking lot.

Katy couldn't ignore the silence between them, each with their thoughts—Katy's full of sorrowful compassion and Derek's overflowing with painful grief.

After they arrived at Christine's, Derek jumped out to retrieve her suitcase and walked her to the door.

She turned to him. "I'm so sorry, Derek." She reached up and pulled him towards her, hugging him tightly. He didn't resist. She thought he might break down again but saw he was beginning to toughen up, Army-ready.

"Thank you for the ride. Let me know if there's anything I can do for you," she said.

"Can you help at the bakery tomorrow? I want to spend the morning with Mrs. Johnson."

"Of course. Don't worry about it. I'll text Mary Beth to let her know." Her hand rubbed his arm and landed on his hand. She squeezed it, gazing into his eyes. *Let me comfort you.*

"Thanks." He let his hand slip out of hers, got into his truck, and drove away.

* * *

Derek glanced at his watch. He still had time to make his meeting tonight and went straight toward the church. Although his body, mind, and spirit were fraught with emotion, being with comrades was the best medicine he knew. Otherwise, he might fall into a bottomless, dark hole.

As he approached the church, he drove past it. He wasn't ready. He couldn't open up in front of everyone. Not yet. He needed to be alone. He kept driving along winding roads, tears falling and his hands gripping the steering wheel. The depth of loss was overtaking him. He could feel it, and he let it. That's what he deserved. He didn't deserve to be happy. Not now. Not ever. Eventually, he found his way home. Pulling into the driveway, he sighed in relief, seeing that Mark's car wasn't there. He couldn't deal yet, and Mark would make him deal.

He dragged himself into the kitchen, grabbed a beer from the fridge, and sat in his recliner. Sitting in the darkness, he drank his brew, thinking about the Nick he knew before the accident. And cried some more.

* * *

Katy scrubbed the wet dough from her fingers, letting the warm water rush over her hands. Hair was falling in her face along with perspiration as she tried to wipe both away with the sleeve of her shirt. She worked alongside the other bakery staff all day, making the infamous gingerbread cakes for the *Hope for Hearts* campaign. Derek had texted earlier, saying he wasn't coming in today. Her heart ached for him, but there was nothing she could do. He was a loner, especially when an incident of this magnitude dropped on him. She would have to wait.

The back door opened, and Katy dried her hands on a towel before checking on who was entering.

Christine stomped her boots and threw her bags into her office as Katy appeared in the doorway. "I'm home!"

Katy hugged her. "So glad you're back! I missed you."

"It was only one day. What are you going to do after Christmas?" She winked at her.

"I don't know. How'd it go with the realtor?"

"The place we want is willing to wait until the end of next week for our down payment. I'm happy with our selection, aren't you?"

"Absolutely. It's a perfect location." Katy sat down in the chair by the table.

"What's going on with Derek? You said it was too much to text."

Katy proceeded to tell her what happened at the veterans' home. "He was so distraught, Christine. My heart breaks for him. It's not just that he was a friend and comrade in arms, but Derek blames himself for everything. The injury, the aftermath, and now his death. That's a lot for one man to shoulder."

"I'm calling Mark. He's his mentor. Maybe he can help."

"Good idea. I doubt he went to his group last night. If he hadn't texted me earlier, I'd be worried."

"About his own life?"

Katy looked down. "Yes."

"Well, we're not going to let that happen. She dug into her purse, searching for her phone, and swiftly hit Mark's number.

He picked up right away. "Hey, Christine. What's up?"

She told him about Nick.

"I wondered why he wasn't in group, and his lights were out when I came home. I have one more patient today, then I'll run over there to check on him. Thanks for the heads up. Don't worry. He'll get through this. I have faith in him. Say a prayer."

Christine closed her eyes. "We will."

"What did he say?"

"He's going to check on him. Don't worry and pray."

Katy nodded.

"Thanks for pitching in today. Some vacation you're getting," Christine said.

"Actually, I find it meditative. Keeps me in the moment. But if you don't mind, I will tackle some emails. I'll hunker down in Derek's office until you're ready to go home."

"Sure. I need to catch up too."

Katy picked up her computer and went next door. She glanced around, taking in the simple décor surrounding the office. A photo of his mom and dad and another one with a bunch of guys in Afghanistan sat on a shelf with business books and cookbooks. An abstract painting hung on one wall which brightened up the room, but the rest was minimal. His desk was clean and organized. She bet his apartment was the same.

He did own an awesome ergonomic chair. *Sweet.* She wiggled her butt onto the chair and opened her computer. She found an email from Simon and started to read it. A heaviness landed in her gut as she read more. *Oh, my god.* The new client was Frosty Mountain. They had probably seen Sweet Ridge's campaign and were racing to do something similar. They had hired Martin and Lewis to handle the account. The muscles in the back of her neck coiled into a knot. This couldn't be happening. She needed to tell Christine right away.

She jumped up from her seat, frantically running to find her. She was out on the floor with the staff, packing the little cakes in cute heart boxes as best she could with her injured wrist. "Christine! Come here." She waved her hand, motioning to follow her to Derek's office.

Christine caught up with her. "What's the matter?"

She grabbed her arm, pulling her to the computer. "Look! My company is representing Frosty Mountain. They want me to work on the campaign." Her eyes widened, her hands shook, and she miraculously kept herself from barfing on the floor. "What am I going to do?"

Christine bent over to read the email from Simon.

Katy watched as the color drained from her face. Her concerned look of distress, caught Katy's eyes, making the nausea worse.

"What do you want to do?"

"I don't know. I have to think. I can't jump in on the campaign. It would be a conflict of interest." She sank down on the chair. "I have to tell them the truth." Wetness began pooling behind her eyes. Why did she feel so sick?

"I support you whatever you want to do." Christine rested her hand on Katy's shoulder.

"I feel no sense of allegiance to Martin and Lewis." A single tear fell down her cheek. "I used to hold the flag higher than anyone in my loyalty to the company. It consumed me. I consumed it. I was on a path to the top." She flipped her hand into the air. "Until I wasn't. My boss is going to be pissed I worked for the competition. Even it was pro bono."

"You didn't know, Katy. This was an accidental coincidence. They'll understand."

"You don't know my boss, William. I need to email Simon immediately, so he's not waiting for me. I'm sure William will call me directly soon afterward."

"I'm here if you need me. I have a few things to do, then let's go home early. Looks like a glass of wine is on our agenda."

"I might need something stronger." She managed a forced grin.

"Anything you want."

Katy leaned back in the chair, staring at the computer screen, formulating her email to Simon in her head. She massaged the kink in her neck, then jumped in, explaining her predicament. Within two minutes of hitting the send button, her ringer went off.

"Hi, Simon."

"Katy! I can't believe this email. What were you thinking? I thought you were on vacation," Simon said.

"I am. My cousin needed help, and that's what I did. Who knew Martin and Lewis were going to end up representing Frosty Mountain? It was an unforeseeable fluke." Pain shot up her neck, inducing a monster headache.

"William won't be happy."

"I know. Listen, I can't help you on the campaign and don't send me any more emails about it for integrity's sake."

"Let me talk to William and see if there's a way around this," Simon said.

Are you crazy? Still trying to squeeze some work out of her even when it was unethical. "I don't think there's much more to say. Good luck, Simon."

"I'll call you later," he said.

Don't bother. "Okay." *Say anything to get off the phone.*

Nothing about Martin and Lewis brought her joy anymore. What was she going to do? She pulled up the bakery's website, scanned through it, and looked for places needing a tweak. She clicked on the video of Mary Beth and Eddie, her eyes misting when it ended. This work gave her joy—helping others build their businesses while giving back to those in need. That's what she wanted to do. Could she still do that at Martin and Lewis?

Christine popped her head in the door. "How'd it go?"

"As expected. Simon even tried to get me to discuss the work I've done for you. He has no scruples."

"Are you ready to leave?"

Katy's ringer went off again. William this time. "Let me take this, and then I'm good to go."

"Hello, Mr. Lewis," Katy said.

"Hello, Miss Flanagan. I've been informed by Simon you completed an entire marketing campaign for our competition. I'm not happy about that."

Are you kidding me? "It was an innocent coincidence, Mr. Lewis. Who knew Frosty Mountain would come to you?"

"You do know you're under exclusive contract with Martin and Lewis and are forbidden to work on rogue projects."

"This was pro-bono, and this was my cousin we're talking about."

A small cyclone of annoyance began to spin in her stomach and chest.

"Either way, I think you need to rethink your priorities to your work and this company. We should have been informed about this campaign."

"But I was volunteering to help my cousin, not start something in competition with you."

"It certainly doesn't look like that, does it?"

Katy knew he was angry, but there was nothing more she could do. Christine was her priority, not William. "I'm sorry you feel that way."

"We'll discuss this more when you return and there may be consequences. I need to consult with my legal department."

"Okay," she said. What else could she say? But legal department? What could they do to her? She didn't know if it was a real threat or bull crap.

After hanging up, she shut down her computer and found Christine. "I need a drink. Let's go home and discuss my life. I think I need to make some changes. I can't wait." She bit her lip, shaking her head in disbelief about her conversations with Simon and William—anything but supportive.

"I've got ya. Let's go home." Christine swept her arm around Katy's shoulder, hugged her, and walked towards her office to get her coat.

Katy needed an evening with her cousin to hash through the tangled feelings consuming her—more so now than ever.

Chapter Twenty-Two

Derek was outstretched, lying on his back across the comforter on his bed, staring at the ceiling. If he closed his eyes, he would see Nick's smiling face for a moment, only to be erased by a mortar hit, where everything went black. He hardly slept a wink last night with images of his friends being hit by a mortar or screaming for help. He had made so much progress, and now he didn't know when he would get a good night's sleep again. His stomach rumbled. He pulled himself up, put two feet on the rug by his bed, stood up, and dragged himself to the kitchen. He opened the refrigerator and sighed. Nothing worth eating.

A knock sounded at the door. *Who could that be?* He wasn't ready to see people yet.

"Hey, Derek, it's Mark. I've got dinner. Open the door."

Of course, it would be Mark. News travels fast in this small town. As he opened the front door, Mark stood there with take-out bags in his hand and two cold beers.

"I heard what happened and missed you at the meeting. But you've gotta eat, man."

"Come on in," Derek said.

Mark went straight to the kitchen, pulling out plates and silverware, dished out the meal, and brought it into the living room.

"Thanks. You didn't have to do this."

"You can't live on pizza. That's what you were going to do, right?" Mark grinned.

"My next move."

Mark patted him on the back. "I knew it. Dig in."

They ate in silence.

Mark leaned back into the sofa after eating, nursing his beer. "I heard you helped Mrs. Johnson with the funeral arrangements. How was it?"

Derek twisted his fingers around the bottle he held, looking down. "It went okay. They had everything arranged since before he left for Afghanistan, just in case. She signed a bunch of papers, and he'll be buried Friday in River Falls with a small service first in their church for friends and family. Her daughter arrives today from California."

Mark nodded. "How are you doing?"

"Not great. Couldn't sleep, and the images of war and him getting injured were more vivid than ever. Every time I close my eyes that's all I see. I feel I'm back at the beginning, Doc. And that scares me." Derek raised his eyes to meet Mark's.

Mark reached over and placed his hand on Derek's knee. "This is a huge trigger for you, Derek. And it might mean you have to go back to the beginning and treat it as such. Visions of war stay in the subconscious for a long time and can resurface at any point, especially with a trigger such as Nick's death." He paused. "I think forgiveness is another element of your healing that needs attention. Everyone in your life has forgiven you for anything you thought you did wrong, but you haven't forgiven yourself. Why?"

Derek tossed his head back against the recliner. "Man, I don't know. I don't know why I can't forgive myself." He fiddled with his dog tags. "That day we switched patrols, I was sick as hell. There's no way I could have been alert or sharp enough to protect myself and my comrades."

"Do you understand that God had another plan for you? Do you believe that?"

He shuffled his feet, crossing and uncrossing them. "Why would God let Nick die and not me?"

Mark took a breath. "I don't think I can answer that one, my friend. Maybe talk to the Reverend about it. But I do know you are alive, you are physically healthy, and you have a great life to live in Maple Ridge with friends and family who love you. Maybe it's time you start focusing on all the good you have in your life. Isn't that what God and Nick would want for you?"

Derek stopped fidgeting. "Yeah, I guess so."

"Look. Nick wouldn't want you moping around and sinking into a dark hole of depression over him and the war. He'd be saying, 'Get out there. Live!' Right?"

"Yep. He was always the first one making us laugh and goof around in camp. He was a jokester." Derek grinned at the thought.

"I know this is tough. You've lost a friend, not once but twice. Take the time to grieve. Be easy on yourself. I'll give you some more techniques I've used for sleeping as well."

"Thanks."

"Give me the info on the funeral, and I'll attend too. Are guys coming from your unit to be pallbearers?"

Derek nodded. "I called them this afternoon for Mrs. Johnson."

"Good. Are you going to work tomorrow?"

"I guess so. I want to be there for Christine in case she needs anything with our project. They make a decision next week."

"Don't feel guilty if you need more time. Because you will need time however you choose to grieve."

"I'll see how I feel tomorrow." Derek leaned forward, raking his fingers through his hair.

"And take a shower. You look like crap."

"Thanks." Derek's lips pressed together, holding back a grin.

Mark stood up. "I'm right next door if you need anything. Do a session with Dr. McPherson too."

"Will do. Thanks for stopping by." Derek walked him to the door.

"You've got this," Mark said. He put his coat on and hugged Derek a little longer than usual. "I'm here for you, man." Then he left.

Derek ambled back to the kitchen, going through the motions of cleaning the dishes, and straightening up. Working was good. Moving was good. He'd get through this. He had to.

* * *

Katy pulled her car into the lot behind the bakery, turned off the ignition, and sat there for a minute. She didn't see Derek's truck; maybe he was taking another day off. Christine had left early in the morning before she had woken up and had been instrumental in helping her the previous night, sorting through the mess in her brain. She laughed. Sometimes she made it more difficult for herself than needed.

Shaking off her boots covered in freshly fallen snow, she found Christine on the phone at her desk. She waved her into the office, and Katy situated herself at the extra table, not wanting to enter Derek's in case he was coming in.

When Christine got off the phone, she turned to her cousin. "That was one of my distributers. He said delivery to New York would be no problem and the extra costs minimal." She clapped her hands together. "But my nerves are beyond keyed-up if you couldn't tell. How am I going to wait another week?" She grinned at Katy.

"One foot in front of the other."

"Is that what you're doing?" Christine asked. "Make any decisions yet?"

"No, I'm waiting to see what my heart wants. But if I'm honest, I already know. I have to quit Martin and Lewis."

"Yeah, I figured. What will you do?"

"Join another agency and hope William doesn't try to sue me for breaking a non-compete clause I signed years ago."

"He can't be that heartless, can he?"

"After the tone of voice he used with me yesterday, anything's possible." She opened her computer. "Is Derek coming in today?"

"Yes. After lunch. I didn't ask him what he was doing. I feel for him. He said the funeral was tomorrow."

"Would you mind if I went?" Katy asked.

"No. I think that would be nice."

"I'll ask him and see if it's alright. But I did make a connection with Nick on our visits. I would like to pay my respects."

Christine nodded and went back to work while Katy checked on their website, sales, and campaign. But the emails and comments about the *Hands-On Beyond* program brought tears to her eyes. She received stories from directors of foster care and orphanage programs all over the country pleading to participate in the campaign, and all their information flooded their inboxes. This is what Alison must have experienced when she first launched the program. Now the organization was getting a second wind with the *Hearts for Hope* campaign. A calmness settled in her soul. She was doing the right thing, at the right time, at the right place. No doubts.

After lunch, she ordered a cappuccino from Mary Beth in the front and looked up to see Derek standing in the doorway, his towering frame and dark brooding eyes staring down at her.

"I'll take one of those too, please," he said.

Katy was inches from him. "Hi." She paused. "Missed you around here." She didn't want to pry.

"Yeah, I helped Nick's mom with funeral arrangements." He grabbed his coffee and headed towards his office.

Katy skipped to catch up with him. "When you have a minute, I want to show you some of the emails we received about the campaign. Might lift your spirit a little." She wanted to reach out and take him in her arms. She wanted to kiss his lips, his face, and everywhere on his body. *Uncontrollable.*

"Give me a few minutes to answer some emails, then come on by," he said.

"Okay." His shoulders drooped; his head hung as she watched him withdraw, trying hard to function. She was beginning to know his moods and how best to interact with them. She had been reading up on PTSD and didn't want to do anything that might trigger him.

She decided to wait a half hour before disturbing him again. Engrossed in emails, she jumped when fingers rapped on her door. "Come in."

His eyes penetrated hers as he stuck his head inside the room. "I'm ready if you are."

"Be right there." She placed her computer in her arms, grabbed her notebook, and followed him.

He pulled up a chair and pointed to his desk, which he had cleared. "Put your stuff here."

Katy arranged everything and sat back in her chair. "First, I need to tell you something that happened yesterday." She clutched her fingers, twisting them against her palm as she relayed her conversations with Simon and William. When finished, she looked at him, hoping for guidance or suggestions. She needed someone to tell her what to do. She trusted him now.

He sat silent for a moment, then met her eye gaze with a softening she craved. An indication that he cared for her, even if it was as a friend. "What are you going to do?"

"I think I will turn in my notice and leave the company. It felt toxic when I was there on Monday, and after working in this environment for the past couple of weeks, I don't want to stay somewhere that doesn't care about me but uses my skills. That's how I feel about Martin and Lewis. It didn't always feel like that." Her eyes shifted downward as she bit her bottom lip.

"And what will you do?"

"Probably get a job with another company, I guess."

"Why don't you start your own company? From what I've seen, you've got all the skills and the passion." He twisted his body around to give her more attention.

"My own company? Where? It's so expensive in New York. That's a big leap." She wrung her hands together in her lap.

Derek reached over and grabbed her hands in his, pulling her closer. "You can do it. I know you can. Start working from your home, gather clients, and when you've made a boatload of money, find an office. Easy peezy."

The touch of his skin against hers discombobulated her brain. In an instant this man could turn her to mush.

"You really think I could?"

A hair slipped down on her face, and Derek reached up, stroking it away. He placed his hand on her cheek. "I think you can do anything you want."

They both became very still. Without warning, he lowered his head slowly, bringing his lips softly to hers. He pulled back and looked into her eyes. "Sorry. I couldn't help myself."

Katy reached up and touched his face as he had done. "No worries. I've been wanting to kiss you."

"I find myself always wanting to kiss you, if I'm honest, but probably not such a great idea since I'm not in the right frame of mind right now for dating. I'm not ready for a relationship and apologize for jumping the gun. My emotions have been all over the place since Nick's death." He pulled away from her and broke the energy between them.

"I understand." But all she wanted to do was throw her arms around him, go somewhere secluded, and dig into the underpinnings of this man, flaws and all.

"I have faith in you, Katy Flanagan. You'll know what to do when the time is right."

"Thanks. I appreciate your support." She paused. "There's one more thing. Would you mind if I went to the service tomorrow? I would like to pay my respects to Nick." She glanced at him to see his response.

"Of course, you can. Do you want to go with me? I can pick you up."

"Yes, that would be great unless you have more responsibilities with the family."

"No, it's alright. Mrs. Johnson's daughter is here now."

"Okay. Just text me a time."

"Will do."

Katy gathered her materials and laptop. "I'm going home. See you tomorrow."

Before she went out the door, he spoke. "Katy, I'm glad I kissed you, but timing is off right now." He paused. "And I don't know how long it's going to take me to be ready for another person in my life. Romantically speaking that is."

"I know, Derek. I know."

Putting on her coat, she pressed her palm against the sick feeling in her stomach. When is the right time for her? She didn't know if love was in the cards for her, and if it ever would be. She pulled her hat and gloves on, walking to the car but could only think about the kiss. And wanted more.

Chapter Twenty-Three

Katy had tossed and turned all night. Nightmares of being fired, dragged to court, and losing everything haunted her. She woke up in a sweat, looked at the clock blazing 5:00 a.m. in red, and decided to get up. What else could she do? Take a hot shower and do some yoga stretches? Maybe that would help.

The hot water beat down on her back and neck, soothing her muscles temporarily. She flashed on the day before her and felt an inkling of sorrow trickling around her heart, thinking of Derek. Would he ever be able to forgive himself? No matter how many people advised him, she knew he needed to come to terms with it himself.

After stretching, she bumped into her cousin making coffee in the kitchen.

"You're up early," Christine said.

"Couldn't sleep."

"Want to talk some more?"

"No. Not really. After coffee, I'm going to take a walk and hope the frigid air knocks some sense into my brain. Or at least, invigorates me." She chuckled. "Derek is picking me up at ten. I hope he's okay with me riding with him."

"I'm sure he is. Any decisions yet?"

"I'm going to scour the internet and research other companies this weekend. It would be nice to have something set up before I quit. My landlord would appreciate that." She grinned.

"I'm here if you need me. Text me later."

"Will do." Katy watched as her cousin picked up her coffee mug and headed out the door to the bakery.

Fresh air filled her lungs as Katy pulled her knitted cap over her ears and stuck her gloved hands into her pockets. She scanned the horizon of rolling hills blanketed in white, tall pines stretching towards a blue sky and the naked forest standing firm in its majesty. She could get used to country living. Besides all the work fiasco, Maple Ridge inspired her. The *Hearts for Hope* campaign resonated with her profoundly and being with Christine reminded her that she had family who cared about her. At least, it had been that way since her mother had died. Being out of New York City and away from the madness of corporate career climbing, she was acutely aware of an emptiness in her gut and soul—a lack of love. Her heart had been opening to the handsome veteran, but last night's declaration had cemented her decision that she needed to pull away too. She didn't want to get hurt and end up in an unrequited love situation.

After the walk, she changed clothes into a navy blue knit dress, put make-up on, and prepared for the funeral. The doorbell rang. She opened it, and goosebumps poured over her skin like a waterfall at the sight of the soldier in his dress blues standing before her.

"Ready?" he asked.

The breath had been knocked out of her for a second as she took in the hotness of this man, dripping in an arousing temptation of male appeal to the max—nothing like a man in uniform.

"Yes. Thanks for picking me up."

"No problem."

They rode in silence, adjusting to the solemnness of the affair. Katy looked straight ahead to keep her chills and butterflies in check. She was there as a friend to support him. Nothing more.

They pulled into the church parking lot, and Katy jumped out of the truck before Derek could open her door. The lot was full, and she noticed a small group of men in uniform, most likely the other pall bearers and comrades in arms.

"I'll meet you afterward by the front of the church." She squeezed his hand and turned away.

Derek walked over to the others, offering hugs and handshakes to the men he had served with in Afghanistan. His unit. They would always remain his family. It was good to see them even if the circumstances were grim.

Derek instructed them on what would happen after the service; they all filed into the church to sit behind Nick's mother and sister. Derek turned his head around, hoping to glimpse Katy, and found her sitting halfway back in the pews. He looked straight ahead again when his heartbeat raced faster at the sight of her. She was a good friend, but underneath all his angst, he wanted more. But also knew he had nothing to give to her. His emotional reserves were empty, and his bandwidth for an intimate relationship was nil. His lustful desires were battling with the truth, making his life more difficult, not easier. Soon she would leave, and he wouldn't have to deal with those sensuous brown eyes, infectious smile, and voluptuous body with curves in all the right places. He needed to pull away from her. That was the only way he could heal himself.

* * *

Katy shivered in the cold as the six men carried the casket down the steps, carefully sliding it into the hearse. She would ride out to the cemetery for a brief service there, and after that, she hadn't even thought of what she would do. Perhaps she should Uber home and let Derek be with his buddies.

As the casket was lowered into the ground, Katy's eyes pooled with tears. She yanked a tissue from her pocket before she started bawling. Looking at all the uniformed men seated next to Nick's mother, an image flashed of how they had given their lives to something greater than themselves. And one of their comrades had paid the highest price—his life. The American flag was folded and presented to Mrs. Johnson as her daughter's arm reached around her shoulders, comforting her the best she could. The sound of taps echoed from the trumpet of another older veteran, letting the melody carry the heaviness of death into the atmosphere with reverence deserved for a fallen soldier. Katy shuddered, listening to the music, signaling the finality of life, and realizing how short it was for everyone.

She waited for Derek to finish talking to Nick's mother, even though her toes were frozen in the silly, fancy boots she had worn.

Derek walked over to her. "We're all going to the Johnson's for food and drink. She insists all of us come. Are you alright with that?"

His gaze bore into hers; she could see the sadness sitting there, not budging. "I can call an Uber if you want to be alone with your friends. No problem."

"No, it's too cold. You're coming with us. Come on." He gently put his hand on her back, guiding her towards the truck.

Katy surrendered and climbed into the truck, thankful for the heat blasting on her feet. They were silent during the drive, but Katy glanced over at him for a brief second. *I'm here as a friend. Remember that.*

Katy followed him inside the house and was surprised at the number of people there. People from his church, high school friends, and his unit. She turned to Derek. "You visit with your friends. I'll be just fine. I want to give my condolences to Mrs. Johnson anyway."

He nodded and moved away from her.

Katy saw Nick's mom seated on the couch and made her way over to her. Nick's sister was standing nearby, so she walked up to her first.

"Hi, I'm Katy. I knew Nick briefly from the veterans' home, and I wanted to tell you how sorry I am for your loss."

"Thank you," she said. "Were you one of his nurses?"

"No. I'm a friend of Derek's. I helped him take cookies and treats from Sweet Ridge Bakery on Friday evenings to him. He was quite the character, even with his injury." Katy smiled at her.

"You should have seen him before he left for his tour. He was always the jokester. I sure am going to miss him." She wiped a tear from her cheek and forced a grin. "Seems I can't stop these lately."

"And no need to." Katy gently tapped her shoulder. When she saw Mrs. Johnson was alone, she made her way over to her.

"Hi, Mrs. Johnson. Remember me? I'm Katy Flanagan. Derek's friend. We met at the facility."

"Oh, yes, dear. Please, sit down." She patted the space next to her on the couch.

Katy lowered herself to the cushion. "I'm so sorry for your loss."

Mrs. Johnson reached her hand out to Katy and tapped her knee. "Thank you. But he would never have wanted to live the way he had been this past year, restrained to a hospital bed, no freedom of his own. God knew what was best for my son, and I trust in that decision. I will miss him terribly, but at least he's not suffering anymore. And I know his soul was suffering. He was too much of a free spirit to live in a nursing home for the rest of his life."

Katy nodded.

She went on. "You talk to Derek quite a bit, right?"

"Yes."

Mrs. Johnson scanned the room until she saw him chatting with his buddies. "I wish there were something more I could say to him about not feeling guilty. He blames himself for Nick's death, and I wish he could heal that pain. I've told him it wasn't his fault, but I can see he carries that burden. I don't know what else I can say. Perhaps you could talk to him?"

"I don't know if I'm the best person, but if I can, I will," Katy said.

Mrs. Johnson patted her knee again. "Good. Someone needs to get through to him." She turned as someone else came to speak to her.

Katy stood up and walked around the house, looking at family pictures.

"You know, we went to the same high school but didn't really know each other until we landed in the same unit."

Katy spun around to see Derek towering over her. This man rocked her insides and there was nothing she could do about it.

"Listen, I'm going to stay longer, help Mrs. Johnson clean up, and hang out with my guys. I found you a ride home with Cynthia, one of the nurses who took care of Nick. She lives close to Christine. I hope you don't mind." He peered down into her eyes with a straight face.

"That's fine. I understand. Thanks for taking care of it."

"Come on, I'll introduce you." Derek turned expecting her to follow.

After introductions were made, Katy put on her coat and stood looking up at Derek. "Guess I'll see you on Monday?"

"Yes, I'll be there. If anything comes up with the project, text me." He abruptly turned and left.

On the drive over to Maple Ridge, the two women chatted, talking about Nick and his last days. Cynthia asked a few questions about Derek, commenting on his dedication to the veterans living in the facility. Probably all the nurses had the hots for him.

That night, as Katy lay in bed, she reflected on the day. Seeing Derek in his uniform reminded her of that other side of him, and it was a big part. One doesn't serve in the military without a degree of dedication, humility, and courage. He seemed sad yet securely at home with his comrades. But looking into his eyes, she knew he was twisted inside, battling invisible demons, and hanging himself from a self-made noose of guilt. Could she get through to him? Could she help him shed this self-hatred that tortured him so? She had no clue but prayed if there was something she could do, she would be shown a sign. And with that, she turned out the light and rolled over to sleep.

* * *

Katy pressed send on her last resume submission and closed her computer. There. She had done it. She had applied to several top marketing companies in New York for a new job. Why didn't she feel better about it?

She was fond of Maple Ridge, and the memories of her childhood came flooding into her consciousness. She didn't want to leave after Christmas. That was her new problem. *Life is never easy, is it?*

She had promised Christine she would volunteer to take goodies to Fairside in the afternoon for their annual Christmas party for the kids. Helping at the orphanage would hopefully take her out of her head and into her heart. She needed that.

She pulled into the parking lot and was surprised to see Derek's truck in the back. Maybe he was going to help too, and she could spend more time with him. Fingers crossed.

The bakery was bustling with extra staff for the holidays, and Katy waved to Derek as she walked through the commotion on her way to getting a cappuccino in the front of the store. He simply nodded in her direction, his focus on the dough in front of him.

Katy waited for her drink and scanned the front tables. Saliva caught in her throat when she spotted Simon sitting in the corner with Alexandra, their assistant. *What is he doing here?*

She walked behind Mary Beth, out of their sight and whispered to her. "How long have they been here?" She pointed in their direction.

"About ten minutes. They ordered lunch. Why? Do you know them?"

"That's my ex-boyfriend, soon to be new boss, and our competition! They must be here doing research. I've got to tell Christine." Katy flew back through the doors and headed straight to Christine's office at a fast clip.

"Christine, come quick. You'll never guess who's in the front." She proceeded to tell her as she grabbed her arm and pulled her towards the swinging doors. On their tiptoes, peeking out the window, Katy pointed out Simon.

Derek approached the two women. "What's going on?"

"Our competition is sitting in the corner," Christine said.

Katy explained further. "Should I go out there?"

"Absolutely," Derek said.

Katy adjusted her sweater, and with shoulders straight, she walked with determination directly to Simon's table.

"Simon! What are doing here?" she asked.

Simon immediately stood up and went in for a hug, but Katy did not reciprocate the fondness and broke away a second later.

"It's so good to see you, Katy. We've missed you right?" He looked down at Alexandra who smiled.

"But why drive all the way up here without letting me know?" Katy knew why but wanted to hear it from his own mouth.

"I think you know why. My client is in competition with this bakery, and we needed to check it out to compare them. We're headed to Vermont later." He pressed his lips together. "I'm sure you did the same thing, right?"

She smirked at him. "Of course."

He suddenly reached out and grabbed her hand. "Look, can we talk somewhere private?"

As he did that, Katy noticed the scowl lurking on Alexandra's face. *Oh my god. Is she into him?*

Katy's shoulders were seizing, writhing in pain. Too much stress. "Not here, Simon."

"Can we take a walk?"

"Let me get my coat." She relented with the hopes of having more closure with this man.

Simon turned to his assistant. "I'll be right back."

Katy wrapped her cashmere scarf tighter around her neck. "Let's go."

Simon followed, staying close beside her. "Listen, I know you're still mad about my promotion, but don't you remember all the conversations we had when we both applied? We vowed to be happy for each other, not hate them. And I feel that's how you feel about me. Am I wrong?"

"I don't hate you, Simon. I was angry you stole my cause marketing ideas for part of your pitch when you know that was all my creation." She turned her gaze towards him with laser sharp intensity. "Admit it, and I'll let it go."

Simon looked away from her, then stopped on the sidewalk. It was too cold to stand outside arguing much longer. "I guess I should have given you partial credit for the ideas in my proposal."

"Partial? Are you kidding me? You never even thought of doing cause marketing for our Krafton case until you saw how successful it was. And William should have known this area of expertise was more in my wheelhouse, not yours. Being shut out from the exclusive men's club was infuriating; the fact that your father has so many connections in the city, didn't help my case either."

Simon was quiet for a moment. "You're right. I was a schmuck for claiming your idea as mine. I'm really sorry, Katy. I'm sorry this broke us up, and I'm sorry you didn't get the recognition you deserved."

"Thank you." The outdoor chill hadn't made a dent on the heat rising in her body from unresolved disgust. She could accept his apology but wasn't ready to forgive him.

"I want you to know that I will be the best boss ever and make sure you have every opportunity to shine in the company with future clients."

Katy looked up at him. She was clear he would never be her boss. Ever. "Let's go back. I'm freezing."

He reached out and touched her arm. "I hope we can be friends again, Katy."

She nodded, wanting to get away from him as soon as possible. When they entered the bakery, she waved at Alexandra once more. "Enjoy your lunch." And turned straight for the doors into the back of the bakery.

"Well?" asked Christine.

Katy plopped down on the chair in her office. Before she opened her mouth, Derek's head peered inside, as his large frame stood in the doorway.

"Is this a private conversation?" he asked.

"No. Come in," Katy said. "They're doing the exact same thing that we did. Research. But they're kind of late unless he comes up with some brilliant idea that they can manifest in two or three days. Knowing Simon and his creative bandwidth, I'm not worried."

Christine studied Katy's face. "Something else is going on. What is it? Do you still have feelings for him?"

Derek shifted his body weight. "Is this a personal conversation? Should I leave?"

"No," Katy said. "I don't mind sharing with you." *In fact, I crave it.* "I'm quitting my position at Martin and Lewis. I'll give my notice on Monday. They're going to be pissed I'm sure, but no way can I handle having Simon as my boss. I've been sending out resumes for the past two days. Something will happen for me—I hope." She smiled at the two of them.

"What about starting your own company? We talked about it, but now might be the time to do it," Derek said. The corners of his mouth lifted, waiting for her response.

His dark eyes pierced through hers and she couldn't look away. This man had faith in her—more than she had for herself. "I don't … don't know," she stammered.

"What are you afraid of?" Christine asked. "You don't think my grandmother was scared out of her wits when she opened up this bakery?"

Katy smiled. "Yeah, you're probably right. I guess I'm afraid of failure. Scared of all the work that would go into opening my own business. And all the questions swarming in my head. Where would I do it? How would I do it? The list goes on and on."

"You'll never know if you don't try," Derek said. "And I can help you. At least with the numbers part."

"Why don't you stay in Maple Ridge and do it here? You can still get clients in New York, even Boston. But you could run your office out of Maple Ridge—much cheaper. Have you thought of that?" Christine asked.

A fluttering in her stomach intensified. Could she stay here? No, there's not enough potential for clients. It's not a big city. But there is the internet, and people do get jobs that way. "I'm not sure I could get the clientele I need to be financially viable."

"Just think about it," Christine said. She looked at her watch. "We've got to load the truck and head out to Fairside for the party. Are you two ready? I can't leave the shop, but I'm sure you two can manage on your own."

Derek looked at Katy. "Coming?"

"Right behind you." Her head was about to explode with the idea of starting her own company. Could she do it? Was Derek offering to help because he wanted her to stay in Maple Ridge? Would he ever heal his damaging wounds enough to be in a healthy relationship? All these questions caused a gnawing headache that was growing by the minute. An afternoon with Fairside kids would get her head straight. At least, she hoped it would.

Chapter Twenty-Four

Derek and Katy carried boxes and trays of assorted Christmas cookies into the Fairside kitchen, ready to be distributed to all the hungry kids in the recreation room. Karen had started a gift exchange last year, where each child or teen had to make a gift for their Secret Santa. Holiday music blared through the speakers, and voices squealed as they unwrapped their surprise presents. Derek and Katy sat in the back and watched the merriment unfold.

Katy leaned over to Derek. "Karen is amazing with these kids."

"Yeah, I know."

Katy's heart expanded inside her chest at the sight before her, and her pulse quickened near Derek. When she saw Simon earlier, no butterflies or chills entered her body—only irritation. She no longer had feelings for him. His actions had destroyed them, and the relationship was unsalvageable. *Is it too soon to take a risk with another man?*

Jolene, Mary Beth's sister, skipped up to them. "Did you guys exchange a present?"

Derek looked at Katy and shook his head. "Were we supposed to?"

"Yes! Everyone needs a gift. Do you want me to see if there are extras? Miss Karen usually does that for those who forgot or can't make anything." She paused. "Or you two can make something on your own and give it to each other before Christmas Eve. What do you say?"

Jolene's big brown eyes nearly melted hers. Katy looked over at Derek. "I guess we could participate, if you're up to it, Mr. Higgins." She grinned.

"Sure. Handmade, huh?" He fidgeted in his seat for a second. "I'll have to think about this one."

Jolene clapped her hands. "Good. You'll have to tell me what you each received next time I see you. Gotta go." She whisked around and joined the others.

Katy laughed. "She's quite the precocious one, isn't she?"

"Yeah."

What is he thinking? Katy reached her hand out and placed it on his knee. "Are you okay?"

"Yeah. Just thinking about these kids and how they ended up here. My stuff seems insignificant compared to them. I need to get over my crap." He wrung his fingers together, back and forth.

"Give yourself a break, Derek. You just lost a good friend, and you're working hard on yourself. That's how I see it from where I'm sitting."

He clasped her hand resting on his leg. "Yeah. You're right."

"I know." She giggled.

Derek looked up and saw Karen motioning to them. "Showtime. Let's go. They're ready for us."

Katy followed along. *I guess this conversation is over for now.*

The two of them became busy dishing out treats and pouring drinks. Katy even forgot about her job woes and let the holiday spirit fill her soul. The kids were anxious to share their gifts. A little boy lifted his model airplane made from popsicle sticks to her and beamed at his prized possession. The simplicity of his joy wrapped around her heart. Oh, how she needed this reminder of the true meaning of Christmas. It was all about giving. And what if her work focused on giving all year round? Simple giving to others as a vocation? *Isn't that what cause marketing is all about?*

Her random thoughts were interrupted when a voice sounded behind her. "Pretty cool, huh? I dig that airplane."

The noise in the room faded out to the background as she circled around and found Derek's face inches from her. She could feel his breath on her cheek, its warmth enticing her to come closer; her voice seemed stuck in her throat. She desperately wanted to kiss him and yearned for time alone, her patience whittling away at her desires. *Pull yourself together, girl.* "Yes, it's quite clever."

He walked away, filling cups with hot cocoa and chatting with the kids.

Seeing Alison helping with Jake at the other end of the room, Katy approached her. "Shouldn't you be doing something to get ready for the wedding?" She laughed.

"Yes, yes. I know. But I think we're all set. I can't believe it's six days from now," Alison said.

"Are you nervous?" Katy asked.

"A little. But I feel so at home here in Maple Ridge; I feel it's just another big party we're throwing. Friends and family are tightknit here and can't wait to celebrate our good fortune. I'm a blessed woman, Katy." She paused. "I wish you were staying here too. Is there any news from the investors yet? We're all rooting for Sweet Ridge and Christine. We all want her to be happy and if living in New York is a possibility for her and Sam, we'll let her go." She laughed. "They were meant for each other."

"No, not yet. We should know by midweek. They promised us they'd tell us before the holidays."

"Any chance you might stay?" Alison asked. "Christine told me you were quitting your job."

"Yes, I am. But I've sent out some resumes to other companies, all in New York."

"I was hoping you'd stay. I see the spark between you and Derek. It's the same spark I had with Jake. Just saying." The edges of her mouth slowly lifted.

"You see it?" she asked.

"Yes. Plain as day." Alison tapped her arm. "Don't let love pass you by. No pressure." She laughed. "Love is complicated but always worth it." She turned and walked away.

Katy stood stunned. Was it that obvious to others how she felt about this man? Even with all his flaws, she found him irresistible. She had her imperfections, so they were evenly matched in that way. She shook her head as a little girl tugged on her shirt, asking for more hot chocolate. "Sure, sweetie. Let me get you a cup."

Derek and Katy helped the adults clean up at the end of the party and watched as the Fairside kids dispersed, laughing, and goofing around with each other.

Katy looked up at him. "I can't believe how much joy exudes from this place when each of these young ones have been dealt a crappy hand in life. Karen is a miracle worker."

"I know. The whole town has taken them under their wing and support her. I've seen it time after time." He rested his hand on her shoulder. "Ready to go?"

"Sure."

"Do you mind stopping by the veterans' home with me on our way back? I missed them yesterday with the funeral and all."

Katy could see the sorrow lingering in his eyes. "Are you sure you want to go there so soon?"

"Nothing's going to change. Nick is gone. I can't bring him back, and I'm not going to disappoint the other veterans who look forward to our baked goods."

She tossed some dirty cups in the trash and turned to him. "I'd love to."

Derek went back into the kitchen, grabbed the remaining empty trays, and motioned for Katy to follow him.

Riding in the truck, Katy glanced over at Derek staring straight ahead, focused on the road. *What is he thinking?* She reflected on Alison's comments. Was it that obvious to others how she felt about this man? Did he feel the same way?

Katy hopped out of the vehicle and Derek handed her a box of cookies. Just two large boxes today—a small one no longer needed. Her heart ached for his loss; she hoped this little trip didn't trigger an emotion he couldn't deal with.

As usual, the men and women were scattered throughout the recreation room and lit up at the sight of Derek and his large pink box.

Wally came over to him and placed his hand on Derek's back. "I'm sorry to hear about your friend, Nick. He was a good guy."

Derek looked down, busying himself with putting cookies on trays. "Yeah, he was." Dishing out cookies he could do. Discussing Nick in this place, he couldn't. He wasn't ready. "How have you been?"

"Same ole, same ole. But I keep moving each day. Can't complain."

Others came up to Derek to give their condolences to him, and he tried his best to brush them away, redirecting the conversations.

Katy made her way over to Betty with a tray of Christmas cookies. "Hello, dear. I didn't know if I'd see you again. How's it going with that man of yours?" Her finger waggled at Derek across the room.

Katy could feel the heat flushing her face. "You mean Derek?"

"Of course, I mean Derek. I may be ninety, but my wits are sharp as a tack. Only the rest of my body is giving out." She chuckled.

"He's fine," Katy said. "Well, not really. Nick's death was quite a blow."

"I'm sure it was. Give him time, dear. Grief doesn't heal overnight." Katy nodded.

"How much longer are you staying in Maple Ridge? Have you considered moving here?"

My, this woman gets right to the heart of the matter, doesn't she? "Not really. Well, maybe. I don't know. I'm quitting my job, but I sent out resumes to other companies in New York."

"You can't set up shop here?" Betty asked.

"Why does everyone keep asking me that? It's a little complicated. I'd have to start my own company and get an investor."

"Then do it." Betty grinned. "I have a feeling about the two of you." She pointed to Derek again. "My hunches are rarely wrong. If you don't mind, I would like another cookie, please. The powdered sugar one." Her feeble fingers reached out to the tray Katy held and grasped the one she wanted. The flaky white powder fell on her sweater as she brought it to her mouth. "See. Life is messy. That's no reason to *not* enjoy it." She winked at Katy.

Katy grinned at her but let the words sink into her gut. She never shied away from messiness at her job. Sometimes she thrived on it, crazy as that seemed. But trusting and relying on a man in a relationship? That terrified her. And she knew the reason why—her father. All the summers and many holidays being shipped off to Maple Ridge had left a hole in her heart when it came to trusting men. She had controlled her relationship with Simon and never let her heart fully open to him. She realized she had been more angry than sad when they broke up. But opening to Derek was scary. He was so unpredictable, vulnerable, and strong all in one package. She knew she could depend on him with business affairs but what about matters of the heart? *Could I depend on him to love me and never desert me?*

She put a smile back on her face and continued her visit around the room to those in wheelchairs or settled in comfy chairs with their walkers by their side. As she stood chatting to another group, a voice sounded behind her. "I'm ready whenever you are."

She spun around, almost tossing the tray into Derek's chest. "Sure. Let me get that last group over there." She motioned with her head to two men playing chess at a table.

"I'll be outside."

"Okay." *He's reached his limit.*

Katy tidied up the table and arranged the leftover baked goods for anyone who wanted them. She put on her coat and made her way out to the parking lot where Derek was sitting in the truck.

She slid into the passenger seat. "Ready."

"Thanks. Sorry I didn't wait for you. I had to get out of there."

She looked at his eyes and noticed they were red and slightly swollen. Most likely he had just finished bawling his eyes out and didn't want her to see. She reached over, touching his hand on the steering wheel. "I understand."

They took off in silence and soon pulled into Christine's driveway. "Thanks for coming with me today," he said.

"I wanted to. I needed to get out of my head." She paused. "Are you attending the tree lighting tonight? Christine wants me to go with her."

"I might walk over. Depends." He stretched his arm out and grasped her hand. "I appreciate that you give me space, Katy. I feel like you have some kind of intuitive sense about me and that means a lot." He squeezed her hand but didn't release it.

Katy sat still. "Yes, I think am getting to know you better." *And I'm starting to trust you.* She squeezed his hand. "I'm happy you're in my life, Derek Higgins." She was flustering at what else to say.

"Ditto," he said. He let go of her hand, leaned over, and drew her in to a solid hug.

Suddenly their faces were touching, side by side. She could feel his breath on her neck and the warmth of his body, even in the awkward position of the front seat, radiating against hers and shooting sparks of heat across her chest.

As they slowly released, their eyes stared into each other's and Derek slowly lowered his lips onto hers, gently caressing her mouth with his own lips. As he pulled back, she looked into his eyes, awaiting a response.

"I'm sorry. I can't seem to help myself when you're that close."

"Don't be sorry. I wanted you to kiss me." She sheepishly grinned at him.

"I'm still not—"

"Don't worry. No promises need to be made here. Let's just leave it as is. For now," Katy said.

"Okay." He reached up and touched her face. "Did I ever tell you what a beautiful woman you are?"

"No." She giggled as heat rose into her cheeks. "Thank you."

He slowly dropped his hand, placing it back on the steering wheel.

"Guess it's time for me to leave. Thanks again for coming with me."

"Always," she said. Katy jumped out of the truck, waved goodbye, and let herself inside the house. *What just happened?*

* * *

Katy glanced at her phone when her text tone sounded. Christine. She was staying in town until after the tree-lighting ceremony and wanted to extend the store's hours, so if anyone wanted a treat, they could get it at Sweet Ridge afterward.

Can you help?

Sure. I'll be there in an hour.
Need to shower and change.

You're the best! Heart emoji.

Katy put down her phone and stared out the window like she had been doing for the last half hour, ever since Derek had dropped her off. Did he kiss her because he was feeling vulnerable and emotional? Or did he have feelings for her like she had for him? He was so hard to read at times.

She opened her computer and scanned emails. Her stomach quivered when she saw one from one of the top marketing firms in New York. "Thank you for your application and letter. We would like to discuss it further with you over the phone on Monday. Please call our office then and ask for Mr. Billings."

Were they going to offer her a job? Excitement grabbed at the possibility, but her heart twisted at the same time. New York was not Maple Ridge. And Derek lived in Maple Ridge. Maybe he could make frequent trips to New York for work with Christine. Then they could see each other more. What was she doing? They hadn't even talked about having a relationship, and she was already living in a pretend one that they had. *Get a grip on reality, girl. One step at a time. Job first. Man second. Stay in control.*

Katy arrived in town in time for the tree-lighting ceremony. She walked out with Christine and stood amongst the town's residents waiting for the big gasp at the end. A school choir sang a few carols, the mayor spoke, and then ta-da! The lights burst into every color of the rainbow, their glittering essence shining onto the square, and everyone cheered.

Katy's eyes swept over the crowd, searching for Derek. She found him in the back and caught her breath as she watched Sophie approach him. He hugged her and smiled. She couldn't tell what they were talking about, but Sophie's batting eyelashes and continuous grinning were obvious signs of her intentions.

Christine pulled on her coat sleeve. "Come on. Let's get inside before the onslaught of hungry and cold masses descend upon the bakery."

Katy turned around and followed. She'd seen enough of Sophie's sensuous ploys on the man who'd just kissed her. *What am I doing?*

"I texted Derek too. He's going to help," Christine said. "I gave Mary Beth the night off to be with Jolene."

"Good. We're going to need it."

Within minutes the shop was packed with families and loud children, excited to indulge in hot chocolate and a cookie. Christine had arranged a beautiful display for the *Hearts for Hope* campaign and made sure the tiny boxes were available for purchase. As Katy reached into the display case, she heard a voice behind her.

"Fancy meeting you here," Derek said.

Katy almost dropped the tongs and cookies she was holding, startled by his closeness. She straightened her back and faced him. "Yes, when Christine calls all hands-on deck, I obey."

He laughed. "What can I do?"

"Maybe help with the drink orders? Mary Beth's replacement is in the back making more cocoa."

"Yes, boss."

My, his mood has changed. Why? "Very funny." She grinned at him.

An hour passed, and the shop quieted down. After the last customer, Christine put the closed sign on the door and the three of them collapsed at a table, sipping their drinks.

"I can't believe we sold out of our heart gingerbread cakes," Christine said. "I know where I'll be tomorrow." She laughed.

"If this takes off, we might have to hire another staff person," Derek said.

"Yeah, I know. Let's relook at everything after the investors make their decision. But for now, I want to enjoy this last week of Christmas celebration." She patted Katy's hand. "I can't believe Alison's wedding is on Friday."

"She looked pretty calm today at Fairside," Katy said. She could feel Derek's eyes on her burning right through any shield she might have put up. She needed to be honest about her future with him. "I got an email today from Carter Marketing and Media Firm. They want to discuss my application on the phone Monday." There she had let him know. She was looking for a job in New York. Why didn't she feel better?

"That's great, Katy," Christine said. "Although I was hoping you'd move here. But I guess if I'm in New York more, we'll still get to see each other. What do you think, Derek?" Christine knew they had been dancing around an obvious chemistry for weeks.

"If that's what you want, go for it. But I still think you'd be awesome starting your own company. Do you want to work for another big corporation that might not have your best interests at heart or understand your dreams?" He stared at her.

Katy fidgeted in the chair, her hands sweaty. He had pressed a button she wasn't ready to look at quite yet. Did she really have the courage to start her own business? "It's just a phone meeting. I haven't made any decisions yet." She looked at him with laser intensity. *If you're interested in me, you better let me know.*

Derek backed off. He stood up, grabbed their empty cups, and headed towards the kitchen. "I'm going home. Long day. See you ladies tomorrow." And he was gone.

Christine looked at Katy. "Do you have feelings for him? More than you're ready to admit?"

Katy shook her head. "I don't know. Yes, I do. But how could it work? It's like you and Sam all over again. Except I'm in New York."

"You could stay here."

"That would take capital, a financial plan, and a lot of work."

"You need to ask yourself, would it be worth it? It seems you have some inner conflict sorting out to do." Christine squeezed her hand. "Hey, I love you. Whatever you choose to do will be great."

"I hope so. Let's go home."

Chapter Twenty-Five

Derek sat on a wooden bench in the side yard of the church scrolling through his phone, waiting for Reverend Michael. They had made an appointment to talk after church when all the parishioners had left, and he could break free.

He stopped on a goofy picture of Katy he had shot in Vermont and grinned. That trip was memorable, creating a bond between the two of them. What direction it would take he had no clue. Were a few kisses the beginning of a relationship? From yesterday's declaration, it sounded like she was going back to New York. Was he capable of a long-distance relationship? He saw the strain it put on Christine. *Not sure I could handle that right now.*

"There's my man," Reverend Michael said.

"Thanks for meeting me."

"That's my job, son. Let's go inside to my office. Too cold out here."

Derek stood, then followed him.

Walking into his office, Michael indicated a sage-green, upholstered sofa in the corner and sat down. "So, what can I do for you today?"

Talking about this was not easy. Derek explained the story about Nick, his injuries, and nursing home care up to his death earlier that week. A moisture drip escaped his forehead; he swiped it away with his sleeve, his stomach tied in a knot. He raised his head to meet the Reverend's eyes without wavering. "Why did God pick him and not me? I should have been the one who was mangled, left to suffer, and eventually die."

Michael paused for a moment. "I don't think God picks one person to die over another, Derek. Each soul has a calling and a purpose on this planet. Whether that's something astronomical like finding a cure for cancer or being the best mother or father a person can be, we each have a life to live independent of each other yet interlinked at the same time, if that makes sense. The bigger question here is, why do you feel guilty?"

"Because it should have been me."

"How does the guilt serve you?"

Derek was quiet. He had never thought about it like that. "I don't know."

"I think you do if you go inside for the answer. Does the guilt protect you from completely grieving the loss of your friend? Does the guilt protect you from getting hurt in other relationships? I definitely see how guilt is keeping you from living a full life, free of worry and pain."

"I know that is true." He squirmed around in his seat, wiping his sweaty palm on the arm of the cushioned couch.

"Grief and guilt go hand in hand, son. Most situations are not in our control and feeling guilty about your buddy is only human. But now that he is gone, are you feeling guilty for being happy again without him?"

"Yes," Derek said. "And I've been angry with God ever since it happened, if you must know."

Michael laughed. "Yes, we all have moments like those." He paused. "I want to help you go through this grief, Derek. Survivor's guilt is a form of grief. Let yourself go through all the emotions; the grieving will eventually heal you. Remember, the depth and experience of your grief do not necessarily indicate a loss of faith. All your emotions, even the hate, are normal reactions to a devastating situation that can coexist with your faith and spirituality. I'm not going to tell you to be grateful for the life you've been left with until you've had a chance to mourn your loss and forgive yourself completely."

"Forgive myself?" Derek asked.

"Yes, forgive yourself. Probably the biggest part of the healing for you. Forgive yourself for being sick that day. Forgive yourself for surviving. Forgive yourself for torturing yourself with all this guilt since the accident happened. No one blames you. Even Nick's mother has tried to tell you that, but you aren't taking it in for some reason. You're not accepting that no one, I said no one, blames you. Nick's mother is grateful you visited him and helped her with all the funeral arrangements. I hope you can soon accept that you have done everything you could have done for this situation and more." Michael reached over, placing his hand on Derek's shoulder.

Moistness trickled down Derek's face until he couldn't hold back the floodgate of tears from falling. His shoulders shook; he dropped his head towards the Reverend, sobbing and collapsing into his arms. He had been holding on to tears for years, swollen with guilt destroying him and despair for his friend's death.

Michael enfolded him into his chest, whispering, "Let the healing begin, son. Time will take care of the rest."

The clock on the wall ticked; their embrace hung in a reverent space. The crying eventually shifted into a soft whimpering from the man who had served his country fearlessly. Derek sat up. "Sorry."

"No need for apologies." Michael handed him a tissue from the table in front of them. "Here you go."

Derek blew his nose, wiped his face, but his eyes remained fixed on his hands in his lap.

Michael placed his hand on his back. "Are you okay?"

Derek nodded, not looking up.

"I'd say you're on the path to healing, son. Your own path, however, you do it. You're going to be alright." He rubbed his back gently.

Derek wiped his eyes again with the tissue and turned to Michael. "Thank you. I don't know what came over me." He felt raw, unable to move.

"I think all that guilt and grief you had locked up inside came bursting through your heart and for the first time, you didn't stop it. You let it go."

Derek's chest rose and fell, his silence resting in the air.

"Listen. Can you do me a favor and do something nice for yourself today? Can you take the day off from work?"

"Maybe."

"This is heavy work you're doing. I want you to absorb it. Maybe go for a short hike on the trails. Be outside in nature even if it's cold; bundle up. Have a conversation with your source of faith. Be extra kind to yourself today. That's all I'm saying."

Derek extended his hand and grabbed Michael's. "Thank you."

"You did the work, not me. Those were your emotions, not mine. But come to me anytime you need to. I'm always here."

Derek stood up, Michael followed, and the two men hugged.

"Remember, anytime," Michael said.

Derek smiled. "Okay."

As he walked out into the yard, he lifted his head, letting the rays of the sun bathe his wounded soul and barely felt the chill in the air. One foot in front of the other, he decided to take the Reverend's advice and go for a walk in the woods. And talk to God.

* * *

Katy tossed her coat on the hook in Christine's office and sat down at the extra desk. Today she was resigning from Martin and Lewis. She had written a letter yesterday and after several edits, she was ready to hit the send button. She decided to include Simon on the email, so he would get it straight from her rather than the company's owners.

She had seen Derek's truck in the lot, so she knew he was either in his office or on the floor. Probably the floor since it was all-hands- on deck now for the *Hope for Hearts* campaign in addition to Alison's wedding on Friday—especially with Christine's wrist still in a cast. In addition to the cake, Christine had offered to make some hors d'oeuvres for the caterer.

Two minutes after she sent the email, her phone pinged. Simon had texted.

Call me!

Soon.

Was she ready for this? *Deep breath.* She punched in his number. *Might as well get it over with.*

"Katy, you can't quit! We need you. We can work something out with William. I know we can."

Simon's frantic voice echoed fear over the line. Katy knew he was freaking out. Now he would see how much she did for both of them with their clients, and finally see her worth. Same with William, who she knew would be calling next.

"I need to move on, Simon, and hope you understand." *Keep it short.*

"I know we can come up with something. Please. Give us another chance. And I mean both our relationship and your job."

"I have thought about it. I'll be in to pick up my things after the holidays."

"There's nothing I can say to change your mind?" he asked.

"No. I'm sorry, Simon. I have to think about what's best for me now. Merry Christmas and take care of yourself."

"Please, Katy," he said.

"I can't. It's over."

Silence hung in the air, thick with the shock of uncertainty. Finally, he spoke. "Okay."

She hung up, her heart racing. The phone rang again. Now, William. "Hello, Mr. Lewis."

"Very disappointed to receive your email, Miss Flanagan."

Trying to keep her emotions in check, Katy embarked on a similar conversation with her boss, resolving in the same conclusion—she wasn't coming back to work at Martin and Lewis.

As she hung up, Christine came through the door. "I thought I heard you here. How's it going?"

"I just finished talking to everyone at my job, and I am officially unemployed!" She laughed.

"Did you call that Carter agency yet?" Christine asked.

"Nope. Next on my agenda."

"Do you need privacy? I need to make a few calls too."

"Is Derek in his office?" Katy asked.

"No. He's busy on the floor."

"I'll go in there and give you privacy." She grinned.

"Whatever works."

Katy grabbed her notepad and pen, jotted down the number, and went into Derek's office. She glanced around at the familiar space, stopping on the photo of him with his buddies, including Nick, in Afghanistan. Hard to believe he had led a life fighting, killing people, and sacrificing himself both physically and mentally in service to his country. A far cry from small town living in Maple Ridge.

She punched in Carter's number and waited until the right person came on the line. While waiting, Derek walked in.

Katy mouthed 'sorry' to him, but he waved his hand and whispered, "No bother." He pulled out a ledger and started working.

"Hello, Mr. Billings. This is Katy Flanagan. I sent the email about a job; you told me to call you today."

"Yes, yes. How are you? I'm very impressed by your work and my colleagues know who you are. Why didn't they give you the creative directorship at Martin and Lewis?"

Right to the jugular—so embarrassing. "They gave it to someone else."

"Well, their loss is our gain. Anyway, we would like to offer you a position, but we need a creative director for one of our satellite offices. Would you be interested in relocating?"

A jolt hit Katy in the gut. A creative director position? Right off the bat? "Of course. I know I'm ready for that kind of responsibility, sir." Her stomach nerves were whirling with giddiness.

"It's for our Chicago office," he said.

Chicago? Oh no, that's so far away from New York, Maple Ridge, and everything she had grown to love these last few weeks.

"Can I think about it over the holidays?" she asked.

"Yes. I wanted to offer it to you now, but we have to be up and running after the new year."

"Yes, I understand. Thank you so much for the opportunity, and I will let you know as soon as possible."

"Good. Carter agency would be lucky to have you. Enjoy your holidays, Katy."

"You too. Thank you again." She hung up.

Derek glanced over to see Katy staring at the wall, no expression on her face. "Good news?" he asked.

"I don't know." She turned to him. The intimacy of their last time together flashed in front of her. She had feelings for him. No denying. She didn't want to leave him. That much she knew.

"What did they say? You look confused."

"They offered me a creative director position."

"That's great." He paused. "Isn't it?"

"In Chicago."

"Oh." He twiddled with his pencil. "What do you want?"

"I don't know." She reached her hand to her temple, rubbing it.

"You can think about it, I guess."

"Yeah. But Chicago? I can't believe he offered me my coveted position straight out of the gate. I would have complete creative autonomy over the office and be able to make a fresh start. It would be everything I ever wanted."

"You don't look so excited about it." He paused. "What's up, Katy?"

"I don't know if I want to be that far away from New York. And

... Maple Ridge." She looked into his eyes for a response.

He turned in his chair, coming closer and reached out for her hand. "I wouldn't like you being so far away either."

She put her other hand over his, gazing up at him. "Is there a reason for me to stay? Are you going to tell me how you feel? About me?" There she had asked. A knot in her stomach tightened, awaiting his response.

He moved closer. "I like you, Katy. I think you know that. We've had enough intimate moments together. But am I going to ask you to stay here to be with me? No. Your career has meant so much to you your entire adult life. I can't interfere with decisions you need to make for yourself. Take me out of the equation, Katy. Do it for yourself. That's the only way you'll be happy."

"Oh." The corners of her mouth drooped slightly. *I wanted you to fight for me.*

Suddenly, his arms were around her, hugging her. He nuzzled his mouth to her ear. "It's going to work out. Have a little faith," he whispered.

He kissed the side of her cheek, but his lips didn't stop until they found hers. She pressed up against him, anxious to be devoured. She needed this kiss. She needed to know what was on the other side of this story. What would she miss if she chose Chicago? She slowly lifted her lips away from his.

She sighed and let her head rest on his shoulder. "I want more of this, Derek. More of us if I'm being honest."

"I know. I want it too but not at the expense of you giving up on your dreams. You would resent me someday. I know it."

The velvety softness of his flannel shirt against her cheek, soothed her angst just a wee bit. She could stay here forever. "Okay. I'll think about Chicago."

"Good." He released her and rolled his chair back to his desk. "I've got some work to do. Go help Christine with the gingerbread cakes. It will help get your head clear. Busy hands keep a busy mind at bay. It works for me. Try it." He grinned at her.

"What about that kiss?" she asked.

"What about it?" He grinned. "Now you know how I feel. I don't know what I can offer in a relationship or if I'll be good at it, but I am attracted to you. I have been since I met you. That's all I've got right now. My emotional well-being is somewhat unstable at this time."

She nodded. Was that enough? Enough to give up her dream job? *Why isn't life easy?* "Got it." She stood, picked up her notepad, pen, and phone, and walked out the door, ready to get her fingers covered with gingerbread and frosting.

* * *

Katy stood at the bakery sink, washing off all the dough between her fingers and hands. Her phone vibrated in her back pocket as she dried her hands with a towel. She pulled it out and gasped, looking at the name. Her father. Was he still coming to New York?

"Dad. Hi," she said. She walked to the back of the bakery for privacy.

"Hello, sweetheart. How are you?"

The lines in Katy's forehead narrowed. "I'm fine. Great actually. Still here in Maple Ridge visiting Christine for the holidays." She acknowledged the tightening in her chest but kept going. "Are you still coming to New York?"

"Listen, I talked to Christine, and I was thinking of joining you for Christmas. Marge and I both. How does that sound?"

Christmas? Here? She paused as shock reverberated throughout her body. When was the last time she spent Christmas with her dad? Junior high school?

"Katy?"

She shook her head. "When are you coming?" She was going to kill Christine for not cluing her in that he might be coming to Maple Ridge.

"We thought we'd drive up Wednesday or Thursday. We're spending a few days in New York, renting a car, and then driving up. Christine gave us the name of an inn in town, and we made reservations there."

Christine had kept all of this from her? "Whatever you want to do, Dad. Just keep me posted."

"We haven't spent many holidays together over the years, Katy, and I'm sorry for that. This will give us a chance to make up for some of them."

Why now? "Sure, Dad." She paused. "It will be nice to see you. Have to run now." She needed to get off the phone. All of this was too much.

"I'll text or call you with our arrival plans."

"Great." She hung up. Great. Her father was making an appearance.

Katy swung around and marched to Christine's office, pushing open the door without knocking. Derek was sitting in the chair next to her desk.

"Why didn't you tell me? I can't believe you kept this from me!" Her hands trembled with overwhelming irritability mounting in her body.

"Tell you what?" Christine asked.

"My father!" Katy practically screamed.

"Oh. That." Christine hung her head for a second not ready for a confrontation with her favorite cousin.

"When were you going to tell me?"

"Probably tonight. Listen, he called me over the weekend. He wanted to see you and spend time with you. I couldn't say, 'No, you can't come.' could I?"

"You should have told me right away." Katy glanced over at Derek who was staring at both of them.

"Maybe. But we've all been so busy."

"Not that busy." Katy was still fuming.

Derek butted in. "Maybe this will be an opportunity to heal some of those issues you have with your father. Did you ever think of that?"

"Now you're both ganging up on me? I can't believe it. My father doesn't give a crap about me. He's never bothered for years, so why now? He's probably getting old and suddenly realizes what a jerk he's been to me all these years. I won't be all sweet and nice just because he's coming. No, he needs to earn my trust back."

She grabbed her coat, purse, and computer. "I'm going home." She flew out the door and into her car, skidding out of the parking lot in a frenzied fit. Tears poured steadily onto her coat, blinding her until she pulled over. Hanging her head over the steering wheel, she wailed and sobbed as all the past hurt came to the surface and flooded the front seat. She was not looking forward to seeing her father. Too much neglect. Too much pain.

Christine looked over at Derek. "I better go home and work this thing out. Do you mind closing tonight?"

"No. No problem." He ran his fingers through his hair. "Is her father that bad?"

"As a teenager, I know she felt abandoned by him when he sent her here for summers and some holidays. He never offered to take her with him on trips that he did with Marge. That hurt. And as time went on, she built a strong fortress around her heart as an adult so as not to be hurt anymore by his actions or lack of actions. I should have realized this would be a shock and would stir up all those emotions she's tried hard to stuff away in the past. She'll have to readjust. But you're probably right. This could be an opportunity for healing, but you can't force forgiveness on a person unless they're ready. I don't know if Katy is ready to forgive her father, and we can't push her. This is her journey."

Derek knew all too well about that journey of healing.

"I'll see you in the morning. Wish me luck," Christine said. She packed up her things and left to whatever awaited her at home.

* * *

Katy made it home and immediately took a shower to calm her nerves. *Derek just saw a nasty part of me, all rage queen in full force.* Now, he knew she wasn't perfect and had flaws too. Not being told about her dad pushed all her buttons around abandonment and loss. Christine had excluded her from some vital information, but should she blame her? She did say she was going to tell her. Maybe she was scared too. Whatever the reason, she didn't like it.

Katy put on her sweats as she heard the front door open. Christine was home. She decided to curl up in her bed even though she was famished. She wasn't ready to face her yet. She needed to cool down.

About fifteen minutes later, a gentle rap sounded on the door.

"Come in," Katy said.

Christine walked in with a bottle of wine, two glasses and cheese and crackers spread out on a tray. "Still mad at me?"

"Yes."

"Glass of wine?"

"Yes."

Christine sat down in the cushioned chair next to a small table, poured Katy a glass, and handed it to her. She poured her own and raised it. "Truce?"

"Maybe." Katy couldn't stay mad at her cousin for long. Never could ever since they were kids. "Tell me everything he said when he called you."

Christine curled her legs up on the chair and smiled. "He called me yesterday afternoon. You were out somewhere. He knew you were here for the holidays, and he asked if he could come join us and would stay at the inn. He didn't say much else, and what could I say? No? After ten or fifteen years of never asking, and out of the blue, he does? I figured maybe you would enjoy it. I was going to tell you today, but you had a lot on your plate, quitting your job, getting an offer for a new one, and so on. Can you forgive me?" Her eyebrows lifted as a grin spread across her face.

"Yes. I forgive you." Katy paused. "I was shocked, I guess. And I'm scared too. Afraid of all the emotion it's going to stir up inside of me because it will all come out. I know it will."

"Then let it flow. Don't be afraid. Maybe it's time to heal this hole in your heart that you have with your dad. It's none of my business, but healing relationships is better than being tortured by them, I say."

"You're right. As usual."

"Stay open. That's all I'm saying."

Katy sipped her wine.

"I don't know about you, but I'm starved. Let's make some real food."

"Right behind you." Katy had no choice but to deal with whatever happened when seeing her father. She prayed for guidance to handle it best for both of them. That's all she could do.

Chapter Twenty-Six

Derek carried a tray of croissants through the bakery door and held it while Mary Beth filled the display for the morning rush.

"That should do it," she said. A daily influx of customers had been floating in and out of the store with the holiday season upon them.

Derek looked up as Alison and another woman entered, laughing and squealing with each other. He waved to her, and she motioned for him to come closer.

"Derek, I want you to meet Jenny, my best friend, and maid of honor."

He reached out a hand not occupied with the tray. "Nice to meet you. No wonder there's a lot of giggling going on between the two of you. Getting excited?"

Jenny squeezed Alison's arm. "Absolutely! We've been waiting for this day forever."

"Christine asked me to meet her to go over the last items on our hors d'oeuvre list," Alison said. "And who doesn't like a latte and scone?" She laughed.

"Take a seat at the corner, and I'll let her know you're here." Derek gave Mary Beth their order and went hunting for Christine.

The back bakery was bustling with extra staff working on the wedding, the *Hearts for Hope* campaign, and their regular orders. Christine was making a nice profit, and Derek was confident the extra workers would help boost their sales by producing a more extensive inventory.

"Hey, Christine. Alison is in the front waiting for you."

She looked up from her desk. "Thanks."

Derek shuffled his feet, looking down. "How's Katy? Did you two work things out?"

"Yep. We can't stay mad at each other for long. It was a shock to hear her father was coming. She's not looking forward to all the pent-up emotions releasing if that happens. I don't think she's going to repress her feelings any more around him, and that scares her."

"I understand. Is she coming in today?"

"Later. She's taking some time for herself this morning, but we'll see her soon. We're all on pins and needles, knowing the fruits of our labor will either explode or dissipate soon."

"You're right. I'll be on the floor if you need me."

"Thanks, Derek. For everything. I don't know what I would do without you. You have helped take my business to a whole other level. You are a blessing for sure."

"As you are to me too." Derek hugged her. "Okay. Enough. Alison's waiting." He grinned and walked away.

Later in the afternoon, Mary Beth approached Derek as he was overseeing the staff packaging the gingerbread. "Derek, there's a woman here to see you. She said she's Nick's mother."

Startled nerves hit his gut instantly, hearing her words. "I'll be right there." He took off his apron, hung it up and walked to the front.

The older woman was seated at a table on the side, away from others, and held a brown paper bag. She waved to Derek.

"Mrs. Johnson, can I get you a coffee?" he asked.

"Oh, no, dear. I just wanted to give you something. I found this picture and thought you might like it." She pulled it out of the bag and handed it to him.

Derek looked down, wetness forming behind his eyes. It was a photo of Nick and him, arms around each other in front of a platoon tent in Afghanistan. They both had a goofy grin on their face, seemingly unconcerned with the danger and leering death surrounding them.

"He emailed me pictures ongoingly, and I remembered this one, so I printed it at the drugstore for you. I put it in a frame I found at home, but you can get a better one."

Derek blinked, forcing the tears not to fall while staring at the photo. "This is very kind of you," he said, not looking up.

"I want you to know that I appreciate how you cared for my son while he was in the facility. You were his best friend, and I know you are still in pain over our loss. But I want you to move on. Keep the memories of his love and make new ones. That is what he would have wanted. That's what I'm going to do. He served his country and lost his life. He knew that could happen as I did. We can't change the past, but we can make a future for ourselves. I don't want to see you feeling guilty anymore. It's time to forgive yourself, Derek. You did nothing wrong. Things happen for a reason, I believe. I came to tell you that again because I didn't think it was getting through to you before." She reached out and squeezed his hand. "I'm his mother. I know best."

Derek grinned. "I guess you do. I'm beginning to let go of my guilt and have been getting counseling, so thank you for this. I'll look at it and remember the good times."

She patted his hand. "Good."

"How are you doing?"

"My daughter is staying another week, so she's helping me clean out things. Having her here is helping with my grieving process. We tell stories to each other; we laugh, and we cry. I'm lucky to have her. I will visit her in January for a few weeks and escape this New England cold!"

"Sounds like a solid plan."

Mrs. Johnson stood up. "I don't want to keep you from your duties here. Come visit anytime."

Derek stood up and hugged the woman. "Thank you again for the photo."

"You're welcome."

Derek stood, mesmerized by the photograph in his hands, his heart throbbing, thinking of his comrade. The guilt was finally relinquishing its rigid grip. He placed the gift back in the bag and returned to his office.

Coming down the hallway, his eyes met Katy's as she emerged from Christine's office. "Hey," he said.

"Hey, yourself." A grin inched its way into her cheeks. "What's in the bag?"

"Nick's mom gave me a gift." He pulled out the photo and showed it to her.

She looked at it and then looked up at Derek. He didn't seem to be shaken or withdrawn when sharing it with her. "Are you okay?"

"Yeah. I'm okay." He put it back in the bag. "Are you okay?" He searched her eyes for an answer.

"Yeah. I'm okay. Sorry, you had to see that ugly side of me yesterday. My emotions can flare when it comes to my father. There's a lot of baggage there I keep to myself—probably a control thing." She lifted her shoulders, raising the palms of her hands with lips pressed together.

"We all have control issues. Nothing new there. I'm here if you want to talk about it. I know you have Christine, but I can always give you a man's point of view if you're interested."

"Thanks. Appreciate that."

"Any decisions on your career yet?"

"No. I want to enjoy the holidays. I'll decide after Christmas."

"Don't let your self-worth be stolen by what your father did or didn't do, Katy. You're an amazing woman who can be anything you want, with or without his support. I think you've been trying to prove that to yourself for years, and maybe it's time to accept how capable and strong you are. I see it. Christine sees it. We all see it. Just saying." The corners of his mouth broadened wide.

Katy felt his eyes piercing hers with an intense gaze—one filled with love and adoration, not judgment. Butterflies cruised around her belly, as spirited as the first day she met this man. He got her. He really did. He accepted her flaws and no longer hid his. *Does he care enough to jump into a relationship with me no matter how messy it might be?*

"That's how I see it anyway. I'll be on the floor if anyone needs me."

She reached out and grabbed his arm as he turned away. "Derek."

He stopped, looking down at her.

"Thank you."

"You're welcome."

Before Derek could get his hands dirty again, Mary Beth approached him. "There's another woman here to see you. Sophie."

"Sophie? What is she doing here?" He pushed through the bakery door and scanned the front for her. She waved when she saw him.

"Sorry, if I interrupted your workday, but I needed a coffee and didn't want to miss a chance to say hello."

"No problem. I've got a minute. What's up?"

"I heard about Nick." She reached her hand across, grasping onto his fingers lying on the table.

Katy whooshed in behind the counter to grab a latte and glanced over at the corner, catching Sophie's move at the exact same time. Derek hadn't seen her, so she backed up out of sight but still able to watch him.

Derek placed his other hand over hers not recoiling from her touch. "Thanks. We were close. Even though he went to the same high school as us, I never really knew him until Afghanistan. Comrades in battle have a special bond." He squeezed her hand and released it.

"If you ever want to talk about anything, I'm here for you." She reached out again, rubbing the flannel shirt on his arm.

"Thanks. Listen I better get back to work. Nice seeing you."

"Don't be a stranger. Maybe come over for dinner after the holidays?"

"Maybe. Text me. Merry Christmas, Sophie."

"Merry Christmas, Derek."

When Katy saw Derek standing up, she flew back into the bakery and back to Christine's office, hiding from him. *Does he still have feelings for Sophie?* Confusion consumed her, but she wasn't even going to live here. She would be in New York or possibly Chicago after the holidays. This maddening little crush would lead to nothing if she left. She placed her hand over her heart as pain pinched her chest.

"What's wrong with you? Are you okay?" Christine looked up from her computer.

"Yeah. I guess so. Sophie came to visit Derek. She was coming on strong with her flirting. I peeked at them from the corner when I went to get my latte."

"Are you stalking him now?" Christine laughed.

"No! It just all happened."

"Right."

"It hit me that I might never have a chance to be in a relationship with him beyond the flirting and occasional kissing we did. That freaks me out." She took a sip of her coffee.

"You could stay here."

"And do what?"

"Start your own company. I know you're scared, but if we get this investment, I will need someone to manage the *Hearts for Hope* campaign, which was your baby. Derek will be too busy with the online business and overseeing things here if I'm in New York most of the time."

Katy rubbed her hand over her heart. *What do I want?* "I have to think about this more."

"What do you want, Katy? What is your heart telling you?" Christine asked.

A rap sounded on the door, and Derek pushed it open. "Hey, ladies. Hope I'm not disturbing anything, but I wanted to let you know I'm heading out early. I need to run an errand, and I have group tonight. Anything else you need?" His eyes caught Katy's, his gaze unwavering.

"No, I'm leaving soon too. I have to do some Christmas shopping before I get swamped with the holiday rush and wedding commitments. Thanks for everything. I guess tomorrow will be the big day. Everyone, say a prayer." She smiled at them both.

"Will do." Derek peered at Katy once more, grinned, and then left.

Christine's gaze pierced Katy's. "Is he worth the risk? That's what you have to ask yourself. In my opinion, yes. He's worth it. He's a better man than you've ever experienced in your life."

"Whoa. Don't hold back." She grinned but knew Christine was right. She had never allowed herself to be in a relationship with a man that would stand by her no matter what. Derek was that kind of man. And one she couldn't control. That's what made him different.

"I'm going to head home too. Maybe do some Christmas shopping. The stores are staying open later, I presume."

"Yep. They are."

Katy's phone pinged with at text. Her father.

Coming in tomorrow. Will be at the inn. Maybe dinner?

She looked up at Christine. "It's Dad. He's coming in tomorrow and wants to have dinner. Will you go with me?"

"Sure," Christine said.

Okay. Text me when you arrive. Safe travels.

Thanks honey. Can't wait to see you.

Katy paused. She didn't feel like sending him a heart emoji, her mind still harboring residual disappointment.

Thumbs up emoji.

Whatever happened she would handle it.

* * *

Derek climbed out of his truck and traipsed up the steps to his apartment. The support group was growing, and Mark had about ten veterans coming together each Tuesday night. Derek was able to share his experience about Nick, his mother, and Reverend Michael without too much anxiety.

Mark had said to him, "Sounds like you're healing inside. We're not in combat anymore, but sometimes it's difficult to stop the war within ourselves. In letting go of guilt and forgiving yourself, you can take healthy footsteps forward to living a full and happy life after the Army. Good job, soldier."

Derek turned the key in the door, tossed his jacket on a nearby chair, and went into his bedroom. He took the photo out of the paper bag and set it on his dresser. His fingers touched it, his heart pounding into his chest. Staring into the mirror above the frame, he caught the reflection of his dog tags, his hands stroking the smooth metal against his skin. Slowly he reached behind his neck and pulled them off, over his head. He held them in his hand, turning them over, staring at his name and service number. He opened the top drawer, and gently placed them inside a wooden box his father had given him years ago, closed the lid, and shut the drawer.

Chapter Twenty-Seven

Katy scrolled through her email sitting at the table in Christine's office. Sam had arrived late last night but stayed at the house to finish up some editing on his computer. She should have done the same except everyone's nerves were on edge, and she didn't want to be alone in the waiting game.

Lost in thought perusing Carter Agency's website she didn't hear the door open.

Derek cleared his throat, announcing his presence.

Katy jumped. "Oh. Hi."

"Sorry if I frightened you." He grinned. "Big day."

"Yes." Nervous jitters twisted in her stomach at the sight of him. "When do you think we'll know?"

"They gave no clue as to how or when. I just know the announcement should come today."

"Okay."

Derek glanced over her shoulder. "Is that the company that offered you a job?"

"Yeah. The Carter agency. They're bigger than my old firm and more established."

"More bureaucracy?"

"Probably."

"Mm-hmm."

"What does that mean?"

"Jumping from the frying pan into the fire? Or maybe you like the security. Nothing wrong with that."

"Bigger company, more opportunities for me." She smirked at him.

"Whatever you say. I'll be out on the floor. Good luck." And he walked out.

Katy stared at the door. That was an unsettling conversation. Would he judge her for taking the job at the slick, fancy firm? Or was that a passive-aggressive attempt to encourage her to stay in Maple Ridge? She shook her head. She wished he would say what he wanted and be done with it. But the truth was, if she didn't know what she wanted, how could she expect him to be clear?

She shut down her computer. She needed some physical activity to settle her mind and joined everyone on the floor.

"Oh, good. Another set of hands. I need help with these pastry cups for the caterer," Christine said.

"No problem. Show me what to do," Katy said.

The morning passed with no sign of the investors online, by phone, or in person. Katy regularly checked Frosty Mountain's website and social media to make sure they weren't celebrating the win. Radio silence everywhere.

Katy's phone pinged as she placed the delicate pastry puffs onto a tray. Wiping her hands on her apron, she pulled out her phone.

Her dad.

> Arriving around four. Will call you after we get settled.

She wrote back.

> Okay.

Katy sensed Derek standing behind her. "Everything okay?" he asked.

She whisked around and gulped her breath, standing within inches of him. "Yeah. My dad comes today. It's stressing me out on top of everything else. I never know how I'm going to react."

He reached both hands out to her shoulders and began to rub them. "You've got some major knots here, Flanagan."

She closed her eyes, melting into his firm touch. She wanted that touch so badly everywhere on her body. Her eyes flew open with the thought. *Oh, God. What am I thinking?* At least she was clear about wanting a physical relationship with this man but knew her heart needed more than that.

She reached up and grabbed one of his hands. "Thanks. I better book a massage after the holidays." Any more contact with him and she would be putty on the floor. Or attacking him with wild abandon.

He broke away from her, smiled and went back to his station to work.

She glanced over at him and caught his eyes staring at her—the connection growing more intense than ever. *What am I going to do?*

Lunchtime came and went, and the unsaid fear thickened in the air. Keeping busy was their only solution until the bakery doors flew open, and Mary Beth came running in.

"They're here! The investors are here!"

All three of them tore off their aprons as fast as they could. Katy and Derek followed Christine out the door.

Christine spoke first. "Mr. Ferguson, nice to see you."

He waved his hand in front of her. "No need for formalities, Miss Boyle. After all, we will be partners very soon."

Christine and Katy shrieked, jumping up and down, hugging

each other. Christine couldn't help herself and hugged Mr. Ferguson, who smiled, unflustered amidst the excitement.

"Let's sit down over there, and I'll explain what comes next." As they sat down, his assistant pulled out an envelope and handed it to Christine. "This is payment for your new rental space and moving expenses. Next week come to my office in New York, and we will review all the details—you and Mr. Higgins. I presume he will continue to be the bookkeeper for both facilities."

Christine looked over at Derek. "Yes. Unless we become so big, we need another person in New York. But Mr. Higgins will be overseeing all my financials." She grinned at him.

"Can I ask you, what made you want to finance our bakery over Frosty Mountain?" Katy asked.

"That's easy. You both have lovely facilities, inside and out, with positive income flow. But your *Hearts for Hope* Campaign won over my board. The quality of marketing for it and the cause behind it touched all of us. I can't wait to see what else you do with it. You will be overseeing that component, correct, Miss Flanagan?"

Katy shuffled her feet underneath the table. She wasn't expecting this. The air caught in her throat.

Christine placed her hand over Katy's. "Of course, she is."

"Yes, I saw you put her in the budget. Smart thinking Mr. Higgins," Mr. Ferguson said.

Katy's eyes flew over to Derek's. He had included her in the business plan, after the holidays? She quickly got it together realizing she hadn't responded to Mr. Ferguson and didn't want to jeopardize anything for Christine. "Yes, I look forward to it."

"Good. We'll sign all the papers next week before the new year when you come to New York. Perhaps Miss Flanagan can come as well and meet with our marketing team. They will help you with anything else you might need as we launch. I want your perspective on my other investments for cause marketing campaigns. I might have a consulting job for you if interested."

Goosebumps spread over her entire body. *What is happening?* "Thank you." She couldn't get any other words out of her mouth.

When they finished, Christine made sure Mr. Ferguson and his assistant walked out with a large box of pastries and cookies for the holidays.

She turned to Derek and Katy as the door shut, hands over her heart. "Thank you. Thank you so much." She grabbed them both, hugging them tightly. "I couldn't have done this without you." Pools of tears were forming in her eyes as one escaped, then another, trickling down her cheek.

Katy, still in shock, rocked in the warmth of her cousin's embrace and the strength of Derek's arm around her. They'd done it. They had won. They had secured a future for Christine and Sam's love to grow, to have a chance and blossom into whatever their hearts desired.

Breaking away, Christine stood back. "We are celebrating tonight! Dinner on me, no buts." She looked at Katy. "Invite your dad. It will be easier for you to have us there as a buffer." She winked at her cousin.

The bells on the door jingled as Sam entered.

"We did it!" Christine screamed. She ran and jumped into his arms, grinning ear to ear.

"I knew you three were unstoppable." Sam released his grasp on Christine and turned to Katy and Derek. "Thank you for helping my amazing woman. I can't wait to spend more time with her without this commute. Believe me, it's no fun."

Katy looked over at Derek. *What is he thinking?* Her heart ached knowing he would not want to engage in a long-distance relationship. He had seen the difficulties Christine and Sam had to endure and wouldn't want any part of that.

Derek's stance relaxed as he reached out and patted him on the back. "No problem. We love a fairy tale ending." He laughed.

"I'm so excited I can hardly breathe," Christine said. "I'm going to call my realtor and give him the good news!" She clapped her hands together and headed towards her office with Sam right behind.

Katy was left standing next to Derek. "Can we talk?" she asked.

"Sure. Let's go to my office."

As Katy sat down in the worn chair next to Derek, she fiddled with a thread on her shirt, twirling it in her fingers, avoiding eye contact.

Derek watched her. "Are you going to tell me what's on your mind?"

She smoothed out her shirt and looked up into his eyes. "Did you have anything to do with Mr. Ferguson's offer for me?"

"No. But I do admit I budgeted money, so we could hire you to continue with the *Hearts for Hope* campaign. I might have listed it as Flanagan Cause Marketing Agency. I guess you could also take it to the Carter agency as your first client."

"Flanagan Cause Marketing Agency? You made that up?"

"Yep. You can change it." His dimples dipped into his cheeks.

"I'll take that into consideration." Stunned by his support, she sat still, her insides quivering in anticipation, until the silence was too heavy to ignore.

"Anything else on your mind?" Derek asked.

"No. It's a lot to take in. And with my dad arriving today, my clarity is nil."

Derek nodded. He rolled his chair closer to her and picked up her hand. "Sometimes these things need a little time. That's all. Believe me, I know."

She let his fingers interlock with hers. Touching his skin, brought an enveloping comfort to her entire body. She wanted more. She lifted her other hand to his chest, rubbing his worn flannel shirt over his heart, staring into his eyes. *Does he want me as much as I want him?*

Derek grabbed her hand on his chest, bringing it to his lips. He kissed her palm, his eyes seemingly searching for a response, and slowly lowered his mouth to hers. She invited the kiss, his tongue gliding around, exploring her openness as they intertwined.

When they separated, Katy looked down. How could she leave this man?

Derek placed his hand underneath her chin, raising it to meet his eye gaze. "What's wrong? I'm sorry if you didn't want to kiss me."

"No, no. It's not you. I wanted to kiss you. I always want to kiss you. I can't help myself, but I'm so torn about my job situation and where I live that I can't open my heart completely to you. That saddens me."

"Come here." He pulled her into his chest. "Don't worry. You'll know what to do when the time is right. If you choose Maple Ridge, I will be here. I'm not going anywhere."

Katy inhaled the sweet air of baked goods which seemed to permeate every inch of the building. His arms around her, she melted into the safety of his strength and caring. No other man had thought enough of her to look out for her future even if it meant they wouldn't be together. He was a selfless, brave man, and he had chosen her. Katy Flanagan. *Can I choose him?*

Katy's ringtone went off and she pulled away. "Sorry." She pulled the phone out of her pocket and saw her dad's name. "I have to take it."

Derek scooted his chair back to his desk.

"Hi, Dad."

"Hi, dear. Marge and I made it to the inn. What time do you want to meet for dinner?"

"I hope you don't mind, but Christine got some good news today, and we're all going out to celebrate at Vinny's. Why don't you join us? I'll explain everything when I see you."

"Sounds terrific. What time?"

"Six? I'll text you the address."

"We'll be there."

"See you then." She hung up.

All the feelings of pleasure and goodness had dissipated as her nerves spiked into overdrive at the thought of being with her father during the holidays.

"Are you okay?" Derek asked.

"I will be. I hope I can be civil tonight."

"You will be. Give him a chance. He did come to you."

"You're right. He did." She stood up. "I'm going back to Christine's to shower and change. See you tonight?"

"Of course. And Katy?"

Standing in the doorway she turned her head. "Yes?"

"You've got this. You're strong, resilient, and loving. He's lucky to have you in his life."

"Thanks."

She grabbed her coat and things in Christine's office and headed to the car. Driving along the countryside laden with snow, Katy prayed for a sign—a sign to help her know what to do and which direction to take. But seeing her father, with all that she'd realized about herself, would she be able to forgive him now?

Chapter Twenty-Eight

Turning around before the mirror, Katy's nerves bounced against her ribs as she moved. She stopped and took one last look at herself. Confident, attractive, and resilient. Even though fear and angst cohabitated alongside her strengths, she would focus on the positive. She had to.

Christine yelled up from the foyer. "Katy! Are you ready?"

"Coming."

Katy hopped into the backseat of Sam's SUV. "Ready to celebrate?"

"Heck, ya!" exclaimed Christine. "Pinch me. I still can't believe this is real."

"Better believe it, girl," Katy said. All three laughed.

"Are you nervous about seeing your dad?" Christine asked.

"Of course. I'm trying to remain open, though. It takes too much energy to keep these walls up. But I'm most nervous that I won't be able to control my anger at him."

"Or your sadness," Christine added.

"Yeah, you're right. There's always hurt and pain underneath the anger I don't want to feel, so we'll see what happens. Hopefully, we can keep the conversation on Sweet Ridge Bakery and your future plans."

Christine and Sam looked at each other, grinning ear to ear.

Katy watched the two of them, their feelings obvious for each other, and sighed. *Why can't I make love a priority in my life?*

As they walked into the restaurant, Katy scanned the room and saw her father and Marge sitting at a table in the back. Derek and Mary Beth were already there with Jolene since she was staying with her sister for the holidays.

She walked behind Christine and Sam, needing a few more seconds to gather herself. Coming face to face with her dad as he stood to greet her, she hugged him. "Hi, Dad."

"Hi, darling. I'm so glad this worked out. I forgot what a lovely little town this is."

Marge stood up, and Katy gave her a quick squeeze. "Nice to see you."

Formalities settled, everyone sat down. Katy's dad was on her left and Christine on her right. Derek was directly in front of her, his face giving her looks of encouragement. She smiled at him.

"Tell me about this project you all have been working on. I want to know why we're celebrating," Mr. Flanagan said.

Christine looked at Katy. "Why don't you tell him?"

Katy looked over at Derek and explained how he had found investors for the bakery expansion and how it turned into a competition. She discussed the cause marketing element added to the package and what the New York site meant for Christine and Sam's relationship. When she finished, the waiter appeared with a chilled bottle of premier champagne her father had ordered before she got there.

"I say this calls for a toast," Mr. Flanagan said.

Champagne flowed, and everyone lifted their glasses, including Jolene and Mary Beth, with flutes of ginger ale. "Thank you. It was a team effort, and we wouldn't have succeeded without each of you playing your part. From the bottom of my heart, I love you all. Here's to success, happiness, and love!" Christine declared.

As she lowered her glass, Katy caught Derek's gaze aimed at her, his smile broadening. He pulled her in, his vibe emanating desire, and she wanted to run out of the restaurant with him, away from the uncomfortableness of being with her dad and into his arms of safety. But she couldn't.

"How's everything going with your job at Martin and Lewis?" her dad asked.

"I quit," Katy said. "Last week." She pretended to peruse the menu, not wanting to engage in more depth, but knew it couldn't be avoided.

"You quit? Why?"

Katy put down the menu and proceeded to tell him the whole story up to her offer for the creative director position in Chicago.

"Is that what you want?" he asked.

When did you care about what I want? "I'm not sure."

"Do you have other options?"

"She could start her own firm," Derek said. "Sorry. I couldn't help butting in your conversation." He grinned.

"Your own firm, huh?" her dad asked.

"It's a long shot. I don't have the capital, and I'm not sure where I would start."

Christine turned around. "She already has one new client with us. Derek put her in our budget to keep managing the *Hearts for Hope* campaign." She fondly touched Katy's shoulder.

"And Ferguson investments wants a meeting with her next week to discuss possible consulting jobs with his other companies," Derek said.

"Alright you guys. Stop. Enough about me. Let's discuss the bakery or anything else but my job conundrum." Katy looked down at her plate, fiddling with her fork.

Christine knew when to back off. She looked up and saw Jake standing at the cash register picking up take-out. She waved to him, and he walked over.

"Hey, guys. Heard the good news. Congratulations," he said. Jake held up his bags. "Dinner for me and the girls. I can hardly believe our wedding is in two days!"

"I'll be working on your cake tomorrow," Christine said. "Most of our hors-d'oeuvres are done, waiting to be picked up from the caterer."

"I'm sure it will all be perfect. I just have to convince Alison of that. I think she's nervous although she won't admit it." He glanced over at Katy's dad and reached out his hand. "Hi, I'm Jake Sanders. Groom-to-be in two days." He laughed.

"Sorry about my manners, Jake. This is my dad, Brian Flanagan and his wife, Marge."

"Nice to meet you. Are you here for Christmas?" Jake asked.

"Yes," Brian said.

"Well, feel free to come to the wedding on Friday night. Everyone else in town is." He grinned. "Christine can give you the details. Family should be together on Christmas Eve." His phone pinged. "Gotta go. The girls are hungry. See you all on Friday!"

Panic struck Katy's gut like a torpedo. Did Jake invite her dad to the wedding? Family should be together on Christmas Eve; someone should have told that to her dad fifteen years ago.

"He seems like a nice man," Brian said.

"He is. He owns the bookstore in town as well as a publishing company with his uncle. You should check out the store tomorrow." Katy picked up her fork and tried to eat something, her tension seeping into every pore of her body. She took another swig of champagne hoping to calm down.

"Did you guys give your presents yet?" Jolene piped up.

Derek and Katy looked at each other, their eyes widened.

"Remember? You had to make something for each other. You have until tomorrow." Jolene was adamant.

Derek smiled. "Okay. We will. Right, Miss Flanagan?"

"Yes. A promise is a promise."

"I'll be in the bakery tomorrow to help my sister, so I'll make sure this happens," Jolene responded.

Everyone at the table laughed, and Katy was grateful for the lightness capturing the moment in the room, releasing the ugly knot in her stomach.

As the evening ended, Christine insisted on paying for the dinner, but Katy's dad fought hard and won the battle. Katy whispered in her ear. "Let him pay. He needs to make up for years of dinners."

Christine squeezed Katy's hand. "Thank you, Uncle Brian. I'll accept your generosity, but this gets you free scones and coffee for the remainder of your stay, just so you know."

Brian chuckled. "Sounds like a good deal."

When they stood up, Katy's dad took her in his arms. "It's been too long since we've spent time together, sweet pea. And I'm sorry for that."

Katy blinked back the wetness in her eyes. She wasn't going to let him see her tears. Not now. Not ever. "That's okay, dad. You're here now."

"I'd like to stop by and see you tomorrow at the bakery. Is that okay?"

"Sure. Just text me."

He kissed her on the cheek and left with Marge at his side.

Derek came up behind her. "Do you want a lift home?"

She glanced over at Christine and Sam. "Yeah. Thanks. I'll leave the two lovebirds alone."

Derek helped Katy with her coat, his fingers grazing her neck. She pulled her collar up tighter, trying to ignore his touch electrifying her body, and moved out into the crisp, frigid air of the evening. The stars were sprinkled across the sky, her sight absorbing their wonder before jumping into Derek's truck.

Derek started the ignition, his hands resting on the steering wheel, and gazed over at her. "Are you okay?"

Katy fiddled with her gloves, head down, debating on whether to speak or not about her father. "I can't believe I'm letting him steal my joy on a day like today. We worked so hard, and I should be elated and celebrating with you and Christine. But my happiness is shrouded by my baggage with my dad. It's annoying." Then she looked over at him for a response.

"Do you want my honest opinion about everything from my perspective?" he asked.

"Of course."

"You may not like it."

"At this point, I don't care. I don't want to be in a funk anymore about this stuff." She sighed.

"First of all, no one can steal your joy. You do that to yourself when you blame the other person for your feelings of discomfort. Yes, that person might be the catalyst for your outrage or hurt, but how you react to it is up to you. You can control that emotion if you want to. But you have to get to a place of acceptance. And forgiveness."

"Forgiveness? For all those years he forgot about me? Sent me up here? Prioritized Marge and his work over his daughter? You want me to forgive him?" She squirmed in her seat.

"Listen, take it from someone who has gone through this. If you don't forgive him, Katy, it will eat you up inside until you're left as an empty shell of decaying resentment."

She pressed her lips together. "That's morbid."

"It's the truth."

Katy crossed her arms in front of her. "I need some time to process this. Let's get out of here."

Derek put the truck in reverse and headed home.

Katy said goodbye to Derek, without a kiss or hug. She wanted to be alone. As she lay awake in her bed that night, she sent up a prayer. *Please, God, help me. Help me know what to say to my father tomorrow. I don't know if I'm ready to forgive him.*

In the stillness, a voice spoke to her. *Why not?*

Chapter Twenty-Nine

Katy sipped her coffee, sitting at the island in Christine's kitchen. The day before Alison's and Jake's wedding, Christine even had Sam working in the bakery. Katy chuckled. She wanted to stay home for an hour or two and work on her website. If Mr. Ferguson was serious about possible consulting jobs, she wanted to update her bio and change the site into one emphasizing cause marketing.

After several hours, she sat back and glanced through her changes. Could she start her own company? She had the skills and one new client. *Is that enough to take a leap? And not take the job in Chicago?* Looking at the clock, her hands sweating with apprehension, she shut down her computer and her thoughts—at least for the moment.

Later she walked into the back of the bakery, threw her things in Christine's empty office, and ventured out to the floor. Christine was busy with the wedding cake, and Sam was decorating cookies. Christmas music flowed over the speakers; she waved to Derek in the corner.

"What can I do?" Katy asked.

"Can you help Derek with packaging the gingerbread hearts?" Christine asked.

"Sure." More time with Derek, more emotions stirred. Why the heck not? What else could torture her?

"Hi," he said. "Can you fold some more boxes and line them up over there?" He paused looking her in the eyes. "How are you feeling today?"

She shrugged. "Sorry, I shut down last night. That's what happens when I'm around my dad. The feelings from the past consume me. Not a pretty picture." She looked down. "But I did think about what you said about forgiveness. You may be on to something." She grinned at him.

Derek laughed. "I'm glad you're starting to see that. Only you will know when you're ready."

"How did you get so dang smart?"

"Experience, hard work, and therapy. You know I'm not perfect, but I am persistent. We're kind of alike in that way."

Katy's phone pinged. She took it out of her pocket. Her dad.

Are you at the bakery?

She texted back.

Yes.

Can I stop by to see you for a few minutes. Alone?

Sure.

See you soon.

"Who was that?" Derek asked.

"Guess who? He wants to speak to me. Alone."

"Hmm. This could be your chance, Katy. And it's okay to tell him how hurt you've been by his actions. Nothing wrong with that at all." He reached over and lightly touched her face, then dropped his hand.

"Thanks. You're probably right."

"I know. Now get to work until he comes. We need to get these out today and put more up front. They keep disappearing."

"Aye, aye, boss."

Fifteen minutes passed, and Mary Beth told Katy that her dad was in the front.

"You can use my office if you like," Derek said. "More privacy."

"Thanks." Katy rolled her shoulders back and strutted to the front of the store.

"Hi, Dad." They hugged briefly.

"Hi, honey. Can we go somewhere private?" The store was lined up with customers, picking up holiday orders, and the crowd was growing as they spoke.

"Yes. Follow me."

Brian waved to Christine as they walked through the commotion of human elves working their magic. Katy opened the door and motioned for him to go in. "This is Derek's office, but we can use it. He's too busy on the floor."

"Yes. I can see this place is bustling. Your mom would have been so happy to be here."

A forlorn look in her father's eyes glazed over momentarily as he spoke about her mom. He rarely mentioned her, and his reaction surprised Katy. A knot expanded, its tentacles spreading across her shoulders and neck. *What does he want?*

They took a seat, and Brian faced his daughter. "Listen. I know we haven't seen each other much over the years, but I want to change that."

"Oh, yeah? How?" Katy asked. *I'm not holding back today. Watch out.*

"I'm sorry, Katy. After your mother died, I was lost. I didn't know how to bring up a daughter by myself. Or at least I didn't think I did. I tried my best, but when Marge came along, I know I ignored some of your needs."

"Some of my needs? Are you kidding? You never were around. And you sent me away every summer and almost every holiday. I was happy to go to college and start my own life. You paid for everything, and I'm grateful for that, but I needed a dad. A dad who truly loved me. I should have come first in your life after Mom died. Not Marge." There. She had said it.

"You're right. You're absolutely right. And I'm sorry."

Katy saw a wetness in her dad's eyes. *Is he genuinely sorry?* Her hands twisted and rubbed together, her fingers constantly moving to keep from trembling.

"I hope you can forgive me someday."

Katy lifted her head to meet his gaze. "Maybe. You hurt me."

"I know. I should have done something sooner. When Christine called and told me everything that was going on with you, I decided I needed to come see you. Support you if I could. I know I can't make up for the years behind us, but I can be here now."

Katy could feel his eyes searching hers for a connection, a sign she might forgive him. But Christine? She had called him? She'd address that issue later.

"Give me time, Dad. I need to process all you've told me." Her heart pounded against her chest as she shifted her position in the chair across from him. She was ready to exit the small room.

"There's a couple more things." He reached inside his coat pocket and pulled out two envelopes. He handed her one. "This letter is from your mother. She is the reason I sent you up here every summer. It was her request, and this letter will explain. I wasn't supposed to give it to you unless there was a strong possibility you might want to move here. And from what Christine told me, that choice might be on the table."

Katy took the envelope, running her fingers across the front where her mother's handwriting outlined her name—Katy. She looked up at her dad, speechless.

"And this envelope has a check in it. I want to invest in your new company. From what I've seen and heard, you will be very successful." He grinned at her as he placed the second envelope in her hand.

Katy's hand shook as she took the envelope and slowly opened it. She gasped at the amount. "Dad! This is too much."

"No, it isn't. This will cover most of your expenses for the first year until you're up and running smoothly. It's the least I can do. Don't think I'm trying to buy my way back into your good graces, but a father should be able to support his daughter in starting a new business. You deserve it. You work hard, and it's time you get the credit for everything you do. I see your passion for cause marketing, and it's also doing good in the world."

Katy looked down at the check once more. It was enough that she could start her own company without stress. She looked up at her dad. "Thank you." Tears pooled in her eyes, and suddenly she was back to being ten years old when both her parents were alive, and they were a happy threesome. She flashed on images of her dad pushing her on the swings in the backyard, her squealing and laughter filling the air.

She dropped the check on Derek's desk and threw her arms around her father. His hands embraced her, holding her close to his chest. One tear slid down her face and soon morphed into sobbing. All the anger and hurt built up in her body and soul over the years came spewing out. She couldn't control it, nor did she want to.

Katy's father stroked her hair as he held her. "I'm so sorry, baby. I'm so sorry." He rocked her from side to side. The weeping poured out, her pain flowing with it until only a muffled whimper shadowed the silence.

Katy sat back in the chair, reaching for a nearby tissue on Derek's desk. She wiped her eyes and blew her nose as her dad sat in silence, watching her. Katy froze, unable to speak.

"I love you, Katy. I always have and always will. It breaks my heart to see how much I hurt you. You're right. I probably don't deserve your love, but at least we've been able to talk about it. Maybe the healing can begin." He squeezed her hand.

Katy nodded. If she was honest, she wanted her dad in her life.

"I'm going to go back to the inn and leave you to read your mother's letter. Call me or text later, alright? Maybe we can have dinner again. Invite that Derek friend of yours if you want. I like him."

"Yes, I like him too." That's all that came out of her mouth.

They both stood up, hugged once more and he left.

Katy closed the door for privacy and plopped down on the chair. She grazed her fingers over her mother's cursive writing on the front of the envelope again, then pulled out the letter.

Dearest Katy,

If you are reading this, you have fallen in love with the town of Maple Ridge as I did. I asked your father to give you this letter only if that happened. I didn't want to influence you regarding how and where to live your life, but if the magic of Maple Ridge has sparked some passion for you, I couldn't be happier. I made your father promise he would send you there every summer and many holidays to stay with your cousin, Christine. I wanted you to know my side of the family and feel a part of something bigger than the three of us. Maple Ridge holds a special place in my heart, and I hope it does for you now. If you settle there, I know you will be happy for the rest of your life. I'm sorry I wasn't around long enough. Your father loves you very much, and I know he will always take care of you. I love you with all my heart, sweet daughter. Stay true to your heart. It will forever guide you down the right path in your life.

Love, Mom

Katy reread the letter two more times, reaching for another tissue. She couldn't stop crying. Her father had sent her to Maple Ridge on her mother's request, not because he wanted to get rid of her. And after time, she had pulled away because she didn't understand. The rift between her father and her was just as much about her as it was him. She couldn't believe it. All these wasted years. *Why didn't he tell me?*

A soft tap sounded on the door as Derek slowly opened it. "Can I come in?"

She blew her nose. "Yes. Of course, it's your office." She grinned at him, her splotchy face and red eyes visible; she couldn't hide from Derek. *Here's the real me, buddy. All blubbery, drowning in an unraveled mess right before your very eyes.*

Derek carefully eased himself into the chair across from her. "Wanna talk about it?"

"I don't know where to start." Still holding her mother's letter, she handed it to him. "Here. Read this. It's from my mother."

Derek read the letter and looked up at her.

"Don't you see. This whole disconnection was as much about me as it was him. Why didn't he tell me?" Katy burst into tears again.

"Oh, baby." Derek reached over, pulling her into his arms as the weeping continued.

They remained embraced until the tears ceased. Katy sat back, picked up the second envelope, and passed it over to him. "Look inside."

Seeing the amount of money written on the check, Derek's jaw dropped.

His questioning eyes flashed up to her gaze. "My dad wants to invest in my company. Should cover my operating expenses for the first year." She waited for a response.

He shook his head side to side. "This is unbelievable, Katy." He grabbed her hand. "Do you have any doubts now of what you should be doing with your career?"

She saw his eyes probing her for an answer. "No. If I stay in Maple Ridge, I'll have to find office space."

"No problem. Jake told me he just lost a tenant in his building on Main Street next to the bookstore. Would be a perfect place."

"Oh, Derek! I could do this." She became quiet. "Do you want me to stay in Maple Ridge?" Suddenly her insecurities were nipping at her heels, and she didn't like it.

"Silly girl. I've always wanted you to stay in Maple Ridge. I didn't want to interfere with your decisions and what your heart told you. But Katy Flanagan, I know my heart wants you."

"As does mine, you," she whispered. Derek pulled her into his arms, bringing his lips down to skim her upper lip, then covering her mouth, his tongue exploring the wetness inside of her. She grasped his shirt, pressing against him as the intensity of the kiss, energized by the realization they could be together, fueled their passionate hunger even more. When their lips separated, their faces remained inches apart, not moving.

"I want to be with you, Katy. I want to be the man you can depend on."

"I want to be with you, Derek. You've already made me a better person, and I can't think of anyone I would like to share this next adventure with other than you."

He embraced Katy again, the heat of his body simmering against her breasts, his lips overtaking her. *Please don't stop.* Where all this energy would go, she didn't care—as long as she was with him.

As they broke away from each other, her eyes held steadfast on his. "I could stay here all day." The puzzle pieces of her life were falling into place, and she was making plans with the man who had touched her with his gentle, giving heart.

"Me too. I guess we should get back to work." He smiled. "Let's tell Christine the good news."

"Yes, but before we do ..." She reached into her bag. "I have your homemade Christmas present." She pulled out a small box wrapped in green shiny paper with a red bow. "Here."

"And I have yours as well." He leaned over to the drawer in his desk and pulled out a box.

"Open yours first. And don't laugh too hard." Katy knew her artistic skills were better on the computer than with crafts.

Derek opened the box, pulling out a handmade pencil holder made from popsicle sticks and painted bright colors. On the back she had even placed a small Army decal to make it personal. "I love it." He placed it on his desk and popped a pen inside of it. "Perfect. Now open yours."

Inside of her box was a larger, gingerbread heart like the ones from their campaign, with a note. She opened the note.

Katy,

> *I made this cake especially for you. You have given my heart hope again. Hope to love, hope that I can be the man I want to be. Whatever happens to us, I want you to know I will hold you in a special place in my heart where love will always live. Love, Derek*

A single tear rolled down her cheek. "Thank you."

He wiped it away, letting his hand rest on her chin. "I've grown to love you, Katy Flanagan."

"I love you too, Derek Higgins."

They hugged until a tap sounded at the door. Christine pushed it open.

"There you guys are! What's going on?" Christine's hands rested on her hips, cocking her head. "Something secret?"

Katy pried herself away from Derek and picked up her dad's check. "Look." She handed it to Christine.

"Oh, my god. What is this?"

"Dad wants to invest in my new company. And this." She handed her the letter from her mom.

Christine looked up after reading it. "Oh, Katy. He sent you here all those times because of your mother, not because he didn't care."

"I know. And I pushed him away when I felt abandoned to protect myself and not be hurt. But pushing away didn't do anything for me. It just dug the hole deeper into pain."

Christine wrapped her arms around Katy. "Perhaps now you can forgive him."

"I think so." Katy squeezed her hand.

"I need to go home early and get ready for the rehearsal dinner. Sam is doing some photography for the happy couple. Derek, can you close? Mary Beth has to leave early too since Jolene is in the wedding party with Annie as flower girls."

"No problem," Derek said.

Christine turned to Katy. "Does this mean you are moving to Maple Ridge?"

A broad smile spread across Katy's face, her eyes shimmering with excitement as she clapped her hands together. "Yes!"

"I've been praying for that to happen even if I'll be in New York most of the time." She grinned. "You can live in my house for as long as you want."

"And you can stay in my apartment as well. I guess we're swapping homes." Katy laughed.

"I guess we are." Christine stood up. "See you two tomorrow."

Katy acclimated into the privacy of the space with Derek once more. "I'm having dinner with my dad tonight. The conversation may get uncomfortable, but do you want to come with me?" Was that too much to ask of him?

"Of course. I told you I want to support you in any way I can, Katy. I would be honored to accompany you."

Her fingers draped over his hand, stroking it gently as she drew nearer. "Is this really happening between us?"

His hands cupped her face on either side, his eyes unwavering. "Yes, Katy. This is really happening." He brought his mouth to hers once more, savoring the lusciousness of her pink lips and the rose-scent of her body drifting into his consciousness. He knew what he wanted, and he wasn't letting go.

Epilogue

Katy tossed back her down comforter and praised the sunlight streaming through her window. Images from the day and night before flowed through her brain. Derek had asked her to be his plus one for the wedding, and the dinner with her father had been long overdue. Tears were shed, apologies offered, and forgiveness was given an open road for healing to begin between them. And Derek had witnessed it all, his rock-steady presence beside her, providing support if she needed it. But she had done it all on her own and was now free. Free to chart a course for her new company. Free to move to Maple Ridge. Free to love Derek.

Derek was picking her up at three and offered to take her dad and Marge with them. A new sense of her future family was coming together more amazingly than she could ever have imagined. *I'm a blessed woman.*

* * *

Katy's eyes were glued to the beautiful woman walking down the aisle. Alison wore a sleeveless, A-line satin wedding dress with lace overlay, her veil flowing down the back just grazing the floor. Jake stood at the altar, his uncle Jim next to him and Annie in front of Jim. Jenny,

Alison's best friend, and Maggy, Jake's cousin, were waiting at the altar holding bouquets of red and ivory roses mixed with baby's breath, and draping greenery hand-tied with scarlet velvet ribbon in the Christmas spirit. Eucalyptus with white rose garlands, holly boughs with crimson berries, and draping white orchids adorned the church, their beauty embellishing the festive atmosphere.

As the two stood before each other saying their vows, Derek's hand slid over Katy's as they sat in the pew. When she felt his touch, she glanced over at him. Their eyes spoke volumes, and she was confident they said the same thing. I love you, and I always will. They watched Jake and Alison declare their love and commitment to each other, and Katy felt hopeful for her own happily ever after with the man seated next to her.

Brookhurst Farms, where the reception was held, was tucked away in a pastoral setting blanketed in snow, its charms revealing an upscale barn conversion hotel with exposed beams and farmhouse aesthetics. Derek and Katy joined Christine and Sam at a table along with Mary Beth, Jolene, Katy's father, and Marge. The happiness permeating the air was all consuming.

Katy leaned over to Christine. "Pinch me. Are we in heaven?"

Christine whispered, "I think so, coz. Except heaven is here on earth."

Champagne toasts were recited, food was devoured, and music played late into the night. As the band struck up a tempting slow song, Derek turned to Katy. "Care to dance?"

"Yes, I do," she said, her lashes lifting in adoration.

Derek took her hand and twirled her onto the dance floor, his eyes never leaving her sight.

As he pressed his body against hers, she could feel his heartbeat pounding against her chest. "Who knew you were quite the dancer?" she teased.

"Baby, you haven't seen anything yet." He pulled her closer.

Katy rested her head on his shoulder and closed her eyes, her body moving to the song's rhythm in sync with Derek. The thoughts in her head that had tortured her for weeks were quiet. No longer was she adrift without purpose in her life. She had a direction, a new home, and an adventure waiting to unfold. Best of all, she had a man who had given his heart to her and filled her with hope. Hope for a future together and a life well lived in love. What else did she need?

Derek whispered in her ear. "Everything okay?"

Katy lifted her head, meeting his gaze. "Everything is perfect."

Acknowledgments

Finding a publishing home with Sands Press has been a treasured blessing. The entire staff works relentlessly to provide its authors with encouragement, marketing skills, social media ideas, and literary support in finishing manuscripts and getting them out into the world.

First and foremost, to Perry Prete, the mastermind behind Sands Press and a true champion of my books. You are always available for questions and concerns and continually help push me into becoming a better writer. Your belief in my work is appreciated beyond words.

To She Rises Studios, the new home for Sands Press. I'm excited to see what our future may bring and am grateful for your support.

To Laurie Carter, you're awesome and make the editing process easy. I always look forward to your input and love learning new skills from you.

To Thomas Shivanand Amelio, an active member of my ARC team and a good friend. This year, your advice on social media issues and growing a reading audience has been invaluable to me.

To my first ARC team, Cathy, Mark, Carol, Anne, Thomas, Steven, and Carrie. Thank you for reading an advance copy of my work before it's published. I respect your input and cherish your reviews.

To all my friends and readers who support me by buying books and making comments on my social media. I appreciate you all.

About the Author

Author, Susan Bagby, spent most of her life working with children and youth as a speech pathologist. After retirement, she moved back to her hometown of Akron, Ohio, and her life-long dream to write romance books came true when she found a home with Sands Press Publishing in 2021. Her debut novel, Christmas Wish Upon a Star, was published in 2022 and was a semi-finalist for the 2023 CIBA Chatelaine Book Awards for Romance Fiction. Her second book, Home for Love was released in October of 2023 and was a second-place winner for the Romance-Wholesome category in the Spring BookFest Awards.

Susan belongs to the Great Lakes Fiction Writers organization and Romance Writers of America (RWA).

She is presently working on a new small-town romance series and loves seeing new characters come to life. When she's not writing, she loves reading, walking in the woods, yoga, Pilates, and playing the piano. She's a firm believer that dreams do come true.

If you enjoyed this book and would like more happily-ever-after stories, I invite you to check out my other novels at https://www.susanbagby.com, sign up for my newsletter at https://susanbagby.com/newsletter/ and follow my writing journey on social media.

Thanks for your support!
Susan xo

https://www.facebook.com/profile.php?id=100077976577802
https://www.instagram.com/susanbagbyauthor/
https://x.com/SBagbyauthor
https://www.tiktok.com/@susanbagby31